The Root of All Evil

J. S. Fletcher

The Root of All Evil

Copyright © 2020 Indo-European Publishing

The present edition is a reproduction of previous publication of this classic work. Minor typographical errors may have been corrected without note; however, for an authentic reading experience the spelling, punctuation, and capitalization have been retained from the original text.

ISBN: 978-1-64439-389-5

CONTENTS

Part the First
Rise

Part The Second
Fall

CONTENTS

PART THE FIRST

RISE

CHAPTER I

Applecroft

Half-way along the one straggling street of Savilestowe a narrow lane suddenly opened out between the cottages and turned abruptly towards the uplands which rose on the northern edge of the village. Its first course lay between high grey walls, overhung with ivy and snapdragon. When it emerged from their cool shadowings the church came in view on one hand and the school on the other, each set on its own green knoll and standing high above the meadows. Once past these it became narrower and more tortuous; the banks on either side rose steeply, and were crowned by ancient oaks and elms. In the proper season of the year these banks were thick with celandine and anemone, and the scent of hedge violets rose from the moss among the spreading roots of the trees. Here the ruts of the lane were deep, as if no man had any particular business to repair them. The lane was, in fact, a mere occupation road, and led to nothing but an out-of-the-way farmstead, which stood, isolated and forlorn, half a mile from the village. It bore a picturesque name—Applecroft—and an artist, straying by chance up the lane and coming suddenly upon it would have rejoiced in its queer gables, its twisted chimneys, in the beeches and chestnuts that towered above it, and in the old-world garden and orchard which flanked one side of its brick walls, mellowed by time to the colour of claret. But had such a pilgrim looked closer he would have seen that here were all the marks of ill-fortune and coming ruin—evident, at any rate, to practical eyes in the neglected gates and fences, in the empty fold, in the hingeless, tumble-down doors, in the lack of that stitch in time which by anticipation would have prevented nine more. He would have seen, in short, that this was one of those places, of which there are so

1

many in rural England, whereat a feckless man, short of money, was vainly endeavouring to do what no man can do without brains and capital.

Nevertheless—so powerfully will Nature assert her own wealth in the face of human poverty—the place looked bright and attractive enough on a certain morning, when, it then being May, the trees around it were in the first glory of their leafage, and the orchard was red and white with blossom of apple and plum and cherry. There was a scent of sweetbriar and mignonette around the broken wicket gate which admitted to the garden, and in the garden itself, ill-kept and neglected, a hundred flowers and weeds, growing together unchecked, made patches of vivid colour against the prevalent green. There were other patches of colour, of a different sort, about the place, too. Beyond the garden, and a little to the right of the house, a level sward, open to the full light of the sun, made an excellent drying ground for the family washing, and here, busily hanging out various garments on lines of cord, stretched between rough posts, were two young women, the daughters of William Farnish, the shiftless farmer, whose hold on his house and land was daily becoming increasingly feeble. If any shrewd observer able to render himself invisible had looked all round Applecroft—inside house and hedge, through granary and stable—he would have gone away saying with emphasis, that he had seen nothing worth having there, save the two girls whose print gowns fluttered about their shapely limbs as they raised their bare arms and full bosoms to the cords on which they were pegging out the wet linen.

Farnish's wife had been dead some years, and since her death his two daughters had not only done all the work of the house, but much of what their father managed to carry out on his hundred acres of land. They bore strange names—selected by Farnish and his wife, after much searching and reflection, from the pages of the family Bible. The elder was named Jecholiah; the younger Jerusha. As time had gone on Jecholiah had become Jeckie; Jerusha had been shortened to Rushie. Everybody in the parish and the neighbourhood knew Jeckie and Rushie Farnish. They had always been inseparable, these sisters, yet it needed little particular observation to see that there was a difference of character and temperament between them. Jeckie, at twenty-five, was a tall, handsome, finely-developed young woman, generous in proportion, with a flashing, determined eye, and a mouth and chin which denoted purpose and obstinacy; she was the sort of woman that could love like fire, but whom it would be dangerous to cross in love. Already many of the young men of the district, catching one flash of her hawk-like eyes, had felt themselves warned, and it had been a

2

matter of astonishment to some discerning folk when it became known that she was going to marry Albert Grice, the only son of old George Grice, the village grocer, a somewhat colourless, tame young man whose vices were non-existent and his virtues commonplace, and who had nothing to recommend him but a good-humoured, weak amiability and a rather good-looking, boyish face. Some said that Jeckie was thinking of Old Grice's money-bags, but the vicar's wife, who studied psychology in purely amateur fashion, said that Jeckie Farnish had taken up Albert Grice in precisely the same spirit which makes a child love a legless and faceless doll, and an old maid a miserable mongrel—just in response to the mothering instinct; whether Jeckie loved him, they said, nobody would ever know, for Jeckie, with her proud, scornful lips and eyes full of sombre passion, was not the sort to tell her heart's secrets to anybody. Not so, however, with her sister Rushie, a soft, pretty, lovable, kissable, cuddlesome slip of a girl, who was all for love, and would have been run after by every lad in the village and half the shop-boys in the neighbouring market town, if it had not been that Jeckie's mothering and grandmothering eye had always been on her. Rushie represented one thing in femininity; her sister typified its very opposite. Rushie was of the tribe of Venus, but Jeckie of the daughters of Minerva.

Something of the circumstances and character of this family might have been gathered from the quality of the garments which the sisters were industriously hanging out to dry in the sun and wind. Most of them were their own, and in the bulk there was nothing of the frill and lace of the fine lady, but rather plain linen and calico. An expert housewife, fingering whatever there was, would have said that each separate article had been worn to thinness. Thus, too, were the sheets and pillow-cases and towels; and of such coarse stuff as belonged to Farnish himself—all represented the underwear and appointments of poor folk. But while there was patching and darning in plenty, there were no rags. If her father allowed a gate to fall off its posts rather than hunt up an old hinge and a few nails, Jeckie took good care that her needle and thread came out on the first sign of a rent; it was harder to replace than to repair, in her experience. And now, as she put the last peg in the last scrap of damp linen, it was with the proud consciousness that if the whole show was poverty-stricken it was at least whole and clean.

"That's the lot, Rushie!" she said, turning to her sister as she picked up the empty linen basket. "A good drying wind, too. We'll be able to get to mangling and ironing by tea-time."

Rushie, who had no such love of labour as her sister, made no answer. She followed Jeckie across the drying-ground and into the house; it was indicative of her nature that she immediately dropped into the nearest chair. The washing had been going on since a very early hour in the morning, broken only by a hastily-snatched breakfast; on the table in the one living-room the dirty cups and plates still lay spread about in confusion. And Jeckie, who had eyes all round her head, glanced at them, and at the old clock in the corner, and at her sister, sitting down, all at once.

"Nay, child!" she exclaimed. "It's over soon for that game! Eleven already, and naught done for dinner. Get those pots washed up, Rushie, and then see to the potatoes. Father'll none be so long before he's home; and there'll be Doadie Bartle and him for their dinners at twelve o'clock. Come on, now!"

"I'm tired," said Rushie, as she slowly rose, and began to clear up the untidy table. "We've never done in this house!"

"So'm I," retorted Jeckie. "But what's that to do with it when there's things to be done? Hurry up now, while I look after those fowls; they've never been seen to this morning."

She caught up a sieve as she spoke, filled it with waste stuff from a tub in the scullery, and, going out through the back of the house, walked into the fold behind, calling as she went to the cocks and hens which were endeavouring to find something for themselves amongst its boulders. None knew better than Jeckie the importance and value of that feathered brood. For three years she had kept things going with her poultry and eggs, and with the milk and butter which she got from the four cows that formed Farnish's chief property. The money that she made in this fashion had found the family in food and clothing, and gone some way towards paying the rent. And as she stood there throwing handfuls of food to the fowls, scurring and snatching about her feet, she had a curious sense that outside them and the cows feeding in the adjacent meadow there was literally nothing about the whole farmstead but poverty. The fold was destitute of manure; half a stack of straw stood desolate in the adjoining stack-garth; there was no hay in the loft nor corn in the granary; whatever produce he raised Farnish was always obliged to sell at once. The few pigs which he possessed were at that moment rooting in the lane for something to swell out their lank sides; his one horse was standing disconsolate by the trough near the well, mournfully regarding its emptiness. And Jeckie, as she threw away the last contents of her sieve and went over to the pump, had a vision of what other possibilities there were on the farm—certain acres of wheat and barley, of potatoes and turnips, the welfare of which, to be sure, depended upon the weather. She had a pretty keen idea of what they would bring in that

4

coming autumn in the way of money; she had an equally good one of what Farnish would have to do with it.

The horse, a fairly decent animal, drank greedily when Jeckie had pumped water into the trough, and as soon as he had taken his fill of this cheap commodity she opened the gate of the fold and let him out into the lane to pick up whatever he could get—that was an equally cheap way of feeding stock. Then, always with an eye to snatching up the potentialities of profit, she began to go round the farm buildings, looking for eggs. Hens, as all hen-wives know, are aggravating creatures, and will lay their eggs in any nook or corner. Jeckie knew where eggs were to be found—in beds of nettles, or under the stick-cast in the orchard, or behind the worn-out implements in the barn. Twice a day she or Rushie searched the precincts of Applecroft high and low rather than lose one of the precious things which went to make up so many dozen for market every Saturday, and when they had finished their labours it was always with the uneasy feeling that some perverse Black Spanish or Cochin China had successfully hidden away what would have brought in at any rate a few pence. But a few pence meant much. Though there were always eggs by the score in the wicker baskets in Jeckie's dairy, none were ever eaten by the family nor used for cooking purposes. That, indeed, would have been equivalent to eating money. Eggs meant other things—beef, bread, rent.

Jeckie's search after the morning's eggs took her up into the old pigeon-cote of the farm—an octagon building on the roof of the granary—wherein there had been no pigeons for a long time. Approached by a narrow, much-worn stone stairway, set between the walls of barn and granary, this cobwebbed and musty place was honeycombed from the broken floor to the dilapidated roof by nests of pigeon-holes. There were scores upon scores of them, and Jeckie never knew in which she might not find an egg. Consequently, in order to make an exhaustive search, it was necessary to climb all round the place, examining every row and every separate chamber. In doing this she had to pass the broken window, long destitute of the thick glass which had once been there. Looking through it, she saw her father coming up the lane from the village. At this, leaving her search to be resumed later, she went down to the fold again, carefully carrying her eggs before her in her bunched-up apron; for Jeckie knew that Farnish had been into Sicaster, the neighbouring market-town, that morning on a question that had to do with money, and whenever money was concerned her instincts were immediately aroused.

Farnish was riding into the fold as she regained it, and he got off his pony as she went towards him, and silently removing its

5

saddle and bridle, turned it loose in the lane, to keep the horse company and find its dinner for itself. Carrying its furniture, he advanced in the direction of his daughter—a tall, lank, shambling man, with a wisp of yellowish-grey whisker on either side of a thin, weak face—and shook his head as he turned into the stable, where Jeckie silently followed him. He flung saddle and bridle into an empty manger, seated himself on a corn-bin, and, swinging his long legs, shook his head again.

"Well?" demanded Jeckie.

Farnish, for a long time, had found it difficult to encounter his elder daughter's steady and questioning gaze, and he did not meet it now. His eyes wandered restlessly about the stable, as if wondering out of which particular hole the next rat would look, and he made no show of speech.

"You may as well out with it," said Jeckie. "What is it, now?"

There was an emphasis on the last word that made Farnish look at his daughter for a brief second; he looked away just as quickly, and began to drum his fingers on his bony knees.

"Aye, well, mi lass!" he answered, in a low tone. "As ye say—now! Ye may as well hear now as later. It's just like this here. Things is about at an end! That's the long and that's the short, as the saying goes."

"You'll have to be plainer than that," retorted Jeckie. "What is it? Money, of course! But—who's wanting it?"

Farnish made as if he swallowed something with an effort, and he kept his eyes steadily averted.

"I didn't make ye acquainted wi' it at the time," he said, after a brief silence. "But ye see, Jeckie, my lass, at t'last back-end I had to borrow money fro' one o' them money-lendin' fellers at Clothford—them 'at advertises, like, i' t'newspapers. I were forced to it!—couldn't ha' gone on, nohow, wi'out it at t'time. And so, course, why, its owin'!"

"How much?" demanded Jeckie.

"It were a matter o' two hundred 'at I borrowed," replied Farnish. "But—there's a bit o' interest, of course. It's that there interest——"

"What are they going to do?" asked Jeckie. Her whole instinct was to get at the worst—to come to grips. "Let's be knowing!" she said impatiently. "What's the use of keeping it back?"

"They can sell me up," answered Farnish in a low tone. "They can sell aught there is. I signed papers, d'ye see, mi lass. I had to. There were no two ways about it."

Jeckie made no answer. She saw the whole of Applecroft and its hundred acres as in a vision. Sold up! There was, indeed, she

6

thought, with bitter and ironic contempt, a lot to sell! Household furniture, live stock, dead stock, growing crops—was the whole lot worth two hundred pounds? Perhaps; but, then there would be nothing left. Now, out of the cows and the poultry a living could be scratched together, but....

"I been into Sicaster to see Mr. Burstlewick, th' bank manager," continued Farnish. "I telled him all t'tale. He said he were very sorry, and he couldn't do naught. Naught at all! So, you see, my lass, that's where it is. An' it's a rare pity," he concluded, with a burst of sentimental self-condolence, "for it's a good year for weather, and I reckon 'at what we have on our land'll be worth three or four hundred pound this back-end. And all for t'want of a hundred pounds, Jeckie, mi lass!"

"What do you mean by a hundred pound?" exclaimed Jeckie. "You said two!"

"Aye, but ye don't understand, mi lass," answered Farnish. "If I could give 'em half on it d'ye see, and sign a paper to pay t'other half when harvest's been and gone—what?"

"Would that satisfy 'em?" asked Jeckie suspiciously.

"So they told me, t'last time I saw 'em," replied Farnish in apparent sincerity. "'Give us half on it, Mr. Farnish,' they said, 'and t'other half and t'interest can run on.' So they said; but it's three weeks since, is that."

Jeckie meditated for a moment; then she suddenly turned, left the stable, and, crossing the empty fold, got rid of her eggs. She went into the kitchen; took something from its place in the delf-ledge, and, with another admonition to Rushie to see to the dinner, walked out into the garden, and set off down the lane outside. Farnish, from the fold, saw her going, and as her print gown vanished he turned into the house with a sigh of mingled relief and anticipation. But as he came in sight of the delf-ledge the sigh changed to a groan. Jeckie, he saw, had carried away the key of the beer barrel, and whereas he might have had a quart in her certain absence he would now get nothing but a mere glass on her problematical return.

7

CHAPTER II

The Tight Lip

Ever since her mother's death, ten years before the events of that morning, Jeckie, as responsible manager of household affairs, had cultivated an instinct which had been born in her—the instinct, if a thing had to be done to do it there and then. As soon as Farnish unburdened himself of his difficulty, his daughter's quick brain began to revolve schemes of salvation. There was nothing new in her father's situation; she had helped him out of similar ones more than once. More than once, too, she had borrowed money for him— money to pay an extra-pressing bill; money to make up the rent; money to satisfy the taxes or rates—and she had always taken good care to see that what she had borrowed was punctually repaid when harvest came round—a time of the year when Farnish usually had something to sell. Accordingly, what she had just heard in the stable did not particularly alarm her; she took her father's story in all good faith, and believed that if he could stave off the Clothford money-lender with a hundred pounds on account all would go on in the old way until autumn, when money would be coming in. And her sole idea in setting off to the village was to borrow the necessary sum. Once borrowed, she would see to it that it was at once forwarded to the importunate creditor; she would see to it, too, that it was repaid to whomever it was that she got it from. As to that last particular, she was canvassing certain possibilities as she walked quickly down the lane. There was Mr. Stubley, the biggest farmer in the place, who was also understeward for the estate. She had more than once borrowed twenty or thirty pounds from him, and he had always had it back. Then there was Mr. Merritt, almost as well-to-do as Mr. Stubley. The same reflections applied to him, and he was a good natured man. And there was old George Grice, Albert's father, who was as warm a man as any tradesman of the neighbourhood. One or other of these three would surely lend her a hundred pounds; she was, indeed, so certain of it that she felt no doubt on the matter, and her only regret at the moment was that her visit to the village might make her a little late for her dinner—no unimportant matter to her, a healthy young woman of good appetite, who had breakfasted scantily at six o'clock. Jeckie took a short cut across the churchyard and down the church lane, and came out upon the village street a little above the cross roads. There, talking to the landlord of the "Coach-and-Four," who stood in his open doorway holding a tray and a glass, she saw Mr. Stubley a comfortable man, who spent all his mornings on a fat old pony, ambling about his land. Stubley saw her coming along the street, and, with a nod to the landlord, touched the pony with his ash-plant switch and steered him in her direction. Jeckie, who had a spice of the sanguine in her temperament, took this as a good omen; she had an idea that in five more minutes she would be with this prosperous elderly farmer in his cozy parlour, close by, watching him laboriously writing out a cheque. And she smiled almost gaily as the pony and its burden came to the side of the road along which she walked.

"Now, mi lass!" said Mr. Stubley, looking her closely over out of his sharp eyes. "What're you doing down town this time o' day? Going to Grice's, I reckon? I were wanting a word or two wi' you," he went on, before Jeckie could get in a word of her own. "A word or two i' private, you understand. You're aware, of course, mi lass," he continued, bending down from his saddle. "You're aware 'at t'rent day's none so far off? What?"

A sudden sense of fear sent the warm flush out of Jeckie's cheeks, and left her pale. Her dark eyes grew darker as she looked at the man who was regarding her so steadily and inquiringly.

"What about the rent-day Mr. Stubley?" she asked. "What do you mean?"

"I had a line from t'steward this morning," answered Stubley. "He just mentioned a matter—'at he hoped Farnish 'ud be ready with the rent; and t'last half-year's an' all. What?"

The hot blood came back to Jeckie's cheeks in a fierce wave. She felt, somehow, as if some man's hand had smitten her, right and left.

"The last half-year's rent!" she repeated. "Do—do you mean that father didn't pay it?"

Stubley looked at her for an instant with speculation in his shrewd eyes. Then he nodded his head. There was a world of meaning in the nod.

"Paid nowt!" he answered. "Nowt at all. Not a penny piece, mi lass."

Jeckie's hands fell limply to her sides.

"I didn't know," she answered, helplessly. "He—he never told me. I'd no idea of it; Mr. Stubley."

"Dare say not, mi lass," said the farmer. "It 'ud be better for Farnish if he'd to tell a young woman like you more nor what he does, seemin'ly. But, now—is he going to be ready this time?"

Jeckie made no answer. She stood looking up and down the street, seeing all manner of things, real and unreal. And suddenly a look of sullen anger came into her eyes and round her red lips.

9

"How can I tell?" she said. "He—as you say—he doesn't tell me!"

Stubley bent still lower, and, from sheer force of habit, glanced right and left before he spoke.

"Aye, well, Jeckie, mi lass!" he said in low tones. "Then I'll tell you summat. Look to yourself—you an' yon sister o' yours! There's queer talk about Farnish. I've heard it, time and again, at market and where else. He'll none last so long, my lass—can't! It's my opinion there'll be no rent for t'steward; nowt but excuses and begging off, and such like; he's hard up, is your father! It 'ud be a deal better for him to give up, Jeckie; he'll never carry on! Now, you're a sensible young woman; what say you?"

There was a strong, almost mulish sense of obstinacy in the Farnish blood, and it was particularly developed in Farnish's elder daughter. Jeckie stood for a moment staring across the road. She looked as if she were gazing at the sign of the "Coach-and-Four," which had recently been done up and embellished with a new frame. In reality she saw neither it nor the ancient hostelry behind it. What she did see was a vision of her own!

"I don't know, Mr. Stubley," she answered suddenly. "My father's like all little farmers—no capital and always short o' ready money. But there's money to come in; come harvest and winter! And I know that if I'd that farm on my hands, I'd make it pay. I could make it pay now if I'd all my own way with it. But——"

Then, just as suddenly as she had spoken, she moved off, and went rapidly down the street in the direction of Grice's shop. The conversation with Stubley had given a new turn to her thoughts. What was the use of borrowing a hundred pounds to stave off a money-lender, when the last half-year's rent was owing and another half-year's nearly due? No; she would see if she could not do better than that! Now was the moment; she would try to take things clean into her own hands. Farnish, she knew, was afraid of her—afraid of her superior common sense, her grasp of things, her almost masculine powers of contrivance and management. She could put him on one side as easily as a child can push aside the reeds on the river bank, and then she could have her own way, and pull things round, and ... she paused at that point, remembering that all this could only be done with money.

Noon was just striking from the church clock as Jeckie came up to the front of Grice's shop. She never looked at this establishment without remembering how it had grown within her own recollection. When she was a child of five, and had gone down the street to spend a Saturday penny on sweets, Grice's shop had been housed in one of the rooms of the old timber-fronted house

10

from which the new stores now projected in shameless disregard of the antiquities surrounding them. Nothing, indeed, could be in greater contrast than Grice's shop and Grice's house. The house had stood where it was since the time of Queen Anne; the shop, built out from one corner of it, bore the date 1897, and on its sign—a blue ground with gilt lettering—appeared the significant announcement: "Diamond Jubilee Stores. George Grice & Son." There were fine things about the house, within and without: old furniture in old rooms, and trim hedges and gay flowers on the smooth, velvety lawns; a mere glance at the high, sloping roof was sufficient to make one think of Old England in its days of calm and leisure; but around the shop door and in the shop itself there were the sights and sounds of buying and selling; boxes and packing-cases from Chicago and San Francisco; the scent of spices and of soap; it always seemed to Jeckie, who had highly susceptible nostrils, that Albert Grice, however much he spruced and scented himself on Sundays, was never free of the curious mingling odours associated with a grocer's apron.

Albert was in the shop when she marched in, busied in taking down an order from Mrs. Aislabie, the curate's wife, who, seated in a chair at the counter, was meditatively examining a price list and wondering how to make thirty shillings go as far as forty. He glanced smilingly but without surprise at Jeckie, and inclined his head and the pen behind his large right ear towards a certain door at the back of the shop. Jeckie knew precisely what he meant— which was that his father had just gone to dinner. They had a custom there at Grice's—the old man went to dinner at twelve; Albert at one; there was thus always one of them in the shop to look after things in general and the assistant and two shop lads in particular. And Albert, who knew that since Jeckie was there in her morning gown and without headgear it must be because she wanted to see his father, added a word or two to his signal.

"Only just gone in," he said. "Go forward."

Jeckie went down the shop to the door, tapped at the glass of the upper panel, pushed aside a heavy curtain that hung behind, and entered upon old Grice as he sat down to his dinner. He was a biggish, round-faced, bald-headed man, bearded, save for his upper lip, which was very large and very tight—folk who knew George Grice well, and went to him seeking favours, watched that tight lip, and knew from it whether he was going to accede or not. He was a prosperous-looking man, too; plump and well-fed; and there was a fine round of cold beef and a bowl of smoking potatoes before him, to say nothing of a freshly-cut salad, a big piece of prime Cheddar and a tankard of foaming ale. The buxom servant-lass who attended to the wants of the widowed father and the bachelor son, was just going out of the room by one door as Jeckie entered by the other. She glanced wonderingly at the visitor, but George Grice, picking up the carving knife and fork, showed no surprise. He had long since graduated in the school of life, and well knew the signs when man or woman came wanting something.

"Hallo!" he said in sharp, businesslike tones. "Queer time o' day to come visiting, mi lass! What's in the wind, now?"

Jeckie, uninvited, sat down in one of the two easy chairs which flanked the hearth, and went straight to her subject.

"Mr. Grice!" she said, having ascertained by a glance that the door leading to the kitchen was safely closed. "I came down to see you. Now, look here, Mr. Grice; you know me, and you know I'm going to marry your Albert."

"Humph!" muttered Grice, busied in carving thin slices of beef for himself. "Aye, and what then?"

"And you know I shall make him a rare good wife, too," continued Jeckie. "The best wife he could find anywhere in these parts!"

"When I were a lad," remarked Grice, with the ghost of a thin smile about his top lip, "we used to write a certain saying in the copybook—'Self-praise is no recommendation.' I'm not so certain of it myself, though. Some folks knows the value of their own goods better than anybody."

"I know the value of mine!" asserted Jeckie solemnly. "You couldn't find a better wife for Albert than I shall make him if you went all through Yorkshire with a small-tooth comb! And you know it, Mr. Grice!"

"Well, mi lass," said Grice, "and what then?"

"I want you to do something for me," answered Jeckie. She pulled the chair nearer to the table, and went on talking while the grocer steadily ate and drank. "I'll be plain with you, Mr. Grice. There's nobody knows I've come here, nor why. But it's this—I've come to the conclusion that it's no use my father going on any longer. He isn't fit; he's no good. I've found things out. He's been borrowing money from some, or one, o' them money-lenders at Clothford. He owes half a year's rent, and there's another nearly due. There's others wanting money. I think you want a bit, yourself. Well, it's all got to stop. I'm going to stop it! And as I'm going to be your daughter-in-law, I want you to help me!"

Grice, carefully selecting the ripest of some conservatory-grown tomatoes from the bowl in front of him, stuck a fork into it, and began to peel it with a small silver knife which he picked up from beside his plate. His tight lip pursed itself while he was

12

engaged; it was not until he had put the peeled tomato on his plate, and added the heart of a lettuce to it, that he looked at his caller.

"What d'ye want, mi lass?" he asked.

"I want you to lend me—me!—five or six hundred pounds, just now," replied Jeckie readily. "Me, mind, Mr. Grice—not him. Me!"

"What for?" demanded Grice, stolidly and with no sign of surprise. "What for, now?"

"I'll tell you," answered Jeckie, gaining in courage. "I want to pay off every penny he owes. Then I'll be master! I shall have him under my thumb, and I'll make him do. I'll see to every penny that comes in and goes out; and you mark my words, Mr. Grice, I can make that farm pay! If you'll lend me what I want I'll pay you back in three years, and it'll be then a good going concern. I know what I'm saying."

"In less nor three years you and my son Albert'll be wed," remarked Grice.

"I can keep an eye on it, and on my father and Rushie when we are wed," retorted Jeckie.

"And there's another thing," said Grice. "When I gave my consent to your weddin' my son, it were an agreed thing between me an' Farnish, a bargain, that you should have five hundred pound from him as a portion. Where's that?"

Jeckie gave him a swift meaning look.

"I might have yet, if I took hold o' things," she answered. "But it 'ud be me 'at would find it, Mr. Grice. My father—Lord bless you—he'd never find five hundred pence! But—trust me!"

Grice carved himself some more cold beef, and as he seemed to be considering her proposal, Jeckie resumed her arguments.

"There'll be a good bit of money to come in this back-end," she said. "And if we'd more cows, as I'd have, we should do better. And pigs—I'd go in for pigs. Let me only clear off what debt he's got into, and——"

Grice suddenly laughed quietly, and, seizing his tankard, looked knowingly at her as he lifted it to his lips.

"The question is, mi lass," he said, "the question is—how deep has he got? You don't know that, you know!"

"Most of it, at any rate," said Jeckie. "I'll lay four or five hundred 'ud clear it all off, Mr. Grice."

"Five hundred pound," observed Grice, "is a big, a very big sum o' money. It were a long time," he added reflectively, "before I could truly say that I were worth it!"

"You're worth a lot more now, anyway," remarked Jeckie. "And you'll be doing a good deed if you help me. After all, I want to set things going right; they're my own flesh and blood up yonder. Now, come, Mr. Grice!"

Grice pushed away the remains of the more solid portion of his dinner, and thoroughly dug into the prime old cheese. After eating a little and nibbling at a radish he turned to his visitor.

"I'll not say 'at I will, and I'll not say 'at I willn't," he announced. "It's a matter to be considered about. But I'll say this here—I'll take a ride up Applecroft way this afternoon, and just see how things stands, like. And then——"

He waved Jeckie towards the door, and she, knowing his moods and temperament, took the hint, and with no more than a word of thanks, hastened to leave him. In the shop Albert was still busily engaged with Mrs. Aislabie, who found it hard to determine on Irish roll or Wiltshire. With him Jeckie exchanged no more than a glance. She felt a sense of relief when she got out into the street; and when, five minutes later, she was crossing the churchyard she muttered to herself certain words which showed that her conversation with Stubley was still in her mind.

"Yes, that's the only way—to clear him out altogether, and let me take hold! I'll put things to rights if only George Grice'll find the money!"

At that moment George Grice, having finished his dinner, was taking out of a cupboard certain of his account books. Before he did anything for anybody, he wanted to know precisely how much was owing to him at Applecroft.

CHAPTER III

THE BROKEN MAN

While Jeckie was busied in the village and Farnish, sighing after the key of the beer barrel, was aimlessly wandering about the farm buildings, there came into the kitchen, where Rushie was making ready the dinner, a tall, blue-eyed, broadly-built youngster, whose first action was to glance inquiringly at the clock and whose second was to go to the sink in the corner to wash his brown hands. This was Joe, or Doadie Bartle, about whom nobody in those parts knew more than that he had turned up as a lad of fifteen at

14

Applecroft some six or seven years previously; had been taken in by Farnish to do a bit of work for his meat, drink and lodging, and had remained there ever since. According to his own account, he was an orphan, from Lincolnshire, who had run away from his last place and gone wandering about the country in search of a better. Something in the atmosphere of Applecroft had suited him, and there he had stayed, and was now, in fact, Farnish's sole help on the farm outside the occasional assistance of the two girls. There were folk in the village who said that Farnish got his labour for naught, but Jeckie knew that he had had twenty pounds a year ever since he was eighteen, and had regularly put by one-half of his wages under her supervision. Doadie Bartle, chiefly conspicuous for his air of simple good nature, had come to be a fixture. Without him and Jeckie the place would have gone to wrack and ruin long since, for Farnish had a trick of sitting down when he should have been afoot, and gossiping in public-houses when his presence was wanted elsewhere. It was because of this—a significant indication, had there been anyone to notice it—that Doadie was always treated to a pint of ale at dinner and supper, while his master was rigorously restricted to a glass.

Doadie Bartle looked again at the clock as he finished wiping his hands on the rough towel which hung from its roller behind the door. His glance ended at Rushie, who was sticking a fork into the potatoes on the hob.

"By gow, it's a warm 'un, this mornin'!" he said. "Where's Jeckie, like? I could do wi' my pint now better nor later."

"You'll have to wait," answered Rushie, who had seen her father's despairing glance at the delf-ledge. "She's gone out, and taken the key with her."

Doadie looked disappointedly in the direction of the beer barrel, which stood on its gantry just within the open door of the larder. Resigning himself to the unavoidable, he walked out into the fold, where Farnish leaned against the wall of the pig-stye, hands in pockets.

"I shall have to do a bit o' mendin' up this afternoon," said Doadie. "Merritt's cows has been i' our clover; there's a bad place i' t'hedge."

"Aye!" assented Farnish. There was no interest in his tone, and little more seemed to be awakened when Rushie appeared at the kitchen window and announced that dinner was ready. He shambled indoors, and, without removing his hat, sat down at the head of his table, and began to cut slices off the big lump of cold bacon, which, with boiled potatoes and greens, made up the dinner.

15

"Jeckie's no reight to run off wi' t'key o' t'ale barrel," he grumbled. "Them 'at tews hes a reight to sup!"

"It's not much tewin' 'at you've been doin', I'll lay!" retorted Rushie, who had long since learned the art of homely repartee from her elder sister. "Ridin' about like a lord!"

"Now then, never mind!" growled Farnish. "Happen I done more tewin' nor ye're aware on, mi lass! There's more sorts o' hard work than one."

Then, all three being liberally supplied, the three pairs of jaws set to work, and the steady eating went on in silence until the sheep-cur, chained outside the door to a dilapidated kennel, gave a short, sharp bark. Rushie, who knew this to be a declaration of friendliness rather than of enmity, ran and put the potatoes and greens on the hob to warm up.

"Jeckie!" she said. "None been so long, after all."

Jeckie came bustling into the kitchen as Farnish, who knew her appetite, pushed a well-filled plate towards her place. Without a word she took a big earthenware jug from its hook, went to the larder, and rummaged in her pocket for the key of the beer barrel. Presently the sound of the gurgling ale was heard in the kitchen. Doadie Bartle's big blue eyes glistened as he went on steadily munching. Farnish looked down at the cloth, wondering if his elder daughter meant to be generous. The roseate hopes set up in Jeckie's mind by her interview with George Grice inclined her for once to laxity. When she came back with the ale she gave her father a pint instead of a glass, and Farnish made an involuntary mutter of appreciation. He and his man seized their measures and drank deep. Jeckie, pouring out glasses for herself and her sister, gave them a half-whimsical look; she had been obliged to tilt the barrel a little to draw that ale, and she knew that its contents were running low, and that the brewer's man was not due for two days yet.

The dinner went on to its silent end; the bacon, greens, and potatoes finished. Rushie cleared the plates in a heap, and, setting clean ones before each diner, produced a huge jam tart, hot and smoking from the oven. Jeckie cut this into great strips and distributed them. Bartle, still hungry, took a mouthful of his, turned scarlet, and reached for his pot of beer.

"Gum! that's a hot 'un!" he said drinking heartily. "Like to take t'skin offen your tongue, is that!" Then, with an apologetic glance in Rushie's direction, and, as if to excuse his manners, he murmured, "Jam's allus hotter nor owt 'at iver comes out o' t'oven, I think, and I allus forget it; you mun excuse me!"

"Save toffee," remarked Farnish, with the air of superior knowledge. "There's nowt as hot as what toffee is. I rek'lect 'at I

16

once burnt t'roof o' my mouth varry bad wi' some toffee 'at mi mother made; they hed to oil my mouth same as they oil machines— wi' a feather."

When the last of the jam tart had vanished the two girls put their elbows on the table, propped their chins on their interlaced fingers, and seemed to study the pattern of the coarse linen cloth. Farnish got up slowly; took down his pipe from the corner of the mantlepiece, and, drawing some loose tobacco from his waistcoat pocket, began to smoke. Bartle, after rising and stretching himself, went over to a drawer in the delf-ledge, and presently came back from it with a paper packet, which he began to unfold. An odour of peppermint rose above the lingering smell of the bacon and greens.

"Humbugs!" he said, with a broad grin, as he offered the packet to the two girls. "I bowt three-pennorth t'last time I were i' Sicaster, and I'd forgotten all abowt 'em. They're t'right sort, these is—tasty 'uns."

Munching the brown and white bull's eyes, the sisters began to clear away the dinner things into the scullery. Presently Rushie called to Bartle to bring her the kettle and help her to wash up. When he had gone into the scullery Jeckie, who was folding up the cloth, turned to her father.

"About what you told me this morning," she said, in low tones. "Something's got to be done, and, of course, as usual, I've got to do it. I've been down to see George Grice."

Farnish started, and his thin face flushed a little. He was mortally afraid of George Grice, who represented money and power and will force.

"Aye, well, mi lass!" he muttered slowly. "Of course there's no doubt 'at Mr. George Grice has what they call th' ability to help a body—no doubt at all. But as to whether he's gotten the will, you know, why——"

"Less talk!" commanded Jeckie. "If he helps anybody it'll be me! And you listen here; we're not going on as we have done. You're letting things go from bad to worse. And you don't tell me t'truth, neither. I met Stubley, and he says you never paid t'last half-year's rent. Now, then!"

"I arranged it wi' t'steward," protested Farnish. "Him an' me understand each other; Mr. Stubley's nowt to do wi' it."

"You had the money," asserted Jeckie. "What did you do with it?"

"It went to them money-lendin' fellers," answered Farnish. "That's where it went; they would have it, choose how! Ye see mi lass——"

"I'll tell you what it is," interrupted Jeckie. "You'll have to let

17

me take hold! I can pull things round. Now, you listen! Mr. George Grice is coming up here this very afternoon, and him and me's going to get at a right idea of how matters stand. And if he helps me to pay all off and get a fresh start I'm going to be master, d'ye see? You'll just have to do all 'at I say in future. You can be master in name if you like, but I shall be t'real one. If you don't agree to that, I shall do no more! If I put you right, in future I shall manage things; I shall take all that comes in, and pay all that goes out. Do you understand that?"

Farnish accepted this ultimatum with an almost tipsy gravity. He continued to puff at his pipe while his daughter talked, and when she had finished he bowed solemnly, as if he had been a judge assenting to an arrangement made between contending litigants.

"Now then," he said, in almost unctuous accents, "owt 'at suits you'll suit me! If so be as you can put me on my legs again, Jecholiah, mi lass, I'm agreeable to any arrangement as you're good enough to mak'. You can tek' t'reins o' office, as the sayin' is, wi' pleasure, and do all t'paying out and takin' in. Of course," he added, with a covert glance in his daughter's direction, "you'll not be against givin' your poor father a few o' shillin's a week to buy a bit o' 'bacca wi?—it 'ud be again Nature, and religion, an' all, if I were left——"

"You've never been without beer or 'bacca yet, that I know of," retorted Jeckie, with a flash of her eye. "Trust you! But now, when George Grice comes, mind there's no keeping aught back. We shall want to know——"

Just then Rushie called from the scullery that the grocer was at the garden gate in his trap, and Farnish immediately got out of his easy chair, ill at ease.

"Happen I'd better go walk i' t'croft a bit while you hev your talk to him, Jeckie?" he suggested. "Two's company, and three's——"

"And happen you'd better do naught o' t'sort!" retorted Jeckie. "You bide where you are till you're wanted."

She went out to the gate to meet Grice, who, being one of those men who never walk where they can ride, had driven up to Applecroft in one of his grocery carts, and was now hitching his pony to a ring in the outer wall. He nodded silently to Jeckie as he moved heavily towards her.

"Much obliged to you for coming, Mr. Grice," she said eagerly. "I take it very kind of you. I've spoken to him," she went on, lowering her voice and nodding in the direction of the kitchen. "I've told him, straight, that if you and me help him out o' this mess that he's got into, I shall be master, so——"

"Take your time, mi lass, take your time!" said the grocer.

"Before I think o' helping anybody I want to know where I am! Now," he continued, as they walked into the fold and he looked round him with appraising eyes, "it may seem a queer thing me living in t'same place, my lass, but I've never been near this house o' yours for many a long year—never sin' you were a bairn, I should think—it's out o' t'way, d'ye see! And dear, dear, I see a difference! What!—there's naught about t'place! No straw—no manure—no cattle—a pig or two—a few o' fowls!—Why, there's nowt! Looks bad, my lass, looks very, very bad. Farnish has nowt—nowt!"

Jeckie's heart sank like lead in a well, and a sickened feeling came over her. "I know it looks pretty bad, Mr. Grice," she admitted, almost humbly. "But it's not so bad as it looks. There's four right good cows, and over a hundred and fifty head o' poultry. I know what the butter and milk and eggs bring in!—and there's more pigs nor what you see, and there's the crops. Come through the croft, and look at 'em. If there's no manure in the fold, it's on the land, anyway—we've never sold neither straw nor manure off this place. Come this way."

It was mainly owing to Jeckie, Rushie, and Doadie Bartle that what arable land Farnish held was clear and free of weeds. The grocer was bound to admit that the crops looked well; his long acquaintance with a farming district had taught him how to estimate values; he agreed with Jeckie that, granted the right sort of weather for the rest of the summer and part of autumn, there was money in what he was shown.

"But then, you know, mi lass," he said as they returned to the house, "it all depends on what Farnish is owing. This here money-lender 'at you spoke of—he ought to be cleared off, neck and crop! Then there's a year's rent. And there'll be other things. There's forty pounds due to me. Before ever I take into consideration doing aught at all for you—'cause I wouldn't do it for Farnish, were it ever so!—I shall want to know how matters stands, d'ye see? I must know of every penny 'at's owing—otherwise it 'ud be throwin' good money after bad. I'll none deny that if what he owes is nowt much—two or three hundred or so—things might be pulled round under your management. But, there it is! What does he owe?—that's what we want to be getting at."

"I'll make him tell," said Jeckie. "We'll have it put down on paper. Come in, Mr. Grice." Then, as they went towards the door of the house, she added in confidential, hospitable tones, "I've a bottle o' good old whisky put away, that nobody knows naught about—you shall have a glass."

Grice muttered something about no need for his prospective daughter-in-law to trouble herself, but he followed her into the kitchen, where Farnish stood nervously awaiting them. The grocer, who felt that he could afford to be facetious as well as magnanimous, gave Farnish a sly look.

"Now then, mi lad!" he said. "We've come to hear a bit about what you've been doing o' late! You seem to ha' let things run down, Farnish—there's nowt much to show outside. How is it, like?"

"Why, you see, Mr. Grice," answered Farnish with a weak smile, "there's times, as you'll allow, sir, when a man gets a bit behindhand, and——"

He suddenly paused, and his worn face turned white, and Grice, following his gaze, which was fixed on the garden outside, saw what had checked his speech. Two men were coming to the front door; in one of them Grice recognised a Sicaster auctioneer who was also a sheriff's officer. He let out a sharp exclamation which made Jeckie, who was unlocking a corner cupboard, swing herself round in an agony of fear.

"Good God!" he said. "Bailiffs!"

The door was open to the sunshine and the scent of the garden, and the sheriff's officer, after a glance within, stepped across the threshold and pulled out a paper.

"Afternoon, Mr. Grice!" he said cheerfully. "Fine day, sir. Now, Mr. Farnish, sorry to come on an unpleasant business, but I dare say you've been expecting me any time this last ten days, eh? Levinstein's suit, Mr. Farnish—execution. Four hundred and eighty-three pounds, five shillings, and sixpence. Not convenient to settle, I dare say, so I'll have to leave my man."

Jeckie, who had grown as white as the linen on the lines outside, stood motionless for a moment. Then she turned on her father.

"You said it was only two hundred!" she exclaimed hoarsely. "You said——" She paused, hearing Grice laugh, and turned to see him clap his hat on his head and stride out by the back door. In an instant she was after him, her hand, trembling like a leaf, on his arm.

"Mr. Grice! You're not going? Stand by us—by me! Before God, I'll see you're right!" she cried. "Mr. Grice!"

But Grice strode on towards his trap; the tight lip tighter than ever.

"Nay!" he said. "Nay! It's no good, my lass. It's done wi'."

"Mr. Grice!" she cried again. "Why—I'm promised to your Albert! Mr. Grice!"

But Mr. Grice made no answer; another moment and he had climbed into his cart and was driving away, and Jeckie, after one

20

look at his broad back, muttered something to herself and went back into the house.

An hour later she and Rushie were mangling and ironing, in dead silence. They went on working, still in silence, far into the evening, and Doadie Bartle, after supper, turned the mangle for them. Towards dark Farnish, who had already become fast friends with the man in possession, stole up to his elder daughter, and whispered to her. Jeckie pulled the key of the beer barrel from her pocket, and flung it at him.

"Tek it, and drink t'barrel dry!" she said, fiercely. "It's t'last 'at'll ever be tapped i' this place—by you at any rate!"

CHAPTER IV

THE DIPLOMATIC FATHER

Grice drove away down the lane in a curious temper. He was angry with himself for wasting a couple of hours of his valuable time; angry with Jeckie for having induced him to do so; angry with Farnish for his incapacity and idleness; still more angry to find that it was hopeless to do what he might have done. He knew well enough that Jeckie had been right when she said that he would never find a better wife for Albert; he also knew that after what he had just witnessed he would never allow Albert to marry her. Jeckie alone would have been all right, but Jeckie, saddled with an incompetent parent, was impossible. "And if you can't get t'best," he muttered to himself, "you must take what comes nearest to t'best! There's more young women i' t'world than Jecholiah Farnish, and I mun consider about findin' one. That 'at I've left behind yonder'll never do!"

Half-way down the lane he came across Doadie Bartle, busily engaged in mending the fence. Grice's shrewd eyes saw how the youngster was working; here, at any rate, was no slacker. He pulled up his pony and gave Doadie a friendly nod.

"Now, mi lad!" he said. "Doin' a bit o' repairing, like?"

"Merritt's cows were in there this mornin'," answered Bartle. "They come up t'lane and got in to our clover, Mr. Grice."

"Aye, why," remarked Grice. "It'll none matter much to you

21

how oft Merritt's cows or anybody else's gets in to Farnish's clover in a day or two, my lad. It's over and done wi' up yonder at Applecroft."

Bartle's blue eyes looked a question, and Grice laughed as he answered it.

"T'bailiffs is in!" he said. "Come in just now. It's all up, lad. Farnish'll be selled up—lock, stock, and barrel—within a week."

Bartle drove the fork with which he had been gathering thorns together into the ground at his feet, and leaning on its handle, stared fixedly at Grice.

"Aw!" he said. "Why, I knew things were bad, but I didn't know they were as bad as that, mister. Selled up, now! Come!"

"There'll be nowt left, mi lad, neither in house nor barn, stye nor stable, in another week!" affirmed Grice. Then, waiting until he saw that his announcement had gone home with due effect, he added, "So you'll be out of a place, d'ye see?"

Bartle let his gaze wander from the old grocer's face up the lane. From where he stood he could see Applecroft, and at that moment he saw Jeckie and Rushie standing together in the orchard, evidently in close and deep conversation.

"Aye," he said slowly. "If it's as you say, I reckon I shall. And I been there six or seven year, an' all!"

"And for next to nowt, no doubt," remarked Grice, with a sly look. "Now, look here, mi lad, I'm wanting a young feller like you to go out wi' my cart—'liverin' goods, d'ye understand? If you like to take t'job on ye can start next Monday. I'll gi' you thirty shillin' a week."

He was quick to see the sudden sparkle in Bartle's eyes, and he went on to deepen the impression.

"And there's pickin's an' all," he said. "Ye can buy owt you like out o' my shop at cost price, and t'job's none a heavy 'un. Two horses to look after and this here pony, and go round wi' t'goods. What do you say, now, Bartle?"

"Much obliged to you, mister; I'll consider on it, and tell you to-morrow," answered Bartle. "But"—he looked doubtfully at Grice, and then nodded towards the farm—"these here folks, what's goin' to become o' them? I've been, as it were, one o' t'family, d'ye see, Mr. Grice?"

"There's no fear about t'lasses," declared Grice, emphatically. "They're both capable o' doin' well for theirsens, and I've no doubt Jeckie's gotten a bit o' brass put away safe, somewhere or other. As for Farnish, he mun turn to, and do summat 'at he hasn't done for years—he mun work. What ha' ye to do with that, Bartle? Look to yersen, mi lad! Come and see me to-morrow."

22

He shook up his pony's reins and drove on. The encounter with Farnish's man had improved his temper; he had been wanting a stout young fellow like Bartle for some time, a fellow that would lift heavy packing cases and make himself useful. Bartle was just the man. So he had, after all, got or was likely to get, something out of his afternoon's excursion—satisfactory, that, for he was a man who objected to doing anything without profit.

But now there was Albert to consider. Of one thing George Grice was certain—there was going to be no marriage between Albert and Jecholiah Farnish. True, they were engaged; true, Albert, following the fashion of his betters, had, despite his father's sneers, given her an engagement ring. But that was neither here nor there. Despite the fact that Albert's name appeared in company with his father's on the powder-blue and gold sign above the Diamond Jubilee Stores, Albert had no legal share in the business—there was no partnership; Albert was as much a paid servant as the shop-boy. Now, in old Grice's opinion, the man who holds the purse-strings is master of the situation, and he had the pull over Albert in more ways than one. Moreover, a shrewd and astute man himself, he believed Albert to be a bit of a fool; a good-natured, amiable, weak sort of chap, easily come round. He had half a suspicion that Jeckie had come round him at some time or other. And now he would have to come round him himself, and at once.

"There'll have to be no chance of her gettin' at him," he mused as he drove slowly down the village street. "He's that soft and sentimental, is our Albert, 'at if she had five minutes wi' him, he'd be givin' way to her. I mun use a bit of statesmanship."

Occasion was never far to seek where George Grice was concerned, and before he had passed the "Coach-and-Four" he had conceived a plan of getting Albert out of the way until nightfall. As soon as he arrived at the shop he bustled in, went straight to his desk, and drawing out a letter, turned to his son.

"Albert, mi lad!" he said, as if the matter was of urgent importance, "there's this letter here fro' yon man at Cornchester about that horse 'at he has to sell. Now, we could do wi' a third horse—get yourself ready, and drive over there, and take a look at it. If it's all right, buy it—you can go up to forty pounds for it, and tell him we'll send t'cheque on to-morrow. Go now—t'trap's outside there, and you can give t'pony a feed at Cornchester while you get your tea. Here, take t'letter wi' you, and then you'll have t'man's address—somewhere i' Beechgate. It's nigh on to three o'clock now, so be off."

Albert, who had no objection to a pleasant drive through the country lanes, was ready and gone within ten minutes, and old

Grice was glad to think that he was safely absent until bed-time. During the afternoon and early evening various customers of the better sort, farmers and farmers' wives, dropped in at the shop, and to each he assiduously broke the news of the day—Farnish had gone smash. One of these callers was Stubley, and Stubley, when he heard the news, looked at the grocer with a speculative eye.

"Then I reckon you'll not be for Farnish's lass weddin' yon lad o' yours?" he suggested. "Wouldn't suit your ticket, that, Grice, what?"

"Now, then, what would you do if it were your case, Mr. Stubley?" demanded Grice. "Would you be for tying flesh and blood o' yours up to owt 'at belonged to Farnish?"

"She's a fine lass, all t'same," said Stubley. "I've kept an eye on her this last year or two. Strikes me 'at things 'ud ha' come to an end sooner if it hadn't been for her. She's a grafter, Grice, and no waster, neither. She'd make a rare good wife for your Albert—where he'd make a penny she'd make a pound. I should think twice, mi lad, before I said owt."

But Grice's upper lip grew tighter than before when Stubley had gone, and by the time of his son's return, with the new horse tied up behind the pony cart, he was ready for him. He waited until Albert had eaten his supper; then, when father and son were alone in the parlour, and each had got a tumbler of gin and water at his elbow, he opened his campaign.

"Albert, mi lad!" he said, suavely, "there's been a fine to-do sin' you set off Cornchester way this afternoon. Yon man Farnish has gone clean broke!"

Albert started and stared in surprise.

"It's right, mi lad," continued Grice. "He's gotten t'bailiffs in—he'll be selled up i' less nor a week. Seems 'at he's been goin' to t'money-lenders, yonder i' Clothford—one feller's issued an execution again him. Four hundred and eighty-three pound, five shillings, and sixpence! Did ye ever hear t'like o' that? Him?"

Albert began to twiddle his thumbs.

"Nay!" he said, wonderingly. "I knew he were in a bad way, but I'd no idea it were as bad as that. Then he's nought to pay with, I reckon?"

"Nowt—so to speak," declared Grice. "Nowt 'at 'll settle things, anyway. And I hear fro' Stubley 'at t'last half-year's rent were never paid, and now here's another just about due. And there's other folk. He owes me forty pound odd. If I'd ha' known o' this yesterday, I'd ha' had summat out o' Farnish for my brass—I'd ha' had a cow, or summat. Now, it's too late; I mun take my chance wi' t'rest o'

24

t'creditors. And when t'landlord's been satisfied for t'rent, I lay there'll be nowt much for nobody, money-lender nor anybody else."

"It's a bad job," remarked Albert.

Grice turned to a shelf at the side of his easy chair, opened the lid of a cigar box, selected two cigars, and passed one to his son.

"Aye!" he assented presently, "it is a bad job, mi lad. Farnish promised 'at he'd gi' five hundred pound wi' Jecholiah. I think we mun ha' been soft i' wor heads, Albert, to believe 'at he'd ever do owt o' t'sort. He wor havin' us, as they say—havin' us for mugs!"

Albert made no answer. He began to puff his cigar, watching his father through the blue smoke.

"Every man for his-self!" said old Grice after a while. "It were an understood thing, were that, Albert, and now 'at there's no chance o' Farnish redeemin' his word, there's no need for you to stand by yours. There's plenty o' fine young women i' t'world beside yon lass o' Farnish's. My advice to you, mi lad, is to cast your eyes elsewhere."

Albert began to wriggle in his chair. His experience of Jeckie Farnish was that she had a will of her own; he possessed sufficient mother-wit to know that she was cleverer than he was.

"I don't know what Jecholiah 'ud say to that," he murmured. "We been keeping company this twelve-month, and——"

"Pshaw!" exclaimed Grice. "What bi that! I'll tell you what it is, mi lad—yon lass were never after you. I'll lay owt there's never been much o' what they call love-makin' between you! She were after my brass, d'yer see? Now, if it had been me 'at had gone broke, i'stead o' Farnish, what then? D'ye think she'd ha' stucken to you? Nowt o' t'sort!"

Albert sat reflecting. It was quite true that there had been little love-making between him and Jeckie. Jeckie was neither sentimental nor amorous. She and Albert had gone to church together; occasionally he had spent the evening at Farnish's fireside; once or twice he had taken her for an outing, to a statutes-hiring fair, or a travelling circus. And he was beginning to wonder.

"I know she's very keen on money, is Jecholiah," he said at last.

"Aye, well, she's goin' to have none o' mine!" affirmed old Grice. He was quick to see that Albert was as wax in his hands, and he accordingly brought matters to a climax. "I'll tell you what it is, mi lad!" he continued, replenishing his son's glass, and refilling his own. "We mun have done wi' that lot—it 'ud never do for you, a rising young feller, to wed into a broken man's family. It mun end, Albert!"

25

"She'll have a deal to say," murmured Albert. "She's an awful temper, has Jecholiah, if things doesn't suit her, and——"

"Now then, you listen to me," interrupted Grice. "We'll give her no chance o' sayin'—leastways, not to you, and what she says to me's neither here nor there. Now it's high time you were wed, mi lad, but you mun get t'right sort o' lass. And I'll tell you what—you know 'at I went last year to see mi brother John, 'at lives i' Nottingham—keep's a draper's shop there, does John, and he's a warm man an' all, as warm as what I am, and that's sayin' a bit! Now John has three rare fine lasses—your cousins, mi lad, though you've never seen 'em—and he'll give a nice bit wi' each o' 'em when they wed. I'll tell you what you shall do, mi lad—you shall take a fortnight's holiday, and go over there and see 'em; I'll write a letter to John to-night 'at you can take wi' you. And if you can't pick a wife o' t'three—why, it'll be a pity!—a good-lookin' young feller like you, wi' money behind you. Get your best things packed up to-night, and you shall drive into Sicaster first thing i' t'mornin' and be off to Nottingham. I'll see 'at you have plenty o' spendin' brass wi' you, and you can go and have your fling and make your choice. I tell yer there's three on 'em—fine, good-looking, healthy lasses—choose which you like, and me and her father'll settle all t'rest. And Nottingham's a fine place for a bit of holidayin'."

Old Grice sat up two hours later than usual that night, writing to his brother, the Nottingham draper, and Albert went away before seven o'clock next morning with all his best clothes and with fifty pounds in his pocket. His father told him to do it like a gentleman, and Albert departed in the best of spirits. After all, he had no tender memories of Jeckie, and he remembered that once, when he had taken her to Cornchester Fair, and wanted to have lunch at the "Angel," she had chided him quite sharply for his extravagance and had made him satisfy his appetite on buns and cocoa at a cheap coffee-shop. It was a small thing, but he had smarted under it, for like all weak folk he had a vein of mulish contrariness in him, and it vexed him to know that Jeckie, when she was about, was stronger than he was.

Grice, left to run the business with the aid of his small staff, was kept to the shop during Albert's absence. But he had compensations. The first came in the shape of a letter from his brother, the draper, the contents of which caused George Grice to chuckle and to congratulate himself on his diplomacy; he was, in fact, so pleased by it that he there and then put up £25 in Bank of England notes, enclosed them in a letter to Albert, bidding him to stay in Nottingham a week longer, and went out to register the missive himself. The second was that Bartle came to him and took

26

charge of the horses and carts and lost no time in proving himself useful beyond expectation. And the third lay in knowing that the Farnish Family had gone out of the village. Just as the grocer had prophesied, Farnish had been sold up within a week of the execution which the money-lenders had levied on his effects. Not a stick had been left to him of his household goods, not even a chicken of his live stock, and on the morning of the sale he and his daughters had risen early, and carrying their bundles in their hands had gone into Sicaster and taken lodgings.

"And none such cheap uns, neither!" said the blacksmith, who gave Grice all this news, and to whom Farnish owed several pounds and odd shillings. "Gone to lodge i' a very good house i' Finkle Street, where they'll be paying no less nor a pound a week for t'rooms. Don't tell me! I'll lay owt yon theer Jecholiah has a bit o' brass put by. What! She used to sell a sight o' eggs and a vast o' butter, Mestur Grice! And them owin' me ower nine pounds 'at I shall niver see! Such like i' lodgins at a pound a week! They owt to be i' t'poorhouse!"

Old Grice laughed and said nothing; it mattered nothing to him whether the Farnishes were lodged in rooms or in the wards of the workhouse, so long as Jeckie kept away from Savilestowe until all was safely settled about Albert. He exchanged more letters with John, the draper; John's replies yielded him infinite delight. As he sat alone of an evening, amusing himself with his cigars and his gin and water, he chuckled as he gloated over his own state-craft; once or twice, when he had made his drink rather stronger than usual, he was so impressed by his own cleverness that he assured himself solemnly that he had missed his true vocation, and ought to have been a Member of Parliament. He thought so again in a quite sober moment, when, at the end of three weeks, Albert returned, wearing lemon-coloured kid gloves, and spats over his shoes. There was a new atmosphere about Albert, and old George almost decided to take him into partnership there and then when he announced that he had become engaged to his cousin Lucilla, and that her father would give her two thousand pounds on the day of the wedding. Instead, he signalised his gratification by furnishing and decorating, regardless of cost, two rooms for the use of the expected bride.

CHAPTER V

THE SHAKESPEARE LINE

The Savilestowe blacksmith had been right when he said to George Grice that Jeckie Farnish had probably put money by. Jeckie had for some time foreseen the coming of an evil day, and for three years she had set aside a certain amount of the takings from her milk, butter, and eggs sales, and had lodged it safely in the Penny Bank at Sicaster in her own name. Her father knew nothing of this nest-egg; no one, indeed, except Rushie, knew that she had it; not even Rushie knew its precise amount. And when Jeckie turned away from watching George Grice's broad back disappear down the lane, and knew that her father's downfall was at last inevitable, she at once made up her mind what to do. She knew a widow woman in Sicaster who had a roomy house in one of the oldest thoroughfares, Finkle Street; to her she repaired on the day following the levying of the Clothford money-lender's execution, and bargained with her for the letting of three rooms. On the morning of the forced sale she routed Farnish and Rushie out of their beds as soon as the sun rose; before six o'clock all three, carrying their personal effects in bundles, were making their way across the fields towards Sicaster; by breakfast time they were settled in their lodgings. And within an hour Jeckie had found her father a job, and had told him that unless he stuck to it there would be neither bite nor sup for him at her expense. It was not a grand job, and Jeckie had come across it by accident—Collindale, the greengrocer and fruit merchant in the Market Place, with whom she had done business in the past, selling to him the produce of the Applecroft orchard in good years, happened to want an odd-job man about his shop, and offered a pound a week. Jeckie led her father to Collindale and handed him over, with a few clearly-expressed words to master and man; by noon Farnish was carrying potatoes to one and cauliflowers to another of the greengrocer's customers. Nor was Jeckie less arduous in finding work for her sister and herself. They were both good needlewomen, and she went round the town seeking employment in that direction, and got it. Before she went to her bed that first night in the hired lodgings, she was assured of a livelihood, and of no need to break into the small hoard in the Penny Bank.

Over the interminable stitching which went on in the living-room of this new abode, Jeckie brooded long and heavily over the defection of Albert Grice. She had believed that Albert would hasten up to Applecroft when he heard the bad news, and while her father and the man in possession drank up the last beer in the barrel, and Rushie and Doadie Bartle finished the mangling of the linen, she went out into the gloom of the falling night and listened for his footsteps coming up the lane. Hard enough though her nature was, it was unbelievable to her that the man she had promised to marry could leave her alone at this time of trouble. But Albert had never come, and next day, she heard that he had gone away for a holiday. She knew then what had happened—this was all part of old Grice's plans; old Grice meant that everything was to be broken off between her and his son. She registered a solemn vow when the full realisation came to her, and if George Grice had heard it he would probably have been inclined to take Stubley's advice and think a little before treating Jeckie so cavalierly. She would have her revenge on Grice!—never mind how long it took, nor of what nature it was, she would have it. And she was meditating on the beginnings and foundations of it when Bartle came to her, wanting advice as to his own course of proceeding.

"I reckon it's all over and done wi', as far as this here's concerned," he said, with a deprecating glance round the empty fold. "And I mun do summat for misen. Now, grocer Grice, he offered me a job yesterday—when he were drivin' down t'lane there, after he'd been here. Wants a man to look after his horses, and go round wi' his cart, 'liverin' t'groceries. Thirty shillin' a week. What mun I do about it?"

Jeckie's eyes lighted up.

"Take it, lad!" she answered, with unusual alacrity. "Take it! And while you're at it, keep your eyes and ears open, and learn all you can about t'business. It'll happen stand you in good stead some day. Take it, by all means."

"All reight," said Bartle. "I'll stan' by what you say, Jeckie. But—there's another matter. What?" he continued, almost shamefacedly. "What about—yoursens? I know it's a reight smash up, is this—what's going to be done? I'm never going to see you and Rushie i' a fix, you know. If it's any use, there's that bit o' money 'at you made me put i' t'bank—ye're welcome to it. What were you thinkin' o' doin' like?"

Jeckie took him into her confidence. Her plans were already laid, and she was not afraid. So Bartle went into Grice's service when Jeckie and Rushie started stitching in Sicaster, and thenceforward he turned up in Finkle Street every Sunday afternoon, to see how things were going on with his old employers. It was characteristic of him that he never came empty-handed—now it was a piece of boiling bacon that he brought as an offering; now a pound of tea; now a lump of cheese. And he also brought news of the village, and particularly of his new place. But for four Sundays in succession he had nothing to tell of Albert Grice but that he was away, still holidaying.

On the fifth Sunday, when Bartle came, laden with a fowl (bought, a bargain, from his village landlady) in one hand, and an enormous bunch of flowers (carefully picked to represent every variety of colour) in the other, Jeckie and her father were away, gone to a neighbouring village to see a relation who was ill, and Rushie was all alone. Bartle sat down in the easiest chair which the place afforded, spread his big hands over his Sunday waistcoat, and nodded solemnly at her.

"There's news at our place, Rushie, mi lass!" he said gravely. "I misdoubt how Jeckie'll tak' it when she comes to hear on't. About yon theer Albert."

"What about him?" demanded Rushie, whom Bartle had found lolling on the sofa, reading a penny novelette, and who still remained there, yawning. "Has he come back home?"

"Come back t'other day, lookin' like a duke," answered Bartle. "Yaller gloves on his hands, and a fancy walkin' stick, and things on his feet like t'squire wears. An' it's all out now i' Savilestowe—he's goin' to be wed, is Albert. T'owd chap's fair mad wi' glory about it."

"Who's he goin' to wed?" asked Rushie.

"A lass 'at's his cousin, wi' no end o' money," replied Bartle. "Owd George is tellin' t'tale all ower t'place. She's to hev two thasand pound, down on t'nail, t'day at they're wed, and there'll be more to come, later on. And Grice is hevin' a bedroom and a sittin'-room done up for 'em, in reight grand style—t'paperhangers starts on to-morrow, and there's to be a pianner, and I don't know what else. They're to be wed in a fortnight."

"She can have him!" said Rushie contemptuously. "He's nowt, is Albert Grice!—I never could think however our Jeckie could look at him."

"Well—but that's how it's to be," remarked Bartle. Then, with a solemn look, he added, twiddling his thumbs, "He's treated Jeckie very bad, has Albert."

Rushie said nothing. She gave Bartle his tea, and later went for a walk with him round the old town; in his Sunday suit of blue serge he was a fine-looking young fellow, and Rushie saw many other girls cast admiring looks at him. He had gone homewards when Jeckie and her father returned, and it was accordingly left to Rushie to break the news of Albert's defection to her sister.

Jeckie heard all of it without saying a word, or allowing a sign to show itself in her hard, handsome face. She went on with her

30

work in the usual fashion the next morning, and continued at it all the week, and when Bartle came again on the following Sunday, with more news of the preparation at Grice's, she still remained silent. But on the next Saturday she went out before breakfast to the nearest newsagent's shop and bought a copy of the Yorkshire Post of that morning. She opened it in the shop, and turned to the marriage announcements. When she had assured herself that Albert Grice had been duly married to his cousin Lucilla at Nottingham two days previously, she put the paper in her pocket, went back to Finkle Street, and ate an unusually hearty breakfast. She had made it a principle from the beginning of the new order of things to see that Farnish, Rushie, and herself never wanted good food in plenty—folk who work hard, in Jeckie's opinion, must live well, and her own country-bred appetite was still with her.

But she was going to do no work that Saturday morning. As soon as she and Rushie had breakfasted she went upstairs to her room and put on her best clothes. That done, she unlocked a tin box in which she kept certain private belongings and took from it the engagement-ring which Albert Grice had given her and a small packet of letters. These all went into a hand-bag with the Yorkshire Post; clutching it in her right hand, with an intensity which would have signified a good deal to any careful observer, she marched downstairs to her sister.

"Rushie," she said, "I shall be out for an hour or two—get on with those things for Mrs. Blenkinsop: you know we promised to let her have 'em to-day. Do as much as you can, there's a good lass—I'll set to as soon as ever I'm back. Never mind the dinner till we've finished."

Then she went out and along the big Market Place and into Ropergate, the street wherein the Sicaster solicitors, a keen and shrewd lot, congregated together, in company with auctioneers, accountants, and debt-collectors. There were at least a dozen firms of solicitors in that street, but Jeckie, though she had never employed legal help in her life, knew to which of them she was bound before ever she crossed the threshold of her lodgings. She was a steady reader of the local newspapers, especially of the police and county court news, and so had become aware that Palethorpe & Overthwaite were the men for her money. And into their office she walked, firm and resolute, as St. Sitha's clock struck ten, and demanded of a yawning clerk to see one or other of the principals.

When Jeckie was admitted into the inner regions she found herself in the presence of both partners. Palethorpe, a sharp, keen-faced fellow sat at one table, and Overthwaite, somewhat younger, but no less keen, at another; both recognised Jeckie as the handsome young woman sometimes seen in the town; both saw the look of determination in her eyes and about her lips.

"Well, Miss Farnish," said Palethorpe, who scented business. "What can we do for you, ma'am?"

He drew forward a chair, conveniently placed between his own and his partner's desk, and Jeckie, seating herself, immediately drew out from her hand-bag the various things which she had carefully placed in it.

"I dare say you gentlemen know well enough who I am," she said calmly. "Elder daughter of William Farnish, as was lately farming at Savilestowe. Father, he did badly this last year or two, and everybody knows he was sold up a few weeks since by a Clothford money-lender. But between you and me, Mr. Palethorpe and Mr. Overthwaite, I've a bit of money put by, and I brought him and my sister into lodgings here in Sicaster—I've got him a job, and made him stick to it. And me and my sister's got good work and plenty of it. I'm telling you this so that you'll know that aught that you like to charge me, you'll get—I'm not in the habit of owing money to anybody! And I want, not so much your advice as to give you orders to do something."

The two partners exchanged smileless glances. Here, at any rate, was a client who possessed courage and decision.

"Everybody in Savilestowe knows that for some time before my father was sold up I was engaged to be married to Albert Grice, only son of George Grice, the grocer," continued Jeckie. "It was all regularly arranged. We were to have been married next year, when Albert'll be twenty-five. Here's the engagement ring he gave me. I was with him when he bought it, here in Sicaster, at Mr Pilbrow's jeweller's shop; he paid four pound fifteen and nine for it, and they gave me half-a-dozen of electroplated spoons in with it as a sort of discount. Here's some letters; there's eight of 'em altogether, and I've numbered and marked 'em, that Albert wrote me from time to time; marriage is referred to in every one of 'em. There's no doubt whatever about our engagement; it was agreed to by his father and my father, and, as I said, everybody knew of it."

"To be sure!" said Overthwaite. "I've heard of it, Miss Farnish. Local gossip, you know. Small world, this!"

"Well," continued Jeckie, "all that went on up to the day that the bailiff came to our place. George Grice was there when he came; he went straight away home, and next day he sent Albert off to Nottingham, where they have relations. He kept him away until we were out of the village; he took good care that Albert never came near me nor wrote one single line to me. He got him engaged to his cousin at Nottingham, and now," she concluded, laying her

32

newspaper on Palethorpe's desk and pointing to the marriage announcements, "now you see, they're wed! Wed two days ago; there it is, in the paper."

"I saw it this morning," said Palethorpe. He looked inquisitively at his visitor. "And now," he added, "now, Miss Farnish, you want——"

"Now," answered Jeckie, in curiously quiet tones, "now I'll make Albert Grice and his father pay! You'll sue Albert for breach of promise of marriage, and he shall pay through the nose, too! I'll let George Grice see that no man's going to trifle with me; he shall have a lesson that'll last him his life. I want you to start on with it at once; don't lose a moment!"

"There was never any talk about breaking it off, I suppose?" asked Overthwaite. "I mean between you and Albert?"

"Talk!" exclaimed Jeckie. "How could there be talk? I've never even set eyes on him since the time I'm telling you about. George Grice took care of that!"

Palethorpe picked up the letters. In silence he read through them, noting how Jeckie had marked certain passages with a blue pencil, and as he finished each he passed it to his partner.

"Clear case!" he said when he had handed over the last. "No possible defence! He'll have to pay. Now, Miss Farnish, how much do you want in the way of damages? Have you thought it out?"

"As much as ever I can get," answered Jeckie, promptly. "Yes, I have thought it out. The damage to me's more nor what folk could think at first thoughts. George Grice is a very warm man. I've heard him say, myself, more than once, that he was the warmest man in Savilestowe, and that's saying a good deal, for both Mr. Stubley and Mr. Merritt are well-to-do men. And Albert is an only child: he'd ha' come in—he will come in!—for all his father's money. I reckon that if I'd married Albert Grice I should have been a very well-off woman. So the damages ought to be——"

"Substantial—substantial!" said Palethorpe. "Very substantial, indeed, Miss Farnish." He glanced at his partner, who was just laying aside the last of the letters. "It's well known that George Grice is a rich man," he remarked. "But, now, here's a question—is this son of his in partnership with him?"

Jeckie was ready with an answer to that.

"No, but he will be before a week's out," she said. "In fact, he may be now, for aught that I know. I've certain means of knowing what goes on at Grice's. George has promised to make Albert a partner as soon as he married. Well, now he is married, so it may have come off. He hadn't been a partner up to now."

"We'll soon find that out," said Palethorpe. "Now, then, Miss

Farnish, leave it to us. Don't say a word to anybody, not even to your father or sister. Just wait till we find out how things are about the partnership, and then we'll move. What you want is to make these people pay—what?"

Jeckie rose, and from her commanding height looked down on the two men, who, both insignificant in size, gazed up at her as if she had been an Amazon.

"Money's like heart's blood to George Grice!" she muttered. "I want to wring it out of him. He flung me away like an old clout! He shall see! Do what you like; do what you think best; but make him suffer! I haven't done with him yet." Then, without another word, she marched out of the office, and Palethorpe smiled to his partner.

"What's that line of Shakespeare's?" he said. "Um—'A woman moved is like a fountain troubled.' This one's pretty badly moved to vengeance, I think, eh?"

"Aye!" agreed Overthwaite. "But she isn't, as the quotation goes on, 'bereft of beauty.' Egad, what a face and figure! Albert Grice must be a doubly damned fool!"

CHAPTER VI

THE GLOVES OFF

The old grocer was not the man to do things by halves, and as soon as he found that Albert's engagement to his cousin Lucilla was an accomplished fact, duly approved by the young woman's father and to be determined by a speedy marriage, he made up his mind to put his son out of the mouse stage and make a man of him. Albert should come into full partnership, with a half-share in the business; he should also have a domicile of his own under the old roof. There were two big, accommodating rooms on the first floor of the house, which hitherto had been used as receptacles for lumber and rubbish. Grice had Bartle and a couple of boys to clear them of boxes and crates, and that done, handed them over to a painter and decorator from Sicaster, with full license to do his pleasure on them. The painter and decorator set his wits to work, and achieved a mighty bill; and when he had completed his labours he remarked sagely to old George that the rooms ought to be furnished

34

according-ly, with emphasis on the last syllable. George rose to the bait, and called in the best upholsterer available, with the result that when Albert and his bride came home they found themselves in possession of two brand-new suites of furniture, solid mahogany in the parlour, and rosewood in the bedroom, with carpets and hangings in due sympathy with the rest of the grandeur. The bride also found a new piano, and delighted her father-in-law by immediately sitting down to it and playing a few show pieces, with variations. In her new clothes and smart hat she went well with the rest of the room, and the next morning George took Albert into town and signed the deed of partnership.

"You're a very different man now, mi lad, fro' what ye were two months since, remember," observed George, as he and his son sat together in the "Red Lion" at Sicaster, taking a glass of refreshment before jogging home again. "You were naught but a paid man then; now you're a full partner i' George Grice & Son, grocers, wholesale and retail, and Italian warehousemen, dealers in hay, straw, and horse corn. An' you're a wed man, too, and wi' brass behind and before, and there's no young feller i' t'county has better prospects. Foller my example, Albert, and you'll cut up a good 'un i' t'end!"

Albert grinned weakly, and said that he'd do his best to look after number one, and George went home well satisfied. It seemed to him that having steered his ship safely past that perilous reef called Jecholiah Farnish he would now have plain and comfortable sailing. Instead of being saddled with a poverty-stricken daughter-in-law and her undesirable family, he had got his son a wife who had already brought him a couple of thousand pounds in ready money, and would have more when death laid hands on the Nottingham draper. So there was now nothing to do but attend to business during the day, look over the account books in the evening, and approach sleep by way of gin and water and the tinkle of Lucilla's piano.

"I were allus a man for doing things i' the right way," mused George that evening as he smoked his cigar and listened to his new daughter-in-law singing the latest music-hall songs, "and I done 'em again this time. Now, if I'd let yon lass o' Farnish's wed our Albert there'd ha' been nowt wi' her, and I should never ha' had Farnish his-self off t'doorstep. It 'ud ha' been five pound here, and five pound there. I should ha' had to keep all t'lot on 'em. An' if there is a curse i' this here vale o' tears, it's poor relations!"

It was no poor relation who was tinkling the new piano in the fine new parlour, nor a useless one, either, George thanked Heaven and himself. Mrs. Albert had already proved an acquisition. She was a capable housekeeper; she possessed a good deal of the family characteristic as regards money, and she could keep books and attend to letters. Moreover, she was no idler. Every morning, as soon as she had settled the household affairs for the day, she appeared in the shop and took up her position at the desk. This saved both George and Albert a good deal of clerical work, for the Grice trade, which was largely with the gentry and farmers of the district, involved a considerable amount of book-keeping. Now, George was painfully slow as a scribe, and Albert had no great genius for figures, though he was an expert at wrapping up parcels. The bride, therefore, was valuable as a help as well as advantageous as an ornament. And a certain gentleman who walked into the shop one afternoon, after leaving a smart cob outside in charge of a village lad who happened to be hanging about, looked at her with considerable interest, as if pretty bookkeepers were strange in that part of the country. Old Grice at that moment was busy down the yard, examining a cartload of goods with which Bartle was about to set off to a neighbouring hamlet: Albert was in the warehouse outside, superintending the opening of a cask of sugar. Mrs. Albert went forward; the caller greeted her with marked politeness.

"Mr. Albert Grice?" said the caller, with an interrogatory smile. "Is he in?"

"I can call him in a minute, sir," replied Mrs. Albert. "He's only just outside. Who shall I say?"

"If you'd be kind enough to ask him if he'd see Mr. Palethorpe of Sicaster, for a moment," answered the visitor. "He'll know who I am."

Mrs. Albert opened the door at the back of the shop, and ushered Palethorpe into the room in which Jeckie Farnish had found George Grice eating his cold beef. She passed out through another door into the yard, came back in a moment, saying that her husband would be there presently, and returned to the shop. And upon her heels came Albert, wiping his sugary hands on his apron and looking very much astonished.

"Good afternoon, Mr. Albert," said Palethorpe, in his pleasantest manner. "I called to see you on a little matter of business. I would have sent one of my clerks, but as the business is of a confidential sort I thought I'd just drive over myself. The fact of the case is I've got a writ for you—and there it is!"

Before Albert had comprehended matters, Palethorpe had put a folded, oblong piece of paper into his hand, and had nodded his head, as much as to imply that now, the writ having slipped into Albert's unresisting fingers, something had been effected which could never be undone.

"Thought it would be more considerate to serve you with it myself," he added, with another smile.

"I dare say you prefer that."

Albert looked from Palethorpe to the writ, and from the writ to Palethorpe. His face flushed and his jaw, a weak and purposeless one, dropped.

"What's it all about?" he asked, feebly. "I—I don't owe nobody aught, Mr. Palethorpe. A writ!—for me?"

"Suit of Jecholiah Farnish—breach of promise—damages claimed, two thousand pounds," answered Palethorpe, promptly. "That's what it is! Lord, bless me!—do you mean to say you haven't been expecting it!"

He laughed, half sneeringly, and suddenly broke his laughter short. George Grice had come in, softly, by the back door of the room, and had evidently heard the solicitor's announcement of the reason of his visit. Palethorpe composed his face, and made the grocer a polite bow. It was his policy, on all occasions, to do honour to money, and he knew George to be a well-to-do man.

"Good afternoon, Mr. Grice!" he said. "Fine day, isn't it—splendid weather for——" Grice cut him short with a scowl.

"What did I hear you say?" he demanded, angrily. "Summat about yon Farnish woman, and breach o' promise, and damages? What d'yer mean?"

"Just about what you've said," retorted Palethorpe. "I've served your son with a writ on Miss Farnish's behalf—you'd better read it together."

Grice glanced nervously at the curtained door which led into the shop. Then he beckoned Palethorpe and Albert to follow him, and led them out of the room and across a passage to a small apartment at the rear of the house, a dismal nook in which his account books and papers of the last thirty years had been stored. He carefully closed the door and turned on the solicitor.

"Do you mean to tell me 'at yon there hussy has had the impudence to start proceedin's for breach o' promise again my son?" he said. "I never knew such boldness or brazenness i' my born days! Go your ways back, young man, and tell her 'at sent you 'at she'll get nowt out o' me!"

Palethorpe laughed—something in his laugh made the grocer look at him. And he saw decision and confidence in Palethorpe's face, and suddenly realised that here was trouble which he had never anticipated.

"Nonsense, Mr. Grice!" exclaimed Palethorpe. "I'm surprised at you!—such a keen and sharp man of business as you're known to be. We want nothing out of you—we want what we do want out of your son!"

"He has nowt!" growled the grocer. "He's nowt but what I——"

"Nonsense again, Mr. Grice," interrupted Palethorpe. "He's your partner, with a half-share in the business, as you've announced to a good many of your neighbours and cronies during the last week or so, and he's also got two thousand pounds with his wife. Come, now, what's the good of pretending? Your son's treated my client very badly, very badly indeed, and he'll have to pay. That's flat!"

Grice suddenly stretched out a hand towards his son.

"Gim'me that paper!" he said.

Albert handed over the writ and his father put on a pair of spectacles and carefully read it through from beginning to end. Then he flung it on the desk at which the three men were standing.

"It's nowt but what they call blackmail!" he growled. "I'll none deny 'at there were an arrangement between my son and Farnish's lass. But it were this here—Farnish were to give five hundred pounds wi' her. Now, Farnish went brok'—he had no five hundred pound, nor five hundred pence! So, of course, t'arrangement fell through. That's where it is."

Palethorpe laughed again—and old Grice feared that laugh more than the other.

"I'm more surprised than before, Mr. Grice," said Palethorpe. "My client has nothing whatever to do with any arrangement—if there was any—between you and her father. Her affair is with your son Mr. Albert Grice. He asked her to marry him—she consented. He gave her an engagement ring—it was well known all round the neighbourhood that they were to marry. He wrote her letters, in which marriage is mentioned——"

Grice turned on his son in a sudden paroxysm of fury.

"Ye gre't damned softhead!" he burst out. "Ye don't mean to say 'at you were fool enough to write letters! Letters!"

"I wrote some," replied Albert sullenly. "Now and then, when I was away, like. It's t'usual thing when you're engaged to a young woman."

"Quite the usual thing—when you're engaged to a young woman," said Palethorpe, with a quiet sneer. "And we have the letters—all of 'em. And the engagement ring, too. Mr. Grice, it's no good blustering. This is as clear a case as ever I heard of, and your son'll have to pay. It's no concern of mine whether you take my advice or not, but if you do take it, you'll come to terms with my client. If this case goes before a judge and jury—and it certainly will, if you don't settle it in the meantime—you won't have a leg to stand on, and Miss Farnish will get heavy damages—heavy!—and you'll

38

have all the costs. And between you and me, Mr. Grice, you'll not come out of the matter with very clean hands yourself. We know quite well, for you're a bit talkative, you know—how you engineered the breaking-off of this engagement and contrived the marriage of your son to his cousin, and we shall put you in the witness-box, and ask you some very unpleasant questions. And you're a churchwarden, eh?" concluded Palethorpe, as he turned to the door. "Come now—you know my client's been abominably treated by you and your son—you'd better do the proper thing, and compensate her handsomely."

Grice had become scarlet with anger during the solicitor's last words, and now he picked up the writ and thrust it into his pocket.

"I'll say nowt no more to you!" he exclaimed. "I'll see my lawyer in t'morning, and hear what he's gotten to say to such a piece o' impidence!"

"That's the first sensible thing I've heard you say," remarked Palethorpe. "See him by all means—and he'll say to you just what I've said. You'll see!"

The calm confidence of Palethorpe's tone, and the nonchalant way in which he left father and son, cost Grice a sleepless night. He lay turning in his bed, alternately cursing Jeckie for her insolence and Albert for his foolishness in writing those letters. He had sufficient knowledge of the world to know that Palethorpe was probably right—yet it had never once occurred to him that a country lass could have sufficient sense to invoke the law.

"She's too damned clever i' all ways is that there Jecholiah!" he groaned. "Very like I should ha' done better if I'd kept in wi' her, and let her wed our Albert. It's like to cost a pretty penny afore I've done wi' it if I have to pay her an' all. There were a hundred pounds for Albert's trip to Nottingham and another hundred for t'weddin' and t'honeymoon, and I laid out a good three hundred i' doin' up them rooms and buyin' t'pianner, and now then, there's this here! An' I'd rayther go and fling my brass into t'sea nor have it go into t'hands o' that there Jezebel! I wish I'd never ta'en our Albert into partnership, nor said owt about his wife's two thousand pound— then, when this came on he could ha' pleaded 'at he wor nowt but a paid man, and she'd ha' got next to nowt i' t'way o' damages. Damages!—to that there!—it's enough to mak' me shed tears o' blood!"

Grice was with his solicitor, Mr. Camberley, in Sicaster, by ten o'clock next morning. He had left Albert at home, judging him to be worse than an encumbrance in matters of this sort. He himself had sufficient acumen to keep nothing back from his man of law; he told him all about the ring and the letters, and his face grew heavier as Mr. Camberley's face grew longer.

"You'll have to settle, Grice," said the solicitor, an oldish, experienced man. "It's precisely as Palethorpe said—you haven't a leg to stand on! You know, I'm a bit surprised at you; you might have foreseen this."

Grice pulled out a big bandanna handkerchief, and mopped his high forehead.

"It never crossed my mind 'at she'd be for owt o' this sort!" he groaned. "I never thowt 'at she'd have as much sense as all that. She's gotten a spice o' t'devil in her!—that's where it is. And you think it's no use fightin' t'case?"

"Not a scrap of use!" said the lawyer. "Stop here while I go round to Palethorpe's and see for myself how things are. They'll show me those letters."

Grice sat grunting and muttering in Camberley's office until Camberley returned. One glance at the solicitor's face showed him that there was no hope.

"Well?" he asked anxiously as Camberley sat down to his desk. "Well, now?"

"It's just as I expected," said Camberley. "Of course they've a perfectly good case; they couldn't have a better. I've seen your son's letters. Excellent evidence—for the plaintiff! Marriage is mentioned in every one of them—when it was to be, what arrangements were to be made afterwards, and so on. There's no use beating about the bush, Grice; you haven't a chance!"

"Then, there's naught for it but payin'?" said the grocer with a deep sigh. "No way o' gettin' out of it?"

"There's no way of getting out of it," answered Camberley. "Nobody and nothing can get you out of it. Here's a perfectly blameless, well-behaved, hard-working young woman, whom you had willingly accepted as your son's future wife, suddenly flung off like an old glove, for no cause whatever! What do you suppose a jury would say to that? You'll have to settle, Grice—and I've done my best for you. They'll take fifteen hundred pounds and their costs."

Grice's big face turned white, and the sweat burst out on his forehead and rolled down his cheeks, and over the tight lip and into his beard.

"It's either that, or the case'll go on to trial," said Camberley. "My own opinion," he added, dryly, "is that if it goes to trial, she'd get two thousand. You'd far better write out a cheque and have done with it. It's your own fault, you know."

Grice pulled out his cheque-book and wrote slowly at Camberley's dictation. When he had attached his signature he handed over the cheque with trembling fingers, and, without another word, went out, climbed heavily into his trap, and drove home. He maintained a strange and curious silence all the rest of that day, and that evening the strains of the new piano failed to charm him. More than once his cigar went out unnoticed; once or twice he shed tears into his gin-and-water.

CHAPTER VII

THE GOLDEN TEAPOT

While George Grice was driving out of Sicaster, groaning and grumbling at his ill-luck, Jeckie Farnish, in the Finkle Street lodging, was contemplating a pile of linen which had just been sent in to her for stitching. Rushie contemplated it, too, and made a face at it.

"Looks as if we should never get through it!" she said mournfully, "And it's such dull work, sewing all day long."

"Don't you quarrel with your bread-and-butter, miss!" answered Jeckie, with ready sharpness. "You'd ought to be thankful we've got work to do rather than grumble at it."

"There's other work nor this that a body can do," retorted Rushie. "And a deal pleasanter!"

"Aye, and what, miss, I should like to know?" demanded Jeckie as she thrust a length of linen into her sister's hands. "What is there that you could do, pray?"

"Herbert Binks says Mr. Fryer wants one or two young women in his shop," answered Rushie, diffidently. "I could try for that if I was only let. And it's far more respectable learning the drapery and millinery than sewing sheets and things all day long."

"Is it?" said Jeckie. "Well, I know naught about respectability, and I do know 'at Mr. Fryer 'ud want a nice bit o' money paying to him if he took you as apprentice. And you mind what you're doing with that Herbert Binks! I've no opinion o' these town fellers; he'll be turning your head with soft talk. You be thankful 'at we've got work to do that keeps us out o' the workhouse. Where should we all ha' been now, I should like to know, if it hadn't been for me?"

Then she sat down in her usual place by the window, and

began to sew as if for dear life, while Rushie, taking refuge in poutings and silence, set to work in languid fashion. Already Jeckie was having trouble with her and with Farnish. The younger sister openly revolted against the interminable sewing. Farnish, whose pocket-money had been fixed at five shillings, found eightpence-halfpenny a day all too little for his beer, and sulked every night when he came home from the greengrocer's. Moreover, Jeckie found it impossible to keep Rushie to heel; she could not always be watching her, and as soon as her back was turned of an evening Rushie was out and away about the town, always with some shop-boy or other in attendance. It was not easy work to manage her or Farnish, and Jeckie foresaw a day in which both would strike. Some folk, she knew, would have said let them strike and see to themselves, but Jeckie was one of those unfortunate mortals who are cursed with an exaggerated sense of personal responsibility, and she worried much more about her father and sister than about herself.

"You stick to what work we've got for a bit, Rushie, my lass!" she said presently, in mollifying tones. "I know well enough it's trying, but there'll very likely be something better to do before long; you never know what's going to turn up!"

Something was about to turn up at that moment, though Jeckie was unconscious of it. One of Palethorpe & Overthwaite's office boys came whistling along the street, and, catching sight of Jeckie at the open window, paused and grinned; Jeckie eyed him over with a sudden feeling of anticipation.

"Are you wanting me?" she demanded.

"Mr. Palethorpe's compliments, and would you mind stepping round to our office, miss?" said the lad. "They want to see you, particular."

"I'll be there in a few minutes," answered Jeckie. She laid aside her sewing when the lad had turned on his heel, and looked at her sister. "Get on with your work while I'm out, Rushie," she said. "I'll be as quick as I can—and, maybe, I'll have some news for you when I come back."

Then she hurried into her best garments and hastened round to Palethorpe & Overthwaite's, wondering all the way what they wanted. The partners smiled at her as she was shown in, and Overthwaite manifested an extra politeness in handing her a chair.

"Well, Miss Farnish!" said Palethorpe, almost jocularly. "We've good news for you. The enemy's capitulated! Never made a bit of a fight, either. Clean beaten!"

Jeckie looked from one man to the other with surprised questioning eyes.

"He's going to pay?" she suggested.

42

Palethorpe pointed to a cheque which lay face downwards on his desk.

"He's paid!" he answered. "Half an hour ago. There's the cheque. I'll tell you all about it in a few words. I served Albert with the writ myself yesterday afternoon. Albert had nothing to say; old George blustered, and said he'd see his solicitor. I said he could do nothing better. He came in first thing this morning, and saw Camberley; Camberley came on to see us. And, of course, he knew they hadn't a leg to stand on, so, as you'd given us full permission to settle on your behalf, he came to terms. And—there's the money!"

Jeckie caught her breath, and looked at the cheque with a glance keen enough, as Overthwaite afterwards remarked, to go through it and the wood beneath it. It was with an obvious effort that she got out two words.

"How much?"

"Fifteen hundred pounds—and our costs," answered Palethorpe. "I hope you're satisfied?"

Jeckie gave him a queer, shrewd, enigmatical look.

"Aye, I'm satisfied!" she said in a low voice. "I should ha' made Albert Grice a rare good wife and George Grice a saving daughter-in-law, but—yes, I'm satisfied. And—I know well enough what I shall do with it—as George Grice'll find out! So—I'm worth fifteen hundred pound? That's one thousand five hundred! Very well! And—I'm much obliged to you."

Palethorpe turned to his partner.

"Write out a cheque for Miss Farnish for one thousand five hundred pounds," he said. "And she'll give us a receipt. Now Miss Farnish," he went on, as Overthwaite produced a cheque-book, "You'll want to bank this money, no doubt? If you like, I'll introduce you to the Old Bank."

"Much obliged to you," answered Jeckie. "I have some money of my own in the Penny Bank, but of course, it's naught much. Yes, I'll go to the Old Bank, if you please, Mr. Palethorpe. And—don't I owe you something?"

"Nothing!" answered Palethorpe, with a smile. "We made Grice pay your costs—every penny."

"I hope you charged him plenty," said Jeckie.

Palethorpe laughed, and presently handing her the cheque, took her off to the Old Bank and introduced her to its manager. Half an hour later, Jeckie, with a virgin cheque-book in her hand, burst in upon Rushie.

"There now, Rushie!" she said, "didn't I tell you there'd happen be better times i' store for us. You can drop that sewing—we've done with it. We'll hand it over to Mrs. Thompson; she'll finish it and be glad o' the job an' all. But—we've done wi' that."

Rushie dropped her needle into the folds of the linen and stared.

"Whatever's happened?" she demanded. "You're all red, like!"

"Never you mind if I'm blue or green," said Jeckie. "I've made them Grices pay!—I never told you, but I put t'lawyers on to Albert for breach of promise. And of course there was no defence, and he's had to pay, or old George has paid for him, and I've got the money, and it's safe in the bank!"

"How much?" asked Rushie eagerly. "A lot?"

"No, I shan't tell!" replied Jeckie, with a firm shake of her head. "Then you won't know when father asks, for I certainly shan't tell him. But now, Rushie, you listen here. Take all this stuff to Mrs. Thompson and ask her if she'll finish it off. And see to your own and father's dinner—I shan't be in for dinner; I've important business to see to, and I shall be out till evening. Now don't go trailing about the town, Rushie—be a good girl, and you'll hear news when I come home."

"Then we aren't going to do any more sewing?" asked Rushie.

"We're going to do no more sewing!" said Jeckie. "Not one stitch! We're going to do something a deal better. You'll see, if you behave yourself—and it'll be a deal better, too, nor going 'prentice to Mr. Fryer."

She gave her sister a decisive nod as she left the house and the colour was still bright in her cheeks as she marched off in the direction of a path across the fields which lay between Sicaster and Savilestowe. It was but a very short time since she and Rushie and Farnish had come along that path, carrying their entire belongings in bundles; now, she reflected, she was retracing her steps with the proud consciousness that she had fifteen hundred pounds of solid money in the bank—the knowledge was all the sweeter to her because it had been wrung out of old George Grice.

"Aye!" she muttered, as she walked swiftly along over the quiet meadows and through the growing cornfields. "And now 'at I've got a start, I'll let George Grice see 'at he's not the only one 'at can play at the game o' makin' money! He's a hard and a healthy old feller, and he'll live a good while yet, and I'd let him see 'at I can make money as cleverly as he's done—aye, and at his expense, too! I'll make him and Albert rue the day 'at they cast me aside—let 'em see if I don't!"

The path across the fields led Jeckie out close by Applecroft, but it was indicative of her mood that she never once turned her head aside to glance at the old place. She marched straight down the lane, crossed the churchyard, and presently turned into Stubley's trim garden. It was to see Stubley that she had come to Savilestowe.

44

Stubley, who had just been round his land, was entering his house when Jeckie came up. He led her inside, and, finding she would drink nothing stronger brought out a bottle of home-made wine; he himself turned to a jug of ale which stood ready on the sideboard.

"And what brings ye here, mi lass?" he asked, eyeing her inquisitively as he sat down in his big elbow chair. "Ye're lookin' uncommon well."

"Mr. Stubley," answered Jeckie, "I've come to see you. I've something to tell you, for you were always a good friend to me. You knew that I was going to marry Albert Grice, and that him and his father threw me away when my father came smash. Well, I've made 'em pay! Old George has paid fifteen hundred pound—and I've got it, all safe, in the bank."

Stubley's face lighted up with undisguised admiration, and he brought his big hand down on his knee with a hearty smack.

"Good lass!" he exclaimed. "Good lass! That's the ticket! An' right an' all—they tret you very bad did them two! Good, that 'ud make old George grunt and grumble! But fifteen hundred pound—that's a sight o' money, mi gel—mind you take care on it."

"Trust me!" answered Jeckie, with a sharp look, "I know the value of money as well as anybody. But now, Mr. Stubley, do you know what I'm going to do with that fifteen hundred pound?"

"Nay, sure-ly!" said the farmer. "How should I know, mi lass?"

"Then, I'll tell you," replied Jeckie. She leaned forward across the table, looking earnestly into Stubley's shrewd eyes. "This!" she said. "I'm going to start a grocery business here in Savilestowe—in opposition to Grice and Son! There!"

Stubley started as if somebody had suddenly trod on a corn. He stared at his visitor, rubbed his chin, and shook his head.

"You're a bold 'un!" he said in accents which were not without admiration. "And a clever 'un, an' all! Aye, there's summat in that notion, mi lass; old George has had his own way i' this neighbourhood i' that line too long, and t'place 'ud be all t'better for a bit o' competition. But—what do ye know o' t'trade?"

"I know how to buy and sell with anybody," asserted Jeckie. "An' I'm that quick at picking things up 'at I shall know all there is to be known before I start. My mind's made up, Mr. Stubley. I've reckoned and figured things. George Grice isn't popular here, as you know; there's lots of folks'll give their custom to me. And I'll warrant you I'll have all t'poor folks away from him as soon as ever I open my doors! He's been hard on them, and his prices is shameful, and he doesn't lay himself out to keep what they want; as it is, most on 'em have to go to Sicaster for their stuff. Now, I'll capture all t'lot of

45

'em, here and in this district; I know what they want, and what they can pay, and I'll provide accordingly. An' I'll cut George Grice's prices wherever I can; I know what I'm about! An' I'm sure and certain that there's lots o' the better sort'll give me their trade; you would yourself, now, Mr. Stubley, wouldn't you?"

"Aye, I think I can say I should, mi lass!" asserted the farmer. "I'm none bound to no George Grice; he's a hard, grasping old feller, and there's no love lost between me and him. But you know ye'd want a likely shop, and——"

"That's just what I've come about," interrupted Jeckie. "I want you to let me that empty house that old Mrs. Mapplebeck had; I know it's yours, and I know what she paid you for it. Those two bottom front rooms'll make a splendid shop, and I'd have 'em fitted up at once. Let it to me, Mr. Stubley, and I'll pay you the first year's rent in advance, just now."

Stubley suddenly smote his knee again, and burst into laughter.

"Good; it's right opposite old George's!" he chuckled. "He'd have t'opposition shop straight before his eyes, right i' front of his nose! They talk about poetic justice, what?—now that would be it, wi' a vengeance. Gow!—I can see t'old feller's face! Ye're a bold 'un, Jeckie, mi lass, ye're a bold 'un!"

"Let me the house!" said Jeckie. "It's just because it's in front of Grice's that I do want it. Don't you see, Mr. Stubley, that one o' my best chances is to be right before his very door? There's many that set out to go to him 'ud turn into me when they saw it was better worth their while."

Stubley chuckled again at his visitor's eagerness, and suddenly he pulled up his chair to the table and became serious.

"Now, then, let's go into matters," he said, gravely. "Ye're a smart lass, you know, Jeckie, but it's a serious thing starting to fight an old-established firm like Grice and Son. Let's hear a bit more about what you propose, like."

Jeckie wished for nothing better. She talked, and explained, and outlined her schemes, and pointed out to the farmer, himself a keen man of business, where Grice & Son were hopelessly out of date and where she could hope to draw a considerable amount of trade away from them. She also showed him that she was thoroughly conversant with certain customs of the trade which she now proposed to take up, and that she had already made herself acquainted with the methods of purchase from wholesale grocers and manufacturers. Stubley was struck by her knowledge.

"You've been meditating this, mi lass?" he said. "You've been preparing for it!"

"Ever since I knew there was a chance of getting money out o' George Grice, I have!" admitted Jeckie. "As soon as ever Palethorpe and Overthwaite told me 'at I'd a good case, and that Albert 'ud have to pay, I determined what I'd do with the money even if it wasn't as much as it's turned out to be. And I shall do well, Mr. Stubley, you'll see!"

Stubley let her the house she wanted, and she paid him a year's rent in advance, and went off, triumphant, to the village carpenter, and, having sworn him to secrecy, told him her plans and gave him orders for the fitting up of the two big ground-floor rooms. He, too, got a cheque on account, and promised to go to work at once and to tell nobody who it was that he was working for. But he was wise enough to know that such work as his could not be done in a corner and that there would be infinite curiosity in the shop across the way.

"Ye'll none get that secret kept long, ye know, miss," he said. "When t'Grices sees 'at I'm fittin' yon place up as a shop they'll want to know what it's all about like. It'll have to come out i'now."

"Not till I let it!" said Jeckie. "You go on as fast as you can with your work, and wait till I say the word."

During the next month the carpenter and his men were busy day by day with counters and shelving, and George Grice, crossing the road to them more than once got nothing but evasive replies in answer to his inquisitiveness. But one day, chancing to look across at the mysterious building, he saw the carpenter coming down a ladder from the moulding over the front door; he had just fixed there a great golden teapot. The strong sunlight fell full on its grandeur, and the village street was suddenly bathed in glory.

CHAPTER VIII

THE BATTLE BEGINS

Up to that moment George Grice had fondly and firmly believed that he knew the secret of the house opposite—he was so certain in his assumption, indeed, that he had taken no particular trouble to get at the real truth about it. For some time there had been a travelling draper, a Scotsman, coming into those parts, and doing a considerable amount of trade; this man had often remarked to the grocer that he had a rare good mind to set up a shop in Savilestowe, and make it the headquarters of a further development. He had not been seen in the neighbourhood since early spring, but George, who prided himself on his deductive qualities, was sure that he was behind all the preparations which were going on over the way, and said so, with a knowing chuckle, to Albert.

"They're close, is them Scotch fellers!" he remarked, as he and his son stood at their shop door one afternoon, watching certain material being carried into the opposite house. "I see how it is—he's doing it all on the quiet—made t'carpenter keep t'secret till all's ready for opening. Then he'll be appearin' on t'scene wi' a cargo o' goods. An' I shall hev no objection, Albert, mi lad—owt 'at keeps trade i' t'village 'll bring trade to us, as long as it doesn't trespass on our line."

Once or twice George Grice endeavoured to sound Stubley, as owner of the house, on the subject of the mystery. Stubley took pleasure in heightening it, and winked knowingly at his questioner.

"Aye, ye'll be seeing summat afore long!" said Stubley. "We'm not always going to be asleep here i' Savilestowe. This is what they call a progressive age, mi lad, and some of you old fossils want wakenin' up a bit. We shall be havin' all sorts o' things i' now. You'll have your eyes opened, Grice. Keep a look out on t'windows opposite—ye'll be seeing summat in 'em at'll make you think!"

"Drapery goods, no doubt," suggested Grice. "An' ready-made clothin'. Happen I can see a bit already."

"I'm sayin' nowt," retorted Stubley. "Ye'll see summat—i' time."

But when George Grice saw the golden teapot elevated above the front door, he experienced very much the same feeling which fills the breast of a mariner, who, having sailed long in fog and mist, sees them lift, and finds before him a rocky and perilous coast. Just as a pestle and mortar denote the presence of a chemist, so a teapot would seem to indicate the presence of a dealer in tea—and in like commodities. And it was in something of a cold sweat, induced by anticipation, that he tucked up the corner of his apron and sallied across the street to find out, once and for all, what that glaring object meant.

"Now, mi lad!" he began, coming across the carpenter at the threshold of the renovated house, "What's t'meanin' o' that thing ye've just fixed up? It 'ud seem to be a imitation of a teapot, if it owt is owt. What's it mean, like? What's this here shop going to be?"

The carpenter, a quiet, meditative man, not without a sense of humour, had received his instructions from Jeckie the night

48

before—at noon that day he was to place the golden teapot in position, affix a sign beneath it, and complete the bold announcement by draping the Union Jack over both. So there was no longer any need for secrecy, and with a jerk of his thumb he motioned Grice within one of the newly-fitted rooms, and pointed to an oblong object which rested, covered with coarse sacking, on the counter.

"Mean, eh?" he said, with a laugh. "Why, it means, Mr. Grice, 'at you're going to hev a bit o' competition, like! They say 'at it's a good thing for t'community, is competition, so yer mo'nt grummle. But if you want t'exact meanin'—why, ye can look at this here, if ye like. It'll be up ower t'door in a few o' minutes, for all t'place to see, but I'll gi' yer a private view wi' pleasure—very neat and tasty it is. I'm sure ye'll admit."

With that the carpenter stripped off the sacking from the oblong object and revealed a signboard, the background whereof was of a light apple-green, the lettering in brilliant gold. And Grice took in that lettering in one glance, and stepped back in sickened amazement. Yet there was only one word on the sign, only a name—but the name was "Farnish."

"Nice bit o' sign-writin', that, Mr. Grice?" said the carpenter, maliciously. "Done at Clothford, was that theer—so were t'golden teapot. She'll ha' laid a nice penny out on them two, will Miss Farnish."

Grice, who was already purple with rage, found his tongue.

"D'ye mean to tell me 'at yon woman's going to start a grocery business reight i' front o' my very door!" he vociferated. "Her! Going to——"

"Aye, and why not, Grice?" said a hard and dry voice behind him. "D'ye think 'at ye've gotten a monopoly o' trade i' t'place, or i' t'district, either? Gow, I think ye'll find yer mistaken, mi lad!"

Grice turned angrily, to find Stubley standing amongst the shavings on the floor of the shop. The farmer nodded defiantly as he met the grocer's irate look.

"I told you yer were wrong, Grice, when you turned yon lass off!" he said. "I told you to count twenty afore you did owt. Ye wouldn't—and now she's goin' to make you smart for it. And—it must be a very nice and pleasant reflection for you!—ye've provided her wi' t'sinews o' war! That there fifteen hundred pound 'at she made you fork out's comin' in very useful to t'enemy—what!"

The deep red flush which had overspread Grice's big face and thick neck died out, and he became white as his immaculate apron. He gave Stubley a glare of venomous hatred.

"So you've been at t'back o' this?" he exclaimed. "It's you 'at's

49

backed her up? What reight have you to come interferin' wi' a honest man's trade 'at he's ta'en all these years to build up? Ye're a bad 'un Stubley!"

"Nowt no worse nor you, ye fat owd mork!" retorted Stubley, who had waited a long time to pay off certain old scores. "If there's been owt bad o' late i' this place, it's been your treatment o' yon lass!—and I hope she'll make yer suffer for it. Ye'll ha' t'pleasure o' seein' trade come into this door 'at used to come into yours, Mr. Grice. That'll touch you up, I know!—that'll get home to t'sore place."

Grice made another effort to speak, but before words reached his lips his mood changed, and he turned on his heel and left the house. He went straight across the street, through the shop, and into his private parlour. He had a bottle of brandy in his cupboard, and he took it out and helped himself to a strong dose with a shaking hand. The brandy steadied him for the moment, but his rage was still there, and had to be vented on somebody, and presently he opened the door into the shop and called his son. Albert came in and stared at the brandy bottle.

"Is aught amiss?" asked Albert. "You're that white."

George fixed his small eyes on his son's expressionless face.

"Do you know what that shop is across t'road, and who's going to open it?" he demanded.

"Me?—no!" answered Albert. "What is it—and who is?"

"Then I'll tell yer!" said George in low concentrated tones. "It's a grocer's shop, and it's yon there she-devil's, Jecholiah Farnish. She going to run it i' opposition to me, 'at's been here all these years! An' it's wi' my money 'at it's bein' started—mind you that! Mi money, 'at I've tewed and scratted for all mi life—my fifteen hundred pound, 'at I hed to pay 'cause you were such a damned fool as to gi' that there ring to her and write her them letters! It's all your fault, ye poor soft thing—if yer'd never given her t'ring nor written them letters, I would ha' snapped mi fingers at her! But yer did—and there's t'result!"

He waved a hand, with an almost imperial gesture, in the direction of the offending shop across the way, and looked at his son with eyes full of angry contempt.

"There's t'result!" he repeated. "A shop reight before wer very noses 'at's bound to do us damage—and all owin' to your foolishness!"

Albert put a hand to his mouth and coughed. There was something in that cough that made George start and look more narrowly at his son. And he suddenly realised that Albert was going to show fight.

50

"I'll tell you what it is!" said Albert, with the desperate courage of a weak nature. "I'm goin' to have no more o' that sort o' talk. You seem to think I'm naught but a mouse, but I'll show you I'm as good a man as what you are. You forget 'at I've half o' this business—it's mine, signed and sealed, and naught can do away wi' that—and me and Lucilla's got her two thousand pounds safe i' t'bank and untouched—we're none without brass, and I can claim to have t'partnership wound up any time, and take my lawful share and go elsewhere, and so I will, if there's any more talk. I did no more nor what any other feller 'ud ha' done when I gave that ring and wrote them letters—and I'm none bound to stop i' Savilestowe, neither. Me an' Lucilla——"

The door from the shop opened and Lucilla came in—and George saw at once what had happened. Between his parlour and the shop there was a hatchment in the wall, fitted with a small window; hastily glancing round he saw that the window was open; Lucilla, accordingly, her cashier's desk being close to the hatchment, had heard all that father and son had said. And there were danger signals in her cheeks as she turned on the old grocer.

"No, we're not bound to stop in Savilestowe!" she exclaimed angrily and pertly. "And stop we shan't if you're going to treat Albert as you do. You've never been right to him since you paid that money to that woman! And it's all your fault—you should have paid her something when you first broke it off; she'd ha' been glad to take five hundred pound then. And, as Albert says, we've got my two thousand pounds, and his share in this business, and I'll not have him sat on, neither by you nor anybody, so there! You stand up to him, Albert. We've had enough of black looks this last month—it's not our fault if he paid that woman fifteen hundred pounds!"

Grice looked in amazement at his muttering son and the sharp-tongued bride—and in that moment learned a good deal that he had never known before.

"An' it were for you 'at I laid out all that brass in furniture, and bowt a bran' new pianner!" he said reproachfully. "Well!—there's neither gratitude nor nowt left i' this world!"

"You leave Albert alone!" retorted the bride, sullenly. "We'll have no more of it." She drew Albert back into the shop, and George, peeping through the window of the hatchment saw them standing together in a corner, talking in whispers. Lucilla wore a determined air, and Albert nodded in response to all she said— clearly, they were plotting something. George drew back and picked up his glass—here, indeed, was a fine situation, opposition across the street, and rebellion in his own house! And the recollection of a certain look in his daughter-in-law's eyes frightened him—he had suddenly seen what she was capable of.

"Nowt but trouble—nowt but trouble!" he muttered. "I should ha' done better if I'd let our Albert stick to Jecholiah Farnish! But—it's done!"

That day the Grice household became divided. George dined alone in his parlour behind the shop, and the bride and bridegroom in their quarters upstairs. Father and son only spoke to each other on matters of business during the day, and when evening came Mr. and Mrs. Albert went off to the theatre at Sicaster, and left George to his reflections. They were not pleasant. In his joy at getting rid of Jeckie Farnish and at providing Albert with a moneyed bride he had been over-generous in the matter of the partnership, and had presented his son with a half-share in the business as it stood. And he knew that Albert's was no vain threat. Albert, if he liked, could have the partnership dissolved at any time, and could insist on having his moiety paid out to him. Now, supposing that Lucilla put her husband up to that? Terrible, terrible trouble!—and there was that she-devil, Jeckie, about to appear on the scene.

Jeckie was the first person George Grice saw when he drew up his blind the following morning. She was at her shop-door, very energetic and businesslike, superintending the unloading of two great wagon-loads of goods. The old grocer turned sick with fury when he saw from the signs on the sides of the wagons that they were from the best wholesale grocers in Clothford. All that day and all the rest of the week other wagons and carts arrived. His practised eye saw that the new shop was going to be as well equipped, if not better, than his own. And as he noted these things and realised that his carefully built-up business was in danger, a deep groan burst from his lips, ever and anon, and it invariably ended up with the bitter exclamation:

"All bein' done wi' mi money!—all bein' done with mi money! I've found t'munitions o' battle, and they're bein' used agen me!"

Grice always paid his employees at noon on Saturday. On the Saturday of this eventful week when he went out into the stable-yard and handed Bartle thirty shillings, Bartle quietly handed it back.

"What's that for?" demanded George, suddenly suspecting the truth. "What d'yer mean?"

"'Stead of a week's notice," answered Bartle. "I'm none comin' o' Monday mornin'."

"Ye're goin' across t'road!" exclaimed George, with an angry sneer. "Goin' back to t'owd lot, what?"

"Aye!" answered Bartle. "Allus meant to, mister, as soon as I

52

knew. Ye'll have no difficulty about gettin' a man i'stead o' me; there's two or three young fellers i' t'village 'at'll take it on. But I mun go."

"All reight, mi lad!" said George. "An' I wonder how long it'll last, ower yonder! What does she know about t'grocerin' business?"

"Why, I understand 'at ye didn't nowt about it yersen when you started," retorted Bartle, who was well versed in village gossip, and knew that George had begun life as a market gardener. "An' if there's anybody 'at has a headpiece i' these parts I reckon it's Jeckie. I'm for her, anyway."

This was another bitter piece of bread for Grice to swallow, for he knew that Bartle had picked up a lot of valuable information while in his employ and would infallibly make use of it.

"Take care you tell no tales about my business!" he growled as he thrust the thirty shillings into his pocket and turned away. "There's such a thing as law i' this land, mi lad!"

"Aye," said Bartle, with a grin. "You've had a bit o' experience on't o' late, Mr. Grice, what?"

The shaft went home, but Grice made no sign that he had received it. Blow after blow was falling upon him, and he knew there were more to come. The village folk were by that time conversant with the true history of the case, and found elements of romance and excitement in it. Jeckie Farnish had made George Grice pay up to the tune of fifteen hundred pounds, and she was using the money to beat him at his own trade! Well, to be sure, everybody must give her a turn. George had had his way with folk long enough.

There was a small room over Grice's shop from which he could see all that went on in the street beneath, and on the Monday morning, which saw the formal opening of Jeckie's rival establishment, he posted himself in its window and watched. When Jeckie's blinds were drawn up it was to display a fine, well-arranged assortment of goods; it was a fine, gaily-painted cart in which Bartle presently drove off and it was filled to its edge with parcels. All that morning Grice watched, and saw many of his usual customers turn into the new shop. Monday was a great shopping day for the village; by noon he realised that his own trade was going to suffer. And at night Albert curtly drew his attention to a fact—at least half of the better class of customers had not sent in their weekly orders; instead of there being thirty to forty lists to make up in the morning there were no more than fifteen.

"They're going across there!" muttered Albert significantly. "They say her prices are lower."

Grice got an indication of Jeckie's game next day, when the squire's wife sailed into the shop carrying a smartly-got up price list in her hand with the name, Farnish, prominent on its blue and gold cover. She tackled George in person, wanting to know how it was that Miss Farnish's prices were in all cases below his own, and suggesting that he should come down. Grice grew short in temper and reply, and the squire's wife, remarking airily that every one must have a chance, walked out and went over the road. The wives of the vicar and the curate had made a similar defection the day before, and that evening the one-time monopolist foresaw a steady fall in his revenues.

CHAPTER IX

THE IRON ROD

There were more reasons than one for the first gush of customers to Jeckie Farnish's smart new shop. One of them George Grice had foreseen as soon as his eyes fell on the golden teapot and the new sign novelty. Folk would always go to whatever was fresh, he said; only time would tell if the influx of trade to the new-comer would be kept up. But of other reasons he knew little. One was that he himself was unpopular in the village; he had abused his monopoly; more than once he had refused temporary credit to old customers who wanted it for a week or a fortnight until funds came in; he had a bad reputation for over-ready recourse to the County Court; he had sold up one man for a debt which might have been paid by instalments; he charged top prices for everything, and was not overscrupulous as to weights and measures. At least two-thirds of the village population found it a thing of joy to turn cold shoulders to the old firm and walk defiantly into the opposition establishment.

But there was another reason for Jeckie's popularity of which Grice knew less than he guessed at the second of the causes of his sudden loss of trade. Jeckie was becoming a strategist; quick to see and realise the possibilities of her campaign, and astute in looking ahead. And two days before the formal opening of her shop she marched up the village in her best clothes, her cheque-book in one pocket, and well-filled purse in the other, bent on doing something which, in her well-grounded opinion, would establish her in high favour. Farnish owed money in Savilestowe; she was going to pay his debts. Not the big ones, to be sure, she said to herself with emphasis; they could go by the board. The money-lender and the landlord and such-like could whistle for their money as far as she was concerned. But the debts in the village were small things—a few pounds here, a few there; a few shillings in one case, a few more in others. Thirty pounds, she had ascertained, would cover the lot. The blacksmith wanted something, and the miller, and the landlord of the "Coach-and-Four"; two or three people wanted the reimbursement of money lent; there were even labourers to whom Farnish was in debt for small amounts. All this she was going to clear off; otherwise, as she well knew, she would have had the various creditors coming to her shop and suggesting that they should take out the amount of their debts in tea and sugar, bread and bacon.

She turned in first at the blacksmith's, who, it being Saturday afternoon, was smoking his pipe at the door of his house and enjoying the cool breezes which swept over the meadows in front. Under the impression that Jeckie had come touting for custom, he received her grumpishly, and eyed her with anything but favour.

"Now then, Stubbs!" said Jeckie, in her sharpest manner. "My father owes you some money, doesn't he?"

"Aye, he does!" growled the blacksmith. "Nine pound odd it is, and been owin' a long time. An' I would like to see t'colour on it, or some on it; it's hard on a man to tew and slave and loise his brass at t'end o' his labours!"

"You're going to lose naught," retorted Jeckie. "Get inside and write me a receipt. I'll pay you. And you'll understand 'at it's me 'at's payin' you—not him! He's naught to pay you with, as you very well know. But I reckon it'll none matter to you who pays, as long as you get it!"

"Aw, why, now then!" said the mollified creditor. "That's talkin', that is! No, it none matters to me. An' I tak' it very handsome o' you; and I wish yer well wi' t'shop, and I shall tell my missus to go theer."

"You'll find I can do better for you than Grice ever did," said Jeckie, as she followed him into his cottage and drew out her cheque-book. "You'll save money by coming to me. There's a price-list. You look it over and you'll see 'at I'm charging considerably less nor Grice does, and for better quality goods, too."

"Now, then, ye shall have my custom!" said the blacksmith. "I'm stalled o' George Grice. He's nowt but a skinflint, and we had some bacon thro' him none so long sin' at wor fair reisty."

Jeckie handed over her cheque and took her receipt, and went on her way. It was a way of triumph, for not one of Farnish's Savilestowe creditors had ever expected to get a penny of what was owing, and unexpected payments, however much they may be overdue, are always more welcome than the settlement of a debt which is certain. Jeckie went away from each satisfied creditor conscious that she had made a friend and a regular customer; she had laid out twenty-eight pounds and some shillings by the time she returned home. Never mind, she said to herself, she would soon have it back in profits. And Farnish would now be able to walk abroad in the village, knowing that he owed nothing to any fellow-villager. As to his bigger creditors, let them go hang!

During the week, furniture, just sufficient to satisfy mere necessities, had arrived at the house, and had been disposed in certain rooms by Jeckie and Rushie, and on the Saturday night, acting on his daughter's orders, Farnish, having finished his week's work at the Sicaster greengrocer's, came creeping into the village after dark, cast a longing eye on the red-curtained windows of the "Coach-and-Four," and slunk into his daughter's back premises. His spirits had been very low during this home-coming; they rose somewhat on seeing that a thirteen-gallon cask of ale stood in the pantry adjoining the kitchen in which his supper was set for him, but became anxious and depressed again when he also saw that the key had been carefully removed from the brass tap. He foresaw the beginning of strict allowance, and of ceaseless scheming on his part occasionally to gain possession of that key. Now and then, he thought, Jeckie would surely forget it, and go out without it. It was painful, in Farnish's opinion, to ask a man to live in the house with a locked beer barrel and led to exacerbation of proper feelings.

Jeckie gave him a pint of ale and a hot supper that night, and presented him with a two-ounce packet of tobacco. And, when Rushie had gone into the scullery to wash up the supper things, she marshalled Farnish into a certain easy chair by the corner of the hearth, and proceeded to lay down the law to him in no purposeless fashion.

"Now then, I want to have some talk to you," she said, sitting down opposite him and folding her hands in her apron. "We're going to start out in a new way, and everybody about me's going to hear what I've got to say about it. You'll understand that this is my house, and my shop, and my business—all mine! I'm master!—and there'll nobody have any say in matters but me. Do you understand that?"

"Oh, aye, I understand that, reight enough, Jecholiah, mi lass," answered Farnish. "Of course I never expected no other, considerin' how things is. And I'm sure I wish you well in t'venture!"

"I shall do well enough as long as I'm boss!" said Jeckie in her most matter-of-fact manner. "And that I will be! I'll have no interference, either from you or Rushie. As long as you're both under my roof, you'll just do my bidding. And now I tell you what you'll do. You may as well know your position first as last. And to start with, I've paid off every penny 'at you owed i' this place—nearly thirty pounds good money I've laid down in that way this very afternoon!—so you can walk up t'street and down t'street and feel 'at you owe naught to nobody. And you'll have a deal o' walking to do, for you can't expect me to throw my money away on your behalf wit'out doin' something for me i' return, so there!"

"I'm sure it were very considerate on yer, Jecholiah," said Farnish humbly. "An' I tak' it as very thoughtful an' all. Willn't deny 'at it were a sore trouble to me 'at I owed brass i' t'place. An' what might you be thinkin' o' puttin' me to, now 'at I am here, like?"

"I'm going to tell you," answered Jeckie. "All's ready to open on Monday morning. Me and Rushie'll attend to the shop; Bartle'll go out with the horse and cart; I've got a strong lass coming in that'll see to the house and the cooking. You'll help wi' odd jobs in the shop, and you'll carry out light goods and parcels in t'village. It'll none be such heavy work, but it must be done punctual and reg'lar— no hangin' about and talkin' at corners, and such like—we've all got to work, and to work hard, too!"

"I'm to be fetcher and carrier, like," said Farnish. "Aye, well, mi lass, it's not t'sort o' conclusion to a career 'at I aimed at, but I mun bow down to Providence, as they call it. Beggars can't be choosers, no how!"

"Who's talkin' about beggars!" retorted Jeckie impatiently. "There's no beggars i' this house, anyway. Beggars, indeed! You'll never ha' been so well off in your life as you will be wi' me!"

"Do you say so, Jecholiah?" asked Farnish timidly. "I'm very glad to hear it, I'm sure. How shall I stand, like, then?"

"You'll stand like this," replied Jeckie. "There's a good and comfortable bedroom all ready upstairs; this place'll be more comfortable nor aught we had at Applecroft when all's put to rights in it; there'll always be plenty to eat, and good quality, too; I shall let you have two pints of beer a day, and give you two ounces of tobacco every Saturday. And once a year you shall have a new suit of good clothes, and your underwear as it wants replacing. I'll see 'at you want for naught to fill your belly and cover your back. If that isn't doing well by you, then I don't know what is!"

"Well, I'm sure it's very handsome, is that, Jecholiah," said Farnish. "It's seems as if I were to be well provided for i' t'way o' food and raiment. But how will it be now"—he paused, and looked at his daughter's erect and rigid figure with a furtive depreciating glance—"how will it be now, mi lass, about a bit o' money? Ye wouldn't hev your poor father walkin' t'street wi'out one penny to rub agen another, I'm sure? A man, ye see, Jecholiah, has feelin's!"

Jeckie's lips tightened. It had been her intention, in laying down a code of rules to Farnish, to tell him that he was not going to have money. But as he spoke, a thought came into her mind—if she kept him penniless, he would certainly do one of two things, possibly both; either he would borrow small sums here or there, or he would pilfer from the till and pocket payments from chance customers. Once more she must look ahead.

"I'll tell you what I'll do," she said suddenly. "I'll give you—" then she paused, made some more reflections and calculations, and reckoned up to herself what precise amount of mischief Farnish could do with the amount she was thinking of—"I'll give you seven shilling a week for spending money—I know well enough there's naught on earth'll stop you from dropping in at t' 'Coach-and-Four,' and a shilling a day's enough, and more than enough, for you to waste there. But I'll give you fair warning—if I hear o' you borrowing any money, or running into debt, at t' 'Coach-and-Four,' or elsewhere, or hanging about publics when you ought to be at your job, I shall stop your allowance—and so there you are!" Farnish, on his part, made a swift calculation. A shilling a day meant three pints of ale at fourpence a pint. He was to have two pints at home—very well, five pints would do nicely. He waved a magisterial hand.

"Now, then, ye shall have no cause to complain, Jecholiah," he said. "It's as well to know how we stand, d'ye see, mi lass? It's none so much t'bit o' money," he continued, still more magisterially, "it's what you may term t'principle o' t'thing. A man mun stand by his principles, and it's agen mine to walk about t'world wi' nowt i' my pocket! It's agen t'Bible, an' all, Jecholiah, as you may ha' noticed i' readin' that good owd Book—there's two passages i' that there 'at comes to my reflection at once. 'Put money in thy purse,' it says i' one place, and 'The labourer is worthy of his hire' it remarks in another. An' I wor browt up to Bible principles—mi mother were a very religious woman—she were a chappiler!"

"I don't believe it says aught at all i' t'Bible about puttin' money i' your purse," said Jeckie contemptuously, "and if your mother was as religious as you make out, she should ha' taught you something 'at is there—'Owe no man anything!' Happen you never heard o' that?"

"Now, then, now then!" answered Farnish. "Let's be friendly! There's a deal said i' t'Bible 'at hes dark meanin's—I've no doubt 'at t'real significance o' that passage is summat 'at ye don't understand, mi lass."

"I understand 'at nobody's going to run up debts while they're under my roof," declared Jeckie. "You get that into your head!"

Farnish retired to his comfortable bedroom that evening apparently well satisfied with his position, and when he had left them Jeckie turned to her sister; it was as necessary to have a proper understanding with Rushie as with their father. And Rushie was amenable enough; the prospect of selling things in the smart new shop, and of conversations with customers, and of all the varying incidents in a day's retail trading, appealed to her love of life and change. Jeckie's proposals as to finding her with board, lodging, and all she wanted in the way of clothes and shoe-leather, and giving her a small but sufficient salary, satisfied her well. But at the end of their talk they hit on a difference of opinion.

"And now about that Herbert Binks," said Jeckie suddenly. "He's after you, Rushie, and you're a fool. He's naught but a draper's assistant, when all's said and done. I'll none have him coming here. What do you want wi' young men?"

Rushie began to pout and to look resentful.

"He's a very nice, quiet, respectable young man, is Herbert," she said, half angrily. "And if he is a draper's assistant, do you think he's always going to be one? He has ambitions, has Herbert, and he aims at having a shop of his own."

"Let him get one, then, before he comes running after you!" retorted Jeckie. "Young men of his age has no business to think about girls—what they want to think about is making money."

"Money isn't everything!" said Rushie.

"Isn't it?" sneered Jeckie. "You'll sing another tune, my lass, when you've seen as much as I have! I know what money's meant to me, and what it's going to mean, and I'll take good care none goes by me so long as I've ten fingers to lay hold of it with!"

It needed no observation on the part of Rushie or of Farnish to see that Jeckie had made up her mind to seek the riches of this world. She was up with the sun, and still out of her bed long after the others had sought theirs; she did the work of three people, and never allowed herself to flag. She taught herself book-keeping, and practised correspondence till she could write smart business letters; before long she purchased a typewriter and mastered its intricacies; she had no time to read the local newspaper any longer, but she read the "Grocer" with eagerness and avidity, and became as glibly conversant with prices as any of the travellers who called on her for orders. A sharp, shrewd woman she was to deal with, said the gentlemen amongst themselves; sharper, far, than old Grice across the way, and certain to rob him of most of his trade. And some of them, who did little business with him, and could well afford to be shyly mutinous at his expense, were not slow to poke fun at George about his rival and her capabilities.

"Sad thing for you, Mr. Grice," they would say, with a wink at the golden teapot on which the sun contrived to focus its rays all day long. "Smart woman across there, sir!—ah, great pity you couldn't amalgamate the two businesses, Mr. Grice. Doing well over there, sir, I believe—knows what she's about! Place too small to carry two good businesses like yours and hers, Mr. Grice—ought to come to some arrangement, sir—limited liability company now, Mr. Grice, what?"

All this was so much gall and wormwood to George Grice, who had an additional cause of intense and mortifying annoyance in a certain habit of Jeckie's which, he said, could only have been developed by a woman who was both a Jezebel and a devil. Every now and then, in the full light of day, Miss Farnish would leave her own shop, stroll calmly across the street, and insolently and leisurely inspect George Grice & Son's newly-dressed windows. She would note down all their prices on a scrap of paper—and then she would go back. And within half-an-hour the same goods which Grice's were offering would be in the Farnish windows—with all the prices cut down to figures which made George despairing and furious.

CHAPTER X

THE ETERNAL FEMININE

All unknown to George Grice, there was a certain young person in his immediate surroundings who was watching the course and trend of events with a pair of eyes which were at least as keen as his own. His daughter-in-law had come to her new life armed with a goodly stock of common sense and no small share of the family characteristics of love of money and astuteness in getting it. Lucilla, indeed, was a worthy daughter of her father, the draper, who was as much of a money-grubber as his brother of Savilestowe, and had implanted in his children—all girls—a thorough devotion to

Mammon. The draper had played no small part in engineering the marriage between Lucilla and Albert. Having read the letter which Albert brought him from George, he had conducted Lucilla into privacy and set forth certain facts before her. One, that his brother George was a very warm man, a very warm man indeed, with the true instinct for scraping money together and sticking to it when it was scraped. A second was that he was now an elderly man, of a plethoric habit, and could not, in all reason, expect to live so very much longer. A third was that Albert was an only child and would accordingly come into his father's property and business; a fourth, that the property was considerable and the business a monopoly. And the fifth, and not least important one, was that Albert was the sort of fellow that any woman could twist round her finger and tie up to her apron strings.

Lucilla made up her mind there and then, and skilfully detaching Albert from her two sisters, to whom she and her father said a few words in private, led him through the by-ways of love to the hymeneal altar. When she had safely conducted him there, she took stock of the new world in which she found herself. A close inspection of her father-in-law convinced her that George Grice had a decided tendency to apoplexy, and might be seized at any time. She foresaw great things for Albert and herself—a few years more of monopolistic trading in Savilestowe, and they would be able to sell the business and goodwill for a handsome sum and retire, to be lady and gentleman for all the rest of their lives. This was Lucilla's ambition. It had been hers when she helped her father in his drapery stores; it remained hers when she began to post up her father-in-law's account-books. Linen and lace, bacon and bread were not, in themselves, objects of interest to Lucilla; they were means to an end. The end was a genteel competency in a smart villa residence, with at least a good horse and a showy dog-cart, two maids, and real silver on the dinner table.

But when the golden teapot rose across the street, set high above the arch of Jeckie Farnish's front door, a flaming reminder to George Grice that the enemy's outworks had been pushed close to his citadel, Lucilla began to foresee much. Her brain was small but sharp, and she had been trained in a shrewd school. It needed little reflection to show her that her father-in-law's monopoly was in a fair way of being broken down, and that Albert's partnership in George Grice & Son was not worth as much as it had been when he and his father set their signatures to the deed. Before the first week of the rival's campaign was over, Lucilla, as bookkeeper, was aware of some stern facts. She drew Albert's attention to them during the temporary absence of old Grice from the shop.

"Look here!" she said, pointing to some figures on a sheet of paper. "The takings for this week are not one-third of what they were last week! That's as regard the cash trade. And look at that!" she went on, indicating a row of small account-books. "Where there used to be thirty-three of those, there's now only seventeen. That means that sixteen good customers, who used to pay their accounts weekly, have gone over yonder. She's driving her knife in pretty deep, Albert, is that old flame of yours!"

Albert had been obliged to tell Lucilla of his former attachment; having secured Albert for herself, she had paid little attention to it; she also had had sweethearts in her maiden days. True, she had felt a sense of great injury when Jeckie Farnish got her fifteen hundred pounds, but she had made up her mind that that was never to be brought into account against Albert—George Grice had broken off the match and he must pay. And her last remark was more jocular than reproachful—something in her made her see the humour of a situation in which George was getting the worst of it.

"Now you reckon up, Albert, and just see for yourself what a falling off like this is going to mean at the end of the year!" she continued. "You'll find it'll be a nice round sum."

Albert, who was not behindhand at mental arithmetic, nodded.

"Aye," he said. "But—will it last? I expected naught else this week—folks will go to aught that's new. But a lot of 'em'll come back."

"Will they?" demanded Lucilla, with a certain grimness of aspect. "We'll see!"

There was a note in her voice which seemed to suggest that she had considerable doubt about Albert's optimism, and as time went on her own fears proved to have been well grounded. The truth was, as Lucilla knew, that George Grice & Son had become old-fashioned. George had got into a rut, and nothing could lift him out of it. Instead of laying in what his customers wanted, or developing new lines of trade, he went on in the way to which he had become accustomed, dealing with the same firms, driving away travellers who wanted to introduce new goods, refusing to march with the times. And nobody knew this better than Jeckie Farnish, who welcomed anything new and up-to-date, studied the likes, pleasures, and convenience of her customers in everything, and, in her shop and in all her dealings, cultivated a suavity and charm of manner which sometimes made Farnish and Rushie wonder if she were the same woman to whose sharp tongue and hard words they were not infrequently treated.

62

"You take good care never to speak to customers as you speak to me," remonstrated Rushie on one occasion. "You're as mealy-mouthed as ever they make 'em when you're in t'shop, even if it's in servin' naught but a pennorth o' pepper! It's all smiles and soft talk then—t'customers is fair fawned on when you're behind t'counter!"

"I'm makin' my money out o' customers!" retorted Jeckie. "I'm makin' none out o' you, mi lass. I should be a fool, an' all, if I didn't do a bit o' soft sawderin' to folks 'at brings brass i' their hands. Pounds or pence, politeness is due to all. It costs naught."

There was more gruffness than politeness across the way, and at the end of six months Lucilla knew that George Grice and Son were seriously affected. Certain old customers had stuck to the old firm; certain of the village folk still came in at the door; there were others who continued to trade with the Grices because they were in debt to them and were paying by instalments. But Lucilla knew—for she kept the books. And without saying anything to Albert, she formed plans and ideas of her own which eventually developed into a project, and one winter afternoon, when George and his son had gone to Clothford on business which required their joint presence, she boldly walked across the street, and, entering the rival establishment, marched calmly up to the mistress at the cash desk.

"Good afternoon, Miss Farnish," she said, in as matter-of-fact tones as she would have employed if she had called in to change a sovereign into silver. "Can I have a word or two with you? You know me, Miss Farnish?—Mrs. Albert Grice."

For once in her life Jeckie was taken aback. She stared at her visitor as if Lucilla had been one of the animals from the menagerie just then being shown at Sicaster, and the vivid colour which always distinguished her healthy cheeks deepened. In silence, and with a glance at Rushie, who was staring open-mouthed at Mrs. Albert, she left the cash desk and ushered the caller into the parlour.

"What do you want?" she demanded with asperity. "I'm busy!"

"You're always busy," said Lucilla. "Anybody can see that. But you'll spare me a minute or two, I'm sure, and I'll sit down, if you please, Miss Farnish," she went on, when Jeckie had ungraciously indicated the chair and had taken one herself—to sit on the extreme edge of it in a severely rigid and disapproving attitude. "Miss Farnish, there's no need for you and me to be enemies, whatever you may be with the men opposite. I'd naught to do with what happened between you and the Grices. I never knew that you and Albert had been engaged when he came to our house at Nottingham. I never knew till we were married. What I know is that I brought Albert Grice a couple of thousand pounds, and that me

63

and my father expected I was marrying into something that was worth having!"

"Isn't it?" demanded Jeckie, with a grim face.

"It's not going to be if things go on as they are!" answered Lucilla, with obvious candour. "I'm all for plain speaking, and truth, and seeing things as they are, I am! And what's the use of endeavouring to conceal things, Miss Farnish? I've kept the books across there ever since I came to this place, and I know how George Grice & Son is situated."

"Well?" said Jeckie, grim as ever. "Well?"

"Well," answered Lucilla, "I should think the plain truth's obvious to anybody that has eyes! Their trade's falling off. Of course, you know that as well as I do. You've got what they've lost. I don't see any use in concealing matters; their turn-over this year'll not be half of what it was last year. Now, Miss Farnish, I put it to you—how long's this going to last?"

Jeckie shifted her stiff position, and began to grow interested.

"I don't know what you mean," she said.

"Why, I mean this," replied Lucilla. "I've been brought up to business, and I know what I'm talking about. Here's two businesses in one place, covering the same district—rival businesses. The probability is that things have got to a settled point now—you've established your business, and very quick, too, and George Grice & Son, if they've lost what you've gained, have got a certain number of customers that'll stick to them. You'll not get any farther in one way and they'll not go farther in the other. Now, what foolishness to have two such businesses in one place, trying to cut one another's throats! Why not come to terms, Miss Farnish? Amalgamate!— that's what's wanted. Call it Farnish & Grice, or Grice & Farnish. Turn the two firms into a limited liability company, if you like, but bring them together! That's what I say, anyway."

"Who sent you?" asked Jeckie.

Lucilla stared.

"Sent—me?" she exclaimed. "Lord, do you think anybody sent me? What, old Grice? or Albert? I should like to see either of 'em send me about anything! No, I came on my own hook. They don't know. It's my idea. But—if you'd agree to what I say I would bring them to it, both of 'em. Albert, of course, he'd do just what I told him to do, and as for his father, well, I could talk him round. But what do you say?"

For the first time since her visitor had entered the parlour Jeckie let her stern features relax into a smile. It was the sort of a smile which might overspread the face of a conqueror who, having his enemy at his feet, is asked, suddenly, to let him off, unscathed.

"What do I say?" she said. "Why, I say 'at you don't know me, or else you'd never come here with such a proposal! Lord bless you! I wouldn't have aught to do with George Grice were it ever so! Why should I? I've not been seven month at this business, and I've made it pay. Aye, nobody but myself knows how well, for all I've cut prices to the last extent. And this is naught to what I intend to do. I'm servin' a radius o' five miles now, but it'll be ten next year. I'm not going to content myself with Savilestowe, you make no mistake! An' you started out by saying, how long's this going to last? I'll tell you how long it's going to last. It's going to last till I've done what I aimed at doing when I started!"

"And what's that?" inquired Lucilla. "What did you aim at?"

"I aimed at forcing George Grice to put up his shutters!" answered Jeckie, in harsh, tense tones. "And—I'll do it!"

Lucilla rose from her chair, staring at the stern eyes and hard mouth.

"Oh, well, in that case," she said, "of course, if you're feeling that way, there's no more to be said about it, and I shall know what to do."

"And what's that?" demanded Jeckie, who was still inquisitive. "What will you do?"

"That's my business," answered Lucilla. "However, I'm obliged to you for making things plainer. I shall know better what course to take. And, as I said, there's no reason why you and me should be enemies; I've nothing against you. I reckon you're doing your best for yourself. So am I!"

Jeckie asked no more questions, and Lucilla marched calmly back across the street, and spent the remainder of the afternoon and evening making a minutely close and accurate examination of the books of George Grice & Son. And that night, in the security of their own parlour, where she and her husband spent all their leisure now that there was a coolness between George and herself, she gave Albert definite orders as to the future. It was in his power to dissolve the partnership and to claim his share at any moment. The moment, in Lucilla's opinion, was at hand. Next year, by that time, the goodwill of the firm would not be worth anything like so much as it was then. The year after that it would be worth still less. In three years, said Lucilla, it would be worth just nothing. Albert gave in, only stipulating that Lucilla should break the news to George and do all the talking. Lucilla was as ready for this as for her breakfast, and within a month George had paid Albert out with six thousand pounds, and stood in his shop a lonely and sour-mouthed man.

It was about this time that Jeckie also came to the waters of bitterness, if not of actual tribulation. Rushie led her to them. In spite of all that her elder sister could say, Rushie would not give up the society and attentions of Mr. Herbert Binks. Herbert was one of those young men who part their hair in the middle, use much pomatum, and are never seen out of doors without gloves; he also wore a tailed coat and a top-hat on Sundays. His chief ideas were centered in the drapery trade, but he was of an innocently amorous nature, and Rushie considered him a perfect gentleman. Not even Jeckie could prevent these two meeting on Sunday afternoons, and as Jeckie would not admit Herbert to her house, he and Rushie took to having tea together at the "Coach-and-Four," whence they invariably proceeded to evensong at the parish church and sang out of the same hymn-book. It was a mark of respectability to go to church, said Herbert, and stood you well in with customers. But the expenditure at the "Coach-and-Four" roused Jeckie's contempt, and hardened her against Rushie's young man.

"A nice sort o' feller you've got!" she said, with one of her grim sneers. "Spending what bit of money he's got in teain' at t' 'Coach-and-Four' every Sunday! I know what they'll charge him for your teas! Ninepence each—such extravagance! Eighteenpence every Sunday. That's three pounds eighteen shillings a year—enough to buy him a new suit o' clothes or you a new gown! And I'll lay my lord must do the grand and put a sixpence in t'plate when you go to church—just to look fine. That's another six-and-twenty shillings! You might as well tell him to chuck his brass i' t'horsepond!"

"We don't have tea at the 'Coach-and-Four' every Sunday in the year!" declared Rushie. "And Herbert doesn't give sixpence at church—he keeps threepenny bits for that. And there'd be no need to have tea at all at the public if you'd behave as you ought and ask him here! But I shall be having a house of my own some day—you'll see!"

"And a fine place it'll be, out o' two pounds a week!" sneered Jeckie. "Nay, I'd ha' summat better nor a feller 'at measures tape and sells pins and needles. Isn't there two or three young fellers abaht 'at has brass? I'd say naught if you'd tak' up wi' young Summers, for instance—he's been looking like a sheep at you this long while, and he's a rare good farm and money i' plenty."

"Never you mind!" retorted Rushie. "Herbert hasn't got a head like a turnip nor a face like a cake with raisins in it. Make up to young Summers yourself!"

Rushie, it was clear, was sentimentally and badly in love with the pomatumed Herbert. But Jeckie had no belief that it would ever come to anything serious until she awoke one morning to discover that her sister had risen much earlier and had departed to Sicaster, where by that time she had become Mrs. Binks.

CHAPTER XI

HUMBLE PIE

Those who were in close touch with Jeckie Farnish on the day of her younger sister's revolt and defection had far from pleasant moments. She drove her father and shop boys about with harsh and impatient words; she was curt and dictatorial with Bartle, one of those conscientious and faithful souls to whom any reasonable employer would have found it impossible to attribute laxity; for the first time since commencing business she was short-tempered with some customers, snappish with others, and openly rude to one or two whose trade was a matter of complete indifference to her. The truth was that Rushie's clandestine marriage had upset more than one of Jeckie's best-laid plans. She had no wish to take in an outsider as principal assistant—outsiders, in her opinion, were never to be trusted, and it was repugnant to her to think that a smart young shopman (for saleswomen were not known in those days) should learn any of the secrets which had already begun to accumulate about the Farnish establishment. Yet the business had already assumed such proportions that assistance was necessary, and Jeckie's first impression was that she would only get it from some young jackanapes who would want the usual wages (or, as he would call it, salary) of his degree, and from whom she would be unable to keep those private details which she had no objection to share with her sister. It was, she considered, a gross piece of ingratitude that Rushie should have preferred Binks to her own flesh and blood, and she made up her mind to say so, plainly and emphatically as soon as the culprit came once more within reach.

But for several days Jeckie had to cherish her wrath in silence and in secret. Rushie and her bridegroom took a short and economical honeymoon at Blackpool; they had been back in Sicaster for forty-eight hours before Jeckie heard of their return. Within an hour of hearing it, however, she appeared at Mr. Herbert Bink's lodgings; it was then nearly noon, and the bridegroom was at his place of employment; the bride, unfortunately, was discovered in idleness, reading her favourite form of fiction, a cheap novelette. She paled and reddened alternately at sight of Jeckie who had cleverly gained admittance without notice, and walked in upon her like an avenging goddess, and her eyes went straight to the cheap clock over the mantelpiece. It was twenty minutes to twelve; and Herbert would not be home until five minutes past; for twenty-five minutes, then, she would have to put up with Jeckie's tantrums. And Jeckie left her no doubt as to what they were to be.

"So this is what you've come to already, my fine madam!" began the elder sister. "Lying there on a sofa, in cheap lodgings, readin' trash in t'very middle o' the day, when you might ha' been and ought to ha' been at honest work—you'll come to find work i' t'poorhouse before you've done! Such idle, good-for-naught ways!"

"You mind what you say, Jecholiah Farnish!" retorted Mrs. Binks. "My husband'll be home before long, and if he catches you—"

"If I'd a husband," said Jeckie, with a contemptuous snort, "I'd be cooking his dinner again his comin' home. But such as you—"

"There's no need to cook our dinner," broke in Mrs. Binks. "Until we start a house of our own, we board and lodge, so——"

"A house o' your own!" exclaimed Jeckie. "When and where are you like to get a house o' your own—a twopenny-halfpenny draper's assistant and an idle wench like you, 'at spends her time readin' that soft stuff? You'll be as poor as church mice all t'days o' your life! He'll never be no more than a shopman at two or three pounds a week—where does such like start houses o' their own? Do you know what you've thrown away, you ungrateful thing?" demanded Jeckie, who was now in full torrent and meant to go on her way unchecked. "If you'd stopped wi' me, your lawful sister, and had done your duty, an' behaved yourself, and kept of all such softness as men and marryin', and shown yourself fit for it, I'd ha' taken you in partnership! An' by the time we'd come to middle life we could ha' done what you'll see I shall do—retire wi' a fortune, and take a fine house at Harrigate or Scarhaven, and keep servants, and have a carriage and pair, and t'best of everything! You've given up all that for this—poor, struggling folk you'll be, all your lives, while I grow up as rich as Creesees, whoever he may ha' been, and happen I shall be a deal richer. All that for a draper's shop-lad!"

"He isn't a draper's shop-lad!" retorted Mrs. Binks, with some spirit. "And him and me loves each other, and——"

"You gr'et soft thing!" exclaimed Jeckie, contemptuously. "Love, indeed!—that's all because you've been wed inside a week! Wait till you've gotten a pack o' screaming childer about you, and you draggle-tailed and down at heel, and see how much you'll talk about love i' them days! You're a fool, Rushie Farnish, and you'll come to rue——"

"My name isn't Farnish!" said Mrs. Binks, "and if Herbert was here, he'd put you out o' this room, and——"

The bride came to a sudden stop. Mr. Binks, impatient to rejoin the recently-secured object of his affection, had contrived to get away from his employer's shop a quarter of an hour earlier than usual, and he had been listening at the keyhole for the last few minutes, his landlady having told him that Miss Farnish had gone up to see her sister. And now he stepped into the room, looking as important and dignified as such a very ordinary young man could. And, not unnaturally, he fell into the language of the drapery department in which he served.

"Oh!" he said. "Miss Farnish, I believe? And what can we have the pleasure of doing for you, ma'am? No previous favours received from your quarter, I believe, Miss Farnish? No transactions between us before—eh, ma'am?"

Jeckie favoured her brother-in-law with a withering glance.

"You impudent young counter-jumper!" she answered. "What do you mean by running away with my sister?—a feller that sells pennorths o' tape and papers o' pins! Answer me that!"

"Better sell anything, Miss Farnish, than be sold up!" retorted Mr. Binks with a grin. "I think that was what had just happened to your family when I first became acquainted with it."

"That's it, Bert!" said Mrs. Binks, glad to give Jeckie something in return for all the scoldings that she herself had suffered. "She's been going on at me dreadfully!"

Jeckie pulled herself up to her full height, and slowly looked from bride to bridegroom.

"I know what you've married on," she said, her voice becoming as calm as it had previously been furious. "You're young fools, and you'll find it out. Don't you ever come to me for anything; if you do you'll find yourselves shown the door! So there; and I've no more to say."

Mr. Binks rubbed his hands.

"That's well, ma'am!" he remarked, almost gaily. "For our bit of dinner's ready downstairs. And you can go away, ma'am, assured that Rushie and me ain't afraid of nothing. You see, we prefer love to money, though we intend to do pretty well in that way, all in good time. No offence, ma'am, but we ain't going to be bullied by you or anybody. If," he concluded, as he opened the door for Jeckie with mock politeness, "if you'd come to our little shop intending to do business on pleasant and friendly lines we might have established a connection, but as you ain't, well, all I've got to say, Miss Farnish, is—nothing doing!"

He felt very proud of himself, this sandy-haired, snub-nosed, commonplace young man, as he uttered this sarcasm; he knew, somehow, that he had got the better of this terrible Jecholiah. And suddenly, as Jeckie was passing through the door, he had an inspiration, and felt it to be clever, very clever.

"But we ain't above or below playing the coals-of-fire game,

Miss Farnish," he said. "You wouldn't ask me into your house to as much as a cup of tea, but if you like to stop you're welcome to your share of as nice a bit of steak and onions as ever you set tooth into! Say the word, ma'am, and take it friendly."

But Jeckie was marching down the stairs in dead and gloomy silence and Mr. Binks turned to his bride.

"I did it proper there, old woman!" he said. "Hand o' friendship, and that sort o' thing—what? Her own fault if she wouldn't take it."

"She's as hard as iron," answered Rushie. "Come down, Bert; the dinner'll be getting cold."

Jeckie drove away from Sicaster feeling that Mr. Binks had somehow got the best of her. He had certainly not been frightened of her; he had poked fun at her. Worst of all, he had actually offered her hospitality, and had been serious when he offered it. And Rushie, when it came to it, had not been afraid of her either. She was surprised at that. Rushie had always been subservient, even if she had occasionally protested. The fact was that Jeckie had driven into the market town under the impression that the erring pair, having irretrievably committed themselves, would beg her forgiveness, and ask her to help them with money so that Binks could set himself up in business. Now Binks's attitude, from the time he walked into the sittingroom to the moment in which he invited her to the steak and onions, was that of cheerful independence. It was beyond Jeckie, who was no psychologist; all that she realised was that though bride and bridegroom knew her to be already a well-to-do tradeswoman they defied her.

She was defied again before night fell, and by her own father. Farnish, so far, had kept his compact with his elder daughter. He was, in fact, in better circumstances than he had ever been in his life. He slept in comfort; he ate and drink his fill at Jeckie's well-provided table; his allowance of money was sufficient to provide him with a few additional glasses of ale at the village inn; moreover, it was added to by occasional tips from the people to whom he carried the Farnish goods. He was waxing fat; he wore a good suit of clothes on Sundays; something of the glory which centered in his successful daughter shone around him, for, after all, he was the parent of the woman who had beaten George Grice and was becoming a power in the village. All this gave him a certain feeling of independence, but there had been no evidence of any Jeshurun-like spirit in him until the evening of the day on which Jeckie paid her visit to the Binks's. Then certain words from Jeckie aroused it.

"There's something I've got to say to you," said Jeckie, suddenly, as she and Farnish sat by the domestic hearth that night after supper. "You know what our Rushie's gone and done?—made a fool of herself?"

"I have been duly informed o' what she's done, Jecholiah," answered Farnish. "As to whether she's made a fool of hersen, I can't say. From what bit I've seen o' t'young feller, he seems a decent, promisin' sort o' chap, and earns a very nice wage at t'drapery business. An' there were a man I met t'other day, a Sicaster chap, 'at told me 'at this here Binks and our Rushie were very much in love with each other, to all accounts, so let's hope it'll come out well."

"Fiddle-de-dee!" sneered Jeckie. "A draper's shopman, earnin', happen, two pound a week! I've been to see 'em to-day and told 'em my mind. I know what they'll be after—they'll be comin' to me for money before long. There'll be bairns comin'—poor folks always has 'em where rich folks won't—and they'll turn to me as t'best off relative they have—I know!"

"Why, why, mi lass!" said Farnish. "I'm sure ye'd none see yer own sister want for owt i' circumstances like them theer. Flesh an' blood, ye know."

"Flesh and blood must agree wi' flesh and blood," retorted Jeckie stolidly. "Our Rushie's set me at naught—me that's done so much for her! She's defied me—and I'll have naught no more to do with her. If she'd been a good gal and behaved herself I'd ha' made a lady on her. But it's done—and neither her nor that counter-jumper's going to darken my doors. And I said I'd a word to say to you, and I'll tell you what it is—I'm not going to have you going there. Don't let me hear tell o' you going to them Binkses, or you an' me'll quarrel. Now then!"

Farnish, who was smoking his after-supper pipe in the easy chair which was his special seat, stared at his daughter for a while in silence. Then he suddenly rose from his place, knocked out the ashes from his pipe, put his hands in his pockets, and shook his head.

"Nay, nay, mi lass!" he said. "Ye're none going to force that on me, neither! I made a bargain wi' you when ye set up this business o' yours, and I've kept it, and you've nowt to complain on, I'm sure, for if ye had had owt I should ha' heard yer tongue afore now. But I'm not going to be telled 'at I'm not to go near mi own dowter! I shall go an' see our Rushie just as often as ever I please, and if it doesn't suit you, why, then ye can find another man to tak' my place. I'm willin' to go on as we have been doin', but if we part I can find work elsewheer. Don't you never say nowt no more to me o' this sort, Jecholiah, or else ye'll see t'back side o' my coat!"

With that Farnish turned and went off to bed, and Jecholiah

stared after him as if he were some wonderful stranger whom she had never seen before. For the second time that day she, the rising and successful tradeswoman, had been defied by poor folk. She ate a considerable amount of humble pie before she laid her head on her pillow that night, and next morning she said no more to her father, and matters went on as usual.

There was another person in Savilestowe who, like Jeckie, was eating humble pie, in even larger slices, about that time. George Grice, left alone since Albert's defection, saw his trade decline more and more. Jeckie, wherever she got it from, had a natural instinct for attracting custom, and an almost uncanny intuition as to suiting their tastes. By that time nearly all the big houses in the neighbourhood were on her books, and the smart cart driven by Bartle had become two. Rushie was replaced by an experienced assistant, carefully selected by Jeckie out of many applicants; two apprentices were taken in; Bartle had another man to help him, and Farnish became foreman of several errand boys. All this meant that trade was steadily flowing from Grice on one side of the street to Farnish on the other. Old George used to stand in his window and watch his former customers pass in and out of the door beneath the golden teapot. His first anger and resentment changed slowly to a feeling of mournful acquiescence in fate, and two new lines were added to those already set deeply on each side of the tight lip. But a new anger arose one morning, when, chancing to gaze across the street, he saw the smart dog-cart which Albert and Lucilla had set up at their villa residence just outside the village arrive at Farnish's, and Lucilla herself descend, bearing in her hand a sheet of paper and her purse. George knew what that meant; his daughter-in-law, who up to that time had traded with him, for very decency's sake, was now going to try the opposition shop. He turned away full of new resentment and mortification.

"Nay, nay," he muttered. "That beats all! One's own flesh and blood! But I might ha' seen how it would be ever since yon young hussy cheeked me to my face wi' her two thousand pound! And I mun think—I mun think! Am I done, or am I not done? That's the question!"

Over his gin-and-water—of which he now, in his solitude, took an increased amount every evening—old George thought hard that night. Between periods of thought he had periods of consultation with his account-books, his banker's pass book, his securities (carefully locked up in a special safe) and with various memoranda relating to the business and private property. When all was over he went to bed, and lay awake half the night, still thinking; he continued to think during most of the next day. And the result of all this thought was that, a night or two later, when shops had closed, darkness fallen, and most of the Savilestowe folk abed, George Grice slunk across the street to his rival's private door.

CHAPTER XII

THE TRIPLE CHANCE

At the beginning of her venture Jeckie had spent all her energies on the business part of her establishment, and had laid out very little money on the furnishing of the private rooms. A living room for meals, bedrooms for herself and Rushie and their father, had seemed to her sufficient for first needs; additions could come later, if the business prospered. The business had prospered, and there came a time when she determined to have at least a parlour into which the better class of customers could be shown if they wanted to see her, as they sometimes did, in private. Accordingly, she gave orders to the best firm of furniture dealers in Sicaster to fit up a room at the side of the house in handsome, if solid, style, having previously had it, and a lobby adjoining it, painted and decorated in corresponding manner. The door of the lobby opened on a little side garden; she ordered it to be painted a rich dark green, and had it fitted with a fine brass knocker which one of the shop-boys kept so constantly polished that its refulgence exceeded that of the golden teapot at the front of the house. It was to this door that George Grice stole, and at this knocker that he sounded his summons, and the time was half-past nine at night.

Jeckie—alone, for Farnish had already retired—wondered who it could be that came knocking there at that late hour. She picked up a hand-lamp and went round to the lobby and opened the door; the light of the lamp fell full on George Grice's round face, and on a certain sheepish and furtive look in his eyes. He lifted his slouched straw hat, and even smiled faintly, but Jeckie frowned in ominous fashion.

"What do you want?" she demanded in her least gracious manner. She had never heard Grice's voice since the afternoon, now long since, on which he had ridden away from Applecroft, turning a deaf ear to her prayers, but she remembered it well enough, and she knew that there was a new note in it when he spoke, a note of something very like meekness, if not of positive humility.

"I could like a word or two wi' you, if you please," said Grice. "A word i' private."

Jeckie knew from the very tone that this man who had once thrown her aside like an old glove, and whom she had fought with the fierceness and tenacity of a tiger, had come to acknowledge himself defeated. Without a word she motioned him to enter, closed the door, led him into the new parlour, lighted a handsome standard lamp that stood on the table, and pointing him to a chair, took one herself and stared at him.

"Well?" she said.

Grice drew out a big handkerchief and mopped his bald head; it was an old trick of his, well remembered by Jeckie, whenever he was moved or excited.

"I made a mistake i' your case," he answered, almost dully. "I—I didn't know it at the time, but I know it now—to my cost."

"Aye, because I've taught you to know it!" said Jeckie. "I've bested you!" Grice looked at her, furtively. He had some knowledge of human nature, and he suddenly realised the woman's hard, determined spirit.

"If I'd ha' known," he burst out suddenly, "what make of woman you are, I'd ha' taken good care that things turned out different! If you'd married our Albert—aye, things would indeed ha' been different! But I went on t'wrong side o' t'road—and he married that niece o' mine, 'at's now made him turn agen' his own father, and I'm left there—alone!"

"Your own fault!" said Jeckie. "Who made your bed but yourself?"

"That makes it no better," replied Grice. "Nay, it makes it worse! I've borne more nor I ever expected to bear. This—(he waved his hand around as if to include his rival's establishment and trade)—this is t'least of it. You fought me fair and square, no doubt; and I'm beaten. But there's a thing I can suggest, even at this stage."

"What?" demanded Jeckie, who was watching him keenly. "What?"

Grice put both hands on his knees and bent forward to her.

"I'm still a well-to-do man," he said, in a low, terse voice. "Accordin' to some standards, I'm a rich man. I had a reckonin' up t'other night o' what I were worth. If I'd to die now I should cut up well. You'd be surprised. And I shan't leave a penny to my son! My son, Albert Grice—not a penny!"

Jeckie continued to stare at him; herself silent, her face fixed.

She saw that her beaten rival had still a lot more to say, and that left to himself he would say it.

"Not one penny to him!" continued Grice with emphasis. "For why? I'll not say 'at if he were a single man or a widow man I shouldn't. But he's wed and to my niece, and after what I've experienced at her hands I'll take care 'at she handles no more money o' mine. It were her 'at forced Albert to dissolve partnership wi' me. I had to pay him out wi' a lot o' money. But they'll never see another penny of what I've got! An' as I said just now, I'm worth, first and last, a good deal."

Jeckie suddenly opened her tightly-shut lips.

"How much?" she asked quietly.

Grice gave her a quick look; from her face his eyes wandered to the door of the parlour, which Jeckie had left open. He suddenly rose from his chair, tiptoed across the floor, and looked out into the lobby.

"There isn't a soul in the house but Farnish, and he's fast asleep, t'other side of the shop," said Jeckie, laconically. "But you can shut the door if you like."

Grice shut the door, slid back to his chair, and once more looked at her.

"Five and twenty thousand pound, at least," he said in a whisper. "One thing and another, five-and-twenty thousand pound!"

Jeckie watched him steadily through another period of silence.

"What did you come here for?" she suddenly demanded. "It wasn't for naught, I'll be bound! You'd an idea in your head!"

Grice leaned an elbow on the table, and began to tap the smart cloth with his thick fingers.

"An idea, aye—a suggestion," he answered, his small eyes still set on the woman who sat bolt upright before him. "And I'll put it to you, Jecholiah, for I know—and I wish I'd known sooner!—'at you're as keen on brass as what I've always been. It's this here, i' one word—marriage!"

Jeckie heard, without moving a muscle of her face nor relaxing the steady stare of her eyes.

"You an' me," she said in a low voice. "You and me—that's what you mean, Grice?"

"Me an' you," asserted Grice, nodding his bald head. "Me an' you—that is what I mean, and I've thought it out careful. Look here! I'm a certain age, but I'm a strong and well-preserved man, and worth at least—only at least, mind you—five-and-twenty thousand pound. Now then, this here business o' yours—and well you've conducted it!—is worth a lot already, goodwill, stock i' hand, and so on. Mine's still worth a good deal—old established, and I've one trade 'at you haven't touched—hay and corn merchant—'at's as good as ever. Now I haven't counted my businesses in that five-and-twenty thousand pound. An', do you see, supposin' you and me were to sell our businesses to a limited liability company, I know how and where they could be sold, and if you want to know, to one o' them firms o' that sort 'at's takin' over village businesses and transformin' 'em into big general stores. If, I say, we were to do that, d'ye see what a lot o' money we should have between us? And—you'll already have saved a good deal, I know!"

"Well, and what then?" asked Jeckie. There was not a trace of anything but hard business dealing in her voice, and her face was as fixed as ever. "What then, Grice?"

Grice put his head on one side, and seemed to be making some mental reflections.

"Taking one thing with another," he said, "what I have, what I can get for my business; what you have, what you can get for this place, I reckon we should be uncommon well off. We'd marry, and take a nice house, wherever you like, and keep a smart trap and horse."

"Smarter than your Albert's?" interrupted Jeckie with a sneer so faint that Grice failed to see it. "What?"

"Aye, a deal!" asserted Grice. "And we'd show 'em how to do it! Albert'll none ever touch a penny o' mine, now! Say the word, and it comes off, and I'll make a will i' your favour as soon as we're wed! What say you?"

Jeckie, still upright and rigid, sat staring at him until he thought she would never speak. Suddenly she rose, moved to the door, and beckoned him.

"Come here, Grice!" she said.

Grice rose and followed her round the end of the lobby into a passage which led to the shop. She opened a door, lighted a lamp, and, standing in the middle of the place, pointed round the heavily-stacked shelves and counters.

"You want to know what I say, Grice?" she said in low, incisive tones that made the old man's ears tingle. "I say this! Did ye ever see your shop stocked like mine, did you ever do as much trade as I'm doing, did you ever take as much brass over your counter in a fortnight as I take in a week? Never! An' I started all this wi' your money—it was your money that gave me my chance o' revenge. An' when I got that chance I said to myself that I'd never rest, body or soul, till I'd seen your shutters come down, and I never will! Go home!" she concluded, moving swiftly across the shop, and

76

throwing open the street door. "Go home!—I'd as lief think o' marryin' the devil himself as o' weddin' a man like you—I shall see you pull your shutters down yet, and—I shall ha' done it!"

Grice went out into the night without a word, and Jeckie stood in her doorway and watched him march heavily across the road. When he had disappeared within his own door, she closed hers, picked up a couple of sweet biscuits out of an open box as she crossed the shop, and went upstairs, munching them contentedly. And not even the delight of revenge kept her from sleep.

There were other men in Savilestowe who had eyes on Jeckie Farnish with a view to marriage. In spite of her strenuous pursuit of money she kept her good looks; continuous work, indeed, seemed to improve them, and if there was a certain hardness about her she remained the handsomest woman in the village. And not very long after her dramatic dismissal of the old grocer she was brought face to face for the second time with the necessity of making a decision. Calling on Stubley one day to pay her rent, the farmer, after giving her a receipt, turned round from the old bureau at which he had written it, and, leaning back in his elbow chair, gazed at her critically. He was a fine-looking, well-preserved man, a bachelor, more than comfortably off, and something in his eyes brought the colour to his tenant's cheeks. For one second she forgot her hardness and her ambitions and felt, rather than remembered, that she was a woman.

"Well, mi lass!" said Stubley. "And how long's this to go on?"

"How long's what to go on?" asked Jeckie.

"All this tewin' and toilin' and scrattin' after brass?" he said, with a half-amused, half-cynical laugh. "You've been at it a good while now, and you've about done what ye set out to do. Grice'll none keep his shutters up much longer. They say his takings have fallen to naught."

"I know they have," assented Jeckie with a flash of her keen eyes. "He's scarce any trade left."

"Aye, and you have it all, and I'll lay aught you've already made a nice little fortune for yourself!" continued Stubley. "So—why go on? What's the use of wasting your life, a handsome woman like you? There's something else in life than all this money-making, you know, lass. Sell your business—and live a bit!"

"Live a bit?" she said. "I—I don't know what you mean?"

Stubley waved his hand towards the window. There was a beautiful and well-kept garden outside, and beyond it a wide stretch of equally well-kept land. And Jeckie knew what the gesture meant.

"You know me," he said quietly. "Here's t'best farm-house and t'best farm in all this countryside. There's naught wanting here, mi

77

lass—it's plenty ... and peace. And there's no mistress to it, and naught to follow me, neither lad nor lass. Say the word, and get rid o' yon shop, and I'll marry you whenever you like. And—you'd never regret it."

Jeckie stood up, trembling in spite of her strength. She thought of the hard, grinding, sordid, unlovely life which she was living in the pursuit of money, and then of what might be as mistress of that fine old farm and wife of an honest, good-natured, dependable man. But as she thought, recollection came back to her—a recollection which was with her day and night. She saw herself standing in the empty, stockless fold at Applecroft, watching George Grice drive away, deaf to her entreaties for help. The old demon of hatred and determination for revenge, and the lust for money and power which had sprung from his workings, rose up again and conquered her.

"No," she said, turning away. "I can't! I'm obliged to you, Mr. Stubley—you're a straight man, and you mean well. But—I can't do it! I've set myself to a certain thing, and I must go on—I can't stop now!"

"What certain thing, mi lass?" asked Stubley. "What're you aimin' at?"

Jeckie looked round her, at the old furniture, the old pictures and framed samplers on the walls of the farm-house parlour, and from them to Stubley, and her eyes grew deep and sombre.

"I'm going to be the richest woman in all these parts!" she whispered. "I've set my mind to it, and it's got to be. I've no time to think of men—I'm after money—money!"

Then she turned and went swiftly out, leaving the farmer staring after her with wonder in his eyes. And he shook his head as he picked up the cheque which she had just given him and locked it in his bureau. He was thinking of the times when Jeckie Farnish could not have put her name to a cheque for a penny piece. But now—

There was yet one more man who wanted to marry the determined, money-grubbing woman. Bartle, who had seen Jeckie Farnish every day of his life since he had first come, seeking a job, to her father's door, a lad of fifteen, and who had served her like a faithful dog from the beginning of her big venture, came to feel that with him it was either going to be all or nothing. He had developed into a fine, handsome fellow, whose steadiness was a by-word in the village; in looks and character he was a man that any woman might well have been proud of. And one Sunday, having occasion to see Jeckie about some business of the ensuing morning, he suddenly

78

spoke straight out, as he and she stood among the flowers in her garden.

"Missis!" he said, his bronzed cheeks taking on a deep blush. "There's a word I mun either say or burst—I cannot hold it longer! I been i' love wi' you ever sin I were a lad, and you a lass, and it grows waur and waur! Will you wed me?—for if you weern't missis, I mun go!"

Jeckie looked at him, and knew the reality of what he had said. And for a moment she felt something remind her that she was a woman—but in the next she had steeled herself.

"It's no good, lad!" she said softly. "No good! Put it away from you."

Bartle turned white as his Sunday shirt, but he stood erect.

"Then you mun let me go, missis, and at once," he said huskily. "I've saved money, and I'll go a long way off—to this here Canada 'at they talk about. But go I will!"

He came to say good-bye to her three days later, and Jeckie put a hundred pounds in banknotes into his hand. It was the only deed of its sort that she ever wanted to do, but Bartle would have none of it. His eyes looked another appeal as he said his farewell, and Jeckie shook her head and let him go. And so he went, white-faced and dry-eyed, and with him went the last chance of redemption that Jeckie Farnish ever had. She had sold herself by then, body and soul, to Mammon.

CHAPTER XIII

DEAD MEN'S SHOES

Had George Grice but known it, the defection of his daughter-in-law, Lucilla, to the rival establishment across the street had more in it than appeared on the surface. Lucilla, after much worry and anxious thought, had come to the conclusion that there was no more to be got out of Albert's father. She had grown doubtful, not very long after her marriage, about the old man's financial position. George, when the bride and bridegroom had fairly settled down, had begun to throw out hints that her portion—two thousand pounds good money—ought to be sunk in the business, and when she had objected, saying that she preferred to control it herself, had grown grumpy and sullen. Then there had been difficulties about paying Albert out of the business when the dissension took place. George had put every obstacle possible in the way, and had delayed settlement until he was forced to it. Finally, he had forbidden Albert and Lucilla to darken his doors again, and the break-up of family ties had seemed complete. But, Lucilla had kept her eyes and ears open, and had seen and heard how the old man's business fell off; and, getting a purely feminine intuition that George was going steadily downhill and only keeping open out of sheer obstinacy and pride, she formed the opinion that he was by no means as well-off as was fancied, and, therefore, worth no more consideration. Hence the grocery book went no more to Grice but to Farnish. It was a final sign of complete separation, wholly due to Lucilla, who, in addition to other things, was actuated not a little by womanish spite and malice. George had told her a few plain truths to her face when the rift opened, and she had no objection to give him a few kicks behind his back. If she had had positive knowledge that the old man was wealthy she would have taken good care to keep in with him, but she had formed the impression that he was on his last legs, and that she and Albert would, from one cause or another, never benefit by him again.

As for Albert, he was now a gentleman; that is to say, he was a gentleman in the sense in which gentility is understood by village folk. He had nothing to do, and money to do it on. He and Lucilla dwelt in a villa residence on the roadside between Savilestowe and Sicaster; the villa was a pretentious affair of red brick with timber facings, there was a white door with an ornamental black knocker, a flower garden with rustic seats in front, a kitchen garden behind, and in a screened yard a coach-house and a stable with a smart dog-cart in one and a good cob in the other. There were two maidservants in the kitchen, and a pet dog in the parlour; in the dressing-room was Lucilla's chief solace, a piano, not so good, to be sure, as that which old George had bought her (that still remained, with the suite of furniture, in the room over the Savilestowe shop), but more showy in appearance. Lucilla ran the entire establishment—everyone in it, from Albert to the pet dog, was under her thumb. Albert read the newspaper after breakfast. He was then allowed to walk into Sicaster and look round the bar-parlours, but it was a strict commandment that he was never to drink anything but bitter beer, and only a little of that. In the afternoon he drove Lucilla out in the dog-cart. In the evening there was another newspaper to read, and he was allowed two glasses of gin-and-water before retiring to rest. It was a simple life, and Lucilla, who managed all the money matters, saved money every year.

Meanwhile old George went his way. It was a way of solitude, but he kept along its centre, looking neither to right nor left. He sold his hay-and-corn business, and devoted himself to the shop. A certain number of his old customers remained loyal to him; there was always sufficient trade to warrant him in keeping open, but in time he could comfortably do all the counter work himself, and his staff was cut down to an errand boy. He had plenty of time to talk to customers now, and, as they chiefly consisted of garrulous old women, he lounged a good deal over his counter. What affected him chiefly was the evening solitude, and, at last, after his fateful interview with Jeckie Farnish, he broke through the rule of a lifetime, and began to frequent the parlour of the "Coach-and-Four" every night, making one of a select circle wherein sat the miller, the butcher, the blacksmith, and the parish clerk. After a few experiences in this retreat he found himself cordially welcomed, for, having his own intentions as regarded the disposal of his money, he was liberal in spending it on liquor and cigars; nay, more, he actually got back some trade by this new departure, for, as the miller said, it was only reasonable that as Mr. Grice was so friendly and sociable-like they should go back to the old shop. For that George cared little by that time. What he chiefly valued was sympathy, and he quickly found that he could get plenty of it by handing round the cigar-box and paying for his cronies' gin-and-water.

"I reckon ye've been uncommon badly treated, Mr. Grice!" said the butcher as the five chief frequenters of the bar-parlour sat together in an atmosphere of cigar smoke and unsweetened gin one night. "It's a nice game, an' all, when a man's attained to t'eminence 'at you had i' this here place, when an upstart comes in and cuts him out! I should feel it mysen, I should indeed, wor it me!"

"Mr. Grice," observed the parish clerk, "has borne it all wi' Christian fortitude, gentlemen. My respects, sir; you haven't fallen off i' my estimation, Mr. Grice—nor, I'm sure, i' that of any of the rest of these here gentlemen."

There was a general murmur of assent; the fact was that old George had shown himself particularly lavish that evening in insisting on paying for everything, saying that it was his birthday.

"Aye, there's a deal i' Christian fortitude," remarked the

blacksmith. "It's one o' them horses 'at'll carry a man a long way wi'out brakkin' down; it 'ud weer out a good many shoes would that theer. Ye been well favoured to be endowed wi' such a quality, Mr. Grice."

"Now then!" said George, mollified and pleased. "Now then, say no more about it! I hev mi faults, and I hev mi qualities. I could say a good deal, but I'll say naught. All on us hes crosses to bear, and I've borne mine, patient. An' I hope all them 'at's deserted me for never mind who'll never have cause to regret it. But i' mi time, 've give away a deal i' charity i' this place—ask t'parson if he ever knew me not to put mi hand i' mi pocket whenever him or his lady, or t'curate come wantin' summat for coals, and blankets, and t'clothing fund and such-like—and I don't hear 'at a certain person ever gives a penny!"

"None she!" exclaimed the miller. "She's as hard as one o' t'stones i' my mill—and if there's owt i' this world 'at's harder, I could like to hear tell on it! No, she'll none give owt away, weern't that! She's set on makkin' all t'brass 'at she can, and what she scrapes together she'll stick to. All t'same, I don't think you'll put your shutters up yet, Mr. Grice, what?"

"Not while I can draw breath!" answered Grice, with a grim look. "She'll none beat me at that, I can tell yer!"

He had made up his mind on that point after Jeckie Farnish had motioned him away from her shop-door on the night of his strange proposal to her. Let come what might, he would keep down the shutters to the very end—they should never be put up until they were put up some day to show that he was dead. Customers or no customers—he would keep the old shop open. There would have to be a day, of course, whereon he would be unable to tie on his apron and take his stand behind the counter, but until that day came....

The day came with sudden swiftness. One morning the woman who did George Grice's housework arrived to find the doors open, an unusual thing, for he usually came down to let her in. She walked through the kitchen into the parlour, and found him lying back in his elbow-chair at the table, dead and cold. The gin and the cigars were on the table; on the carpet at his feet lay an old account-book which he had evidently been reading when death came upon him; it referred to the days wherein the firm of George Grice & Son had been at the height of its prosperity. So Grice's last thoughts in this world had been of money.

The woman followed the instincts of her sort, and after one horrified glance at the dead man, ran out into the street, eager to spread the news. The first person she set eyes on was Jeckie Farnish, who, always up with the sun, was standing in the roadway outside her shop, vigorously scolding one of her shop-boys for his carelessness in sweeping the sidewalk. Upon her objurgations the woman broke, big with tidings and already half breathless.

"Miss Farnish! Eh, dear—such a turn as it's given me!—Miss Farnish! There's Mr. Grice—there in his parlour—sittin' i' his chair, Miss Farnish, an' wi' his bottle o' sperrits i' front o' him, and all—such an end, to be sure!—and dead—aye, and must ha' died last night, for he's as cowd as ice. An' will you come back wi' me, Miss Farnish?—I'm fair feared to go in agen by misen!"

Jeckie turned and looked down at the woman—a little wizened creature—with an incredulous stare.

"What do you say?" she demanded sharply. "Grice? Dead?"

"Dead as a door-nail, Miss Farnish, as sure as I'm here—and sittin' i' t'easy chair at his table——"

Jeckie looked round at the offending shop-boy; even then she considered her own affairs first.

"You get another pail o' water, and swill them flags again this minute!" she commanded. "And mind you do it right, or else——"

She broke off at that, and without another word to the agitated woman who was staring at her with affrighted eyes, marched straight across the street, through George Grice's yard and in at the side-door of the house. She knew her way about that house as well as its late master, and she turned at once into the parlour in which she had never set foot since that morning, years before, on which she had gone there to beg Grice's help. She saw at one glance that Grice himself was now beyond all human help, and for a moment she stood and looked at his dead face with keen, critical eyes. Death, instead of smoothing the lines of his naturally sly and crafty countenance, had deepened them; it was not a pleasant sight that Jeckie looked at. And the woman, who had crept in after her, spoke in a half-frightened whisper.

"Lord save us!—he don't mak' a beautiful corpse, trew-ly, does he, Miss Farnish?" she said. "He looks that hard and graspin', same as he did when a poor body wanted summat and——"

"He must have had a stroke and died in it," remarked Jeckie, in matter-of-fact tones. "And I should say, as he died all alone, 'at there'll have to be an inquest, so don't you touch aught 'at there is on that table. You go round and tell the policeman to come here at once for he'll have to let the coroner know. Don't say aught to anybody else till he's been, and I'll go and send one of my lads for Mr. Albert."

The woman hurried away, and Jeckie, waiting there with the dead man until the policeman arrived, hated him worse than ever. For she had never seen the shutters go up in his lifetime—he had held out to the end, and cheated her of her cherished revenge. Yet never mind—the Grice business was over; that she knew very well; henceforth she was a monopolist. And when the policeman had come and had taken charge of matters, she went across to her stables, where her van-man was just putting a horse into a light cart.

"Here!" she said, "you're going up to t'top o' t'village, Watkinson. Drive on, as soon as you've delivered those parcels, to Mr. Albert Grice's—tell him his father's dead."

The old man opened his mouth and stared.

"What, t'owd man, missis?" he exclaimed. "Nay!—I seed him all right last night."

"He's dead," repeated Jeckie, turning unconcernedly away. "Tell Mr. Albert he'd better come down."

Albert came within an hour, and Lucilla with him, and the smart cob and smart dog-cart were housed in the dead man's stable. Presently, he himself was laid out in decency on his own bed, and all the blinds were drawn, and the shutters were up in the shop, and Albert and Lucilla, having found George's keys, began to go through his effects. But before they had fairly entered on this congenial task, interruption came in the shape of a Sicaster solicitor, Mr. Whitby, accompanied by a well-known Sicaster tradesman, Mr. Cransdale, who drove up in a cab, evidently in haste, and walked uninvited into the house, to find Albert and Lucilla busied at the dead man's desk. Whitby immediately pulled out some papers.

"Good morning, Mr. Grice—good morning, Mrs. Grice," he said, with a certain amount of disapproval shown behind a surface pleasantness. "Busy, I see, already! I'm afraid I must ask you to hand those keys over to us, Mr. Grice, and to leave all my late client's effects to the care of Mr. Cransdale and myself—we're the executors and trustees of his will——"

"What?" exclaimed Lucilla, whose tongue was always in advance of her husband's. "Then he made a will?"

"Here's the will," answered Whitby, producing a document and folding it in such a fashion that only the last paragraph or two could be seen. "There is the late Mr. George Grice's signature; there are the signatures of the witnesses, and there—you may see that much—is the clause appointing Mr. Cransdale and myself executors and trustees. All in order, Mr. Grice!"

"What's in the will?" demanded Lucilla.

84

"All in good time, ma'am!" responded Whitby. "You'll hear everything after the funeral. In the meantime—those keys, if you please. Now," he continued, as Albert sullenly handed over the keys, "nothing whatever in this house will be touched—no papers, no effects, nothing! You understand, Mr. and Mrs. Grice? Mr. Cransdale and I are in full power. We shall arrange everything."

"So you turn my husband out of his father's house!" exclaimed Lucilla indignantly. "That's what it comes to!"

"I don't think he troubled his father's house very much of late," said Whitby dryly. "But I repeat—Mr. Cransdale and I are in full power. After the late Mr. Grice's funeral the will shall be read."

Albert and Lucilla had to retire, and they spent the next three days in wondering what all this was about. Lucilla's father arrived from Nottingham on the evening before his brother's obsequies; he, too, was full of wonder. He was as busy a man as George had been in his palmiest days, and knew little of what had been going on at Savilestowe. And when his daughter told him the story of recent events he frowned heavily.

"It'll be well if you haven't made a mistake, my girl!" he said. "My brother George was as deep and sly as ever they make 'em. The probability is that he'll cut up a lot better than you think, in spite of everything. You should have kept in with him, whatever came. You wait till that will's read, and I hope you and Albert won't get a nasty surprise!"

Lucilla was surprised enough when she saw the curious assemblage which, duly marshalled by Whitby, gathered together in the dead man's parlour, after he himself had been laid in the grave, which many years before had received his wife's body, and was surmounted by a handsome and weighty obelisk, whereon his own name was now to be cut in deep gilt letters. There were the relatives; herself, her husband, her father; there were also the vicar, the squire, and Stubley, the last three all plainly wondering why they were asked to be present. But their wonder was not to last long. In five minutes the will had been read and everybody there had grasped the meaning of its provisions. George Grice had left everything of which he died possessed in trust to Whitby and Cransdale, who were to realise the whole of his estate, and with the proceeds to build and endow a cottage hospital at Savilestowe, to be known forever as the George Grice Memorial Home, and the vicar, the squire, and Stubley were asked to co-operate with the trustees in carrying out the initial arrangements. For anything and anybody else—not one penny.

When all was done Lucilla's father drew Whitby aside.

"Between you and me," he said, with a knowing look, "what might my brother's estate be likely to come to?"

"As near as I can make out," answered Whitby, "about thirty thousand pounds."

The inquirer followed his daughter and Albert out of the house, and gave them a good deal of his tongue on the way home, and for once in her life Lucilla had nothing to answer. Moreover, she now foresaw trouble between her and Albert.

And that afternoon, before leaving the village, the executors and trustees of George Grice deceased walked across the street to see Miss Jecholiah Farnish. Their conversation with her was of a brief sort as far as time was concerned, but its upshot was of an important nature. Jeckie agreed, there and then, to buy the goodwill of the business which she had set out to ruin, and she took care to get it dirt cheap.

End of the First Part

PART THE SECOND

FALL

CHAPTER I

AVARICE

Five years after George Grice had been gathered to his fathers, by which time Jeckie Farnish had achieved her ambition and become the richest woman in Savilestowe, there walked into the stone-flagged hall of the "Coach-and-Four" one fine spring morning, a gentleman who wore a smart suit of grey tweed, a grey Homburg hat, ornamented by a black band, and swung a handsome gold-mounted walking cane in his elegantly-gloved fingers. There was an air of consequence and distinction about him, though he was apparently still on the right side of thirty; the way in which he looked around as he stepped across the threshold, showed that he was one of those superior beings who are accustomed to give orders and have them obeyed, and Steve Beckitt, the landlord, who chanced to be in the hall at the time, made haste to come forward and throw open the door of the best parlour. The stranger, who was as good-looking as he was well-dressed, smiled genially, showing a set of fine teeth beneath a carefully trimmed dark moustache, and removed his hat as he walked in and glanced approvingly at the old-fashioned furniture. "You the landlord?" he asked pleasantly, and with another smile. "Mr. Beckitt, then?—I had your name given me by the landlady of the 'Red Lion' at Sicaster, where I've been staying for a week or two. I've just walked out from there—and, to begin with, I should like a glass or two of your best bitter ale, Mr. Beckitt. Bring a jug of it—I know you've always good ale in these country inns!—and join me. I want to have a word or two with you."

Beckitt, a worthy and unimaginative soul, full of curiosity, fetched the ale and poured it out; the stranger, producing a handsome silver case, offered him a cigar and lighted one himself. And when he had tasted and praised the ale, he dropped into an easy chair and swinging one leg over the other, looked smilingly at the landlord, whom he had waved to a seat.

"My name's Mortimer," he said, with almost boyish ingenuousness, "Mallerbie Mortimer—I'm from London. I've been having a holiday in the North here, and for the last fortnight I've been staying in Sicaster—at 'the Red Lion.' Now, I've a fancy to stay a bit longer in these parts, Mr. Beckitt, and I have heard in Sicaster that this is a very pretty and interesting neighbourhood. So I walked out this morning to see if you could put me up for a week or two at the 'Coach-and-Four'? How are you fixed?"

Beckitt, who was sure by that time that his visitor was a moneyed gentleman, put his thumbs in the armholes of his waistcoat—a sure sign that he was thinking.

"Well, sir," he replied, "it isn't oft 'at we're asked for accommodation o' that partik'lar nature, but, of course, twice a year we do entertain t'steward—a lawyer gentleman—when he comes to collect t'rents. He has this room for a parlour, and there's a nice big bedroom upstairs—he's allus expressed his-self as very well satisfied wi' all 'at we do for him. Of course, it's naught but plain cookin' at we can offer—but t'steward, he allus takes to it."

"And so should I," affirmed the caller, who was evidently disposed to like anything and everything. "Good, plain, homely fare and cooking, Mr. Beckitt—that's all I want. And for whatever I have, I'll pay you well—now, supposing you call your good lady, and let me see the bedroom, and have a talk to her about my meals?"

Within ten minutes of his entrance Mr. Mallerbie Mortimer had settled matters with the host and hostess of the "Coach-and-Four." He was evidently a man who was accustomed to arrange affairs in quick time; he told Mrs. Beckitt precisely what he wanted in a very few sentences, and then offered her for board and lodging a certain weekly sum which was about half as much again as she would have asked him. Immediately on her acceptance of it, he pulled a handful of loose gold out of his trousers pocket, paid his first week's bill in advance, and turning to the landlord, asked him to send somebody with a trap to Sicaster to fetch his luggage—three portmanteaux and two suit-cases. Then, arranging for a mutton-chop at half-past one, he went out and strolled down the village street, his Homburg hat at a jaunty angle, and his cane swinging lightly in his gloved hand. The folk whom he met wondered at him, and Jeckie Farnish, who happened to be standing at the door of her shop, wondered most of all. Strangers were rare in Savilestowe, and this one was evidently a man of far-off parts.

But before twenty-four hours had gone by, Mr. Mallerbie Mortimer had made himself known to most people in the village. He was an eminently sociable person, and after his first dinner at the "Coach-and-Four"—a roast chicken, the cooking of which he praised unreservedly—he went into the bar-parlour and fraternised with the select company which assembled there every evening. He was generous in the matter of paying for drinks and cigars; he was also an adept in drawing men out. Within a night or two, he knew all the affairs of the place, and all the principal inhabitants by name; also, he had heard, from more than one informant, the full story of Jeckie Farnish and George Grice. He showed himself possessed of pleasant and ingratiating manners, and might be seen chatting in the blacksmith's forge, or lounging in the carpenter's shop, or exchanging jokes with the miller, or hanging about the churchyard with the sexton; he talked farming with Stubley, and smoked an afternoon pipe with Merritt. And when he was not doing any of these things, he was all over the place—farmers met him crossing fields and going about meadows, and along the side of hedgerows; thus encountered, Mr. Mallerbie Mortimer always showed his white teeth and his engaging smile, and said he hoped he wasn't trespassing, but he had a mania for going wherever his fancy prompted when he was in the country. Nobody, of course, objected to so pleasant a gentleman going wherever he pleased, and by the end of the week he had thoroughly explored the parish. And had anybody been with him on these solitary excursions they would have observed that the stranger took a most curious interest in the various soils over which he walked, and that in certain places he would linger a long time, closely inspecting marl and loam and clay and sandstone and outcropping limestone. But the Savilestowe folk saw nothing of this; all they saw was a very smart young gentleman who wore a different, apparently brand-new, suit every day, put on black clothes and a dinner jacket every evening, received piles of letters and bundles of newspapers each morning, and, in spite of his grandeur and his money—his abundant possession of which was soon made evident—had no snobbishness about him, and was only too willing to be hail-fellow-well-met with everybody from the parson to the ploughman.

Mr. Mortimer informed Mrs. Beckitt, at the end of his first week's stay at Savilestowe, that he was so well satisfied with his quarters that he had decided to remain where he was for a while longer—he might, he further informed her, be having a friend down from London to stay for a week or so in this truly delightful spot. Beckitt and his wife were only too pleased; Mr. Mortimer was not only a very profitable lodger, but free of his money in the bar-parlour, where he made a practice of spending his evenings after his seven o'clock dinner. He was in that parlour every night until nearly

89

the second week of his visit had gone by. Then, one night, instead of crossing the hall from his sitting room to join the company which had grown accustomed to his genial presence, he waited until night had fallen, put a light overcoat over his evening clothes, drew on a soft cap, and taking some papers from a dispatch-box which he kept, locked, in his bedroom, slipped out of the "Coach-and-Four" and strolled down the village street. Five minutes later found him knocking gently at the private door of Jeckie Farnish's house.

Jeckie, by this time, kept a couple of maidservants. But it was growing late, and they had gone to bed, and it was Jeckie herself who opened the door and shone the light of a hand-lamp on the caller. Now up to that time Jeckie was about the only person in Savilestowe to whom Mr. Mallerbie Mortimer had not introduced himself; he had passed her shop scores of times, but had never entered it. She stared wonderingly at him as he removed his cap with one hand and offered her a card with the other.

"May I have a few minutes' conversation with you, Miss Farnish—in private?" he asked, favouring Jeckie with the ingratiating smile. "I came late purposely—so that we might have our talk all to ourselves—you are, I know, a very busy woman in the day-time."

Jeckie looked at the card suspiciously. Mr. Mallerbie Mortimer, M.I.M.E., 281c, Victoria Street, London, S.W. The letters at the end of the name conveyed nothing to her. "You're not a traveller?" she asked abruptly, showing no inclination to ask the caller in. "I only see travellers on Fridays—three to five. I can't break my rule."

"I am certainly not a traveller—of that sort," laughed the visitor. "I am a professional man—staying here for a professional purpose. Don't you see, ma'am, what I am, from my card?—a member of the Institute of Mining Engineers? I want to see you alone, on a most important business matter."

Jeckie motioned him to enter.

"I didn't know what those letters meant," she said, with emphasis on the personal pronoun. "But come in—though upon my word, mister, I don't know what you want to see me about, mister! This way, if you please."

Mortimer laughed as he followed her into a parlour where there was a bright fire in the grate—coal was cheap in that neighbourhood—and a lamp burning on the centre table. He closed the door behind him, and when Jeckie had seated herself, dropped into an easy chair in front of her.

"I'll tell you why I've come to see you, Miss Farnish," he said in low suave tones. "There's nothing like going straight to the point.

I came to you because, having now been in Savilestowe, as you're aware, for close on a fortnight, I know that you're the richest person in the place—man or woman! Eh?"

Jeckie had heard this sort of thing before, more than once. It usually prefaced a demand on her purse, and she looked at Mortimer with increased suspicion.

"If it's a subscription you're wanting," she began, and then stopped, seeing the amusement in her visitor's face. "What do you want, then?" she demanded. "You said business."

"And I mean and intend business!" answered Mortimer. "You're a business woman, and I'm a business man, so we shall understand each other if I speak freely and plainly. Look here! Since I came to stay at the 'Coach-and-Four,' nearly a fortnight ago I've heard all about you, Miss Farnish. How you beat that old fellow Grice, drove him out, and all the rest of it. You're a smart woman, you know; you've brains, and go, and initiative, and determination—you're just the person I want!"

"For what?" demanded Jeckie, who was not insensible to flattery. "What's it all about?"

Mortimer edged his chair nearer to hers, and gave her a knowing look. The hard and strenuous life she had lived had robbed Jeckie of some of her beauty, but she was a handsome woman still, and there was recognition of that undoubted fact in the man's bold eyes.

"You're one of the sort that wants to get rich quick!" he said. "Right! so am I. There's a bond between us. Now, as I said, I know for a fact you're the richest person in this place, leaving the squire out of the question. You know that's so! but only yourself knows how well-off you are. Yet, how would you like to be absolutely wealthy?"

"I believe in money," said Jeckie. She saw no use in denying the truth to this persistent and plausible stranger. "I've worked for money, naught else! What do you mean?"

"Supposing I told you of how you could make money in such a fashion that what you're making now would be as nothing to it?" said Mortimer, still watching her keenly. "Would you be inclined to take the chance?"

Jeckie gave her visitor a good, long look before she replied. And Mortimer added another word or two.

"I'm talking sense!" he affirmed. "I mean what I say."

"If I saw the chance o' making money in the way you speak of," answered Jeckie, at last, "it 'ud be a queer thing if I didn't take it. I never missed a chance yet!"

"Don't miss this!" said Mortimer. "Listen! You don't know

why I'm here; you don't know what I mean; you don't know what I've come to see you about. I'll tell you in one word if you'll promise to keep this to yourself?"

"If it's aught about business and money you can be certain I shall," asserted Jeckie. "I'm not given to talking about my affairs."

"Very good," continued Mortimer. "Then, do you know what there is under this village of Savilestowe, under its fields and meadows, aye, underneath where you and I are sitting just now. Do you?"

"What?" demanded Jeckie, roused by his evident enthusiasm. "What?"

Mortimer leaned forward, laid a hand on her arm, and spoke one word—twice.

"Coal!" he said. "Coal?"

Jeckie stared at him, silently, for awhile. And Mortimer kept his eyes fixed on hers, as if he were exercising some hypnotic influence on her. She stirred a little at last, and spoke, wonderingly.

"Coal?" she said, in a low voice. "You mean——"

"I mean that there's no end of coal beneath our feet!" said Mortimer. "Listen! You know—for you must have heard—how the coal-mining industry's been increasing and developing in this part of Yorkshire during the last few years. Now, I'm a mining expert; here's a pocketful of references and testimonials about me that I'll leave with you, to look over at your leisure; and I came over to Sicaster three weeks or so ago to have a look round this neighbourhood. From something I saw one day when I was out for a walk in this direction I decided to come here and go carefully over the ground. I've been carefully over it—every yard of this village! I tell you, as an expert, there's no end of coal under here—no end! And whoever works it'll make—a huge fortune!"

Jeckie sat, almost spellbound, listening; such imagination as she possessed was already stirred. And when she spoke it seemed to her that her voice sounded as if it came from a long way off.

"But—it's down there!" she said.

"But—it is there!" exclaimed Mortimer. "All that's wanted is for man to get it out! I know how to do that. All that's wanted is money! capital!"

He got up from his chair, thrust his hands in his pocket, and jingled the loose coins which lay in them, looking down at Jeckie with a significant smile.

"Capital!" he repeated. "Capital! I'm so certain of what I say that I'm willing to find a good lot myself. But not all that's wanted. And what I want to know is—are you coming in, now that I've told you? Look here, for every ten thousand that's put into this business there'll be a hundred thousand within a very short time of getting to work. I'll stake my reputation—not a bad one, as you'll learn from these papers—that this'll be one of the richest mines, in quantity and quality, in England. A regular gold mine! I know!"

"But—the land?" said Jeckie. "You've to buy the land first, haven't you?"

Mortimer laughed, and picked up his cap.

"I know how to do that in this case," he said. "Not another word now: I'll come and see you again to-morrow evening, same time. In the meantime—strict secrecy. But take my word for it, if you come in with me at this I'll make you a richer woman than you've ever dreamed of being. And I think you've had some ambitions that way—what?"

Then, with a brief, almost curt, good-night, he went away, and Jeckie, after letting him out and fastening her door, read through the papers which he had left with her. There was a banker's reference, and a solicitor's reference, and numerous testimonials to the great ability of Mr. Mallerbie Mortimer as a mining expert. Jeckie knew enough of things to estimate these papers at their proper value, especially the banker's reference, and she went off to bed with new ideas forming in her brain. Coal!—there, beneath her feet—black, shining stuff that could be turned into yellow gold. It seemed to her that she hated the green fields and red earth that lay between it and her avaricious fingers.

CHAPTER II

THE BIT OF BAD LAND

Mortimer was at Jeckie Farnish's private door to the minute on the following evening, and Jeckie hastened to admit him and to lead him to her parlour. He went straight to the point at which he had broken off their conversation of the night before.

"You were saying that before ever starting on the project I mentioned it would be necessary to buy the land," he said, as he settled himself in an easy chair. "Now, Miss Farnish, let's be plain and matter-of-fact about one thing. Most of the land in this parish of Savilestowe belongs to the squire. But we're not going to have him in at this business! I don't want him even to know that anything's afoot until matters are settled, and in full working order. For not all the land is his!—which is fortunate. A good deal of it, as you know, is glebe land. Then, Stubley owns a bit, and I understand those two fields by the mill are the freehold property of the miller. And, very fortunately for my scheme and ideas, there's a considerable piece of land here which belongs to a man who, I should say, would be very glad to sell it—I mean the piece down there beyond the old stone quarry, which you villagers call Savilestowe Leys."

"Worst bit o' land in the place!" exclaimed Jeckie. "There's naught grown there but the coarsest sort o' grass and weeds and such-like; it's more like a wilderness than aught!"

Mortimer showed his white teeth and his eyes sparkled.

"All the better for us, my dear lady!" he said. "But it's under there that we shall find the richest bed of coal! I know that! Seams, without doubt, spread away from that bed in several directions, but the real wealth of this place lies under that bad bit of land, half-marsh, half-wilderness, as you say. Now, I understand that that particular property—forty acres in all—belongs to that little farmer at the Sicaster end of the village. You know the man I mean—Benjamin Scholes?"

"Yes," assented Jeckie. "It's been in Ben Scholes's family for many a generation."

Mortimer leaned forward, gave Jeckie a sharp, meaning look, and tapped her wrist.

"The first thing to be done is to buy these forty acres of land from Scholes—privately," he said. "That land's the front door to a store-house of unlimited wealth! And—you must buy it."

Jeckie shook her head.

"I say you must!" asserted Mortimer. "There's nobody but you who can do it. It'll have to be done on the quiet. You're the person!"

"It's not that," said Jeckie. "You're a stranger; you don't know our people. Ben Scholes is a poor man; he'd be glad enough of the money. But that land's been in their family for two or three hundred years; he'll none want to part with it, were it ever so. Poor as it is, the squire wanted to buy it from him some time since; he'd a notion of planting it with fir and pine. But Ben wouldn't sell. And, besides, what excuse could I make for buying it?—poor land like that! He'd be suspicious."

"I've thought of all that," answered Mortimer. "I'm full of resource, as you'll find out. Everybody knows what an enterprising woman you are, so that what I'm going to suggest you should do would surprise nobody if you do it—as you must. Go and see

94

Scholes; tell him you want to start a market garden and a fruit orchard, and that his land will just suit your purposes when it's been thoroughly drained and prepared. Offer to buy it outright; stick to him till you get it. Never you mind about his refusal to the squire; you've got a better tongue in your head than the squire has from what I've seen of him, and you'll get round Scholes. You ought to get the forty acres, such bad land as it is, for two or three hundred pounds. But look here—go up to that. You see, I'm not asking you to find the money."

He drew out a pocket-book, extracted a folded slip of paper from it, unfolded it, and dropped it on the table at Jeckie's elbow. Jeckie looked down and saw a cheque, made payable to herself, for five hundred pounds.

"You'll get it for less than that if you go about it the right way," continued Mortimer. "And, of course, when you buy it, and the conveyancing's done, you'll have all the papers made out in your name. I shan't appear in it at all. You and I can settle matters later—but—there's the money. And if this chap Scholes stands out for more you've nothing to do but ask me. Only—but! At once!"

"And if he will sell?—if I get it?" asked Jeckie. "What then?"

"Then we've got forty acres of worthless stuff on top, and many a thousand tons of coal beneath!" said Mortimer. "It'll take a good time to exhaust what there is beneath the forty acres. And we can get to work. As for the rest of the land in the place—well, as need arises we shall have to come to terms with the other property owners. We should pay them royalties; that's all a matter of arrangement. We might lease their land—mineral rights, you know—from them for a term of years. All that can be settled later. What we want is a definite standing as owners; to begin with—owners! We might have leased Scholes's forty acres for twenty-one, forty-two, or sixty-three years, but it's far best to buy. Then it's ours. Go and see Scholes at once—to-morrow."

Jeckie picked up the cheque, and seemed to be looking at it, but Mortimer saw that she did not see it at all; her thoughts were elsewhere.

"And if I buy this bit o' land?" she said, after a pause. "What then?"

"Then, my dear madam, we'll get the necessary capital together, and proceed to make our mine!" replied Mortimer, with a laugh. "But there'll be things to be done first. First of all, so as to make assurance doubly sure, we should do a bit of prospecting—dig a drift into the seam (if I find an out-crop, as I may) to prove its value, or sink a trial pit, or do some boring. It'll probably be boring;

and when that takes place you'll soon know what to expect in the way of results."

"I should want to know a lot about that before I put money into it," affirmed Jeckie. "I'm not the sort to throw money away."

"Neither am I!" laughed Mortimer. He rose in his characteristically abrupt fashion. "Well!" he said. "You'll see Scholes?—at once! Get hold of his forty acres, and then—then we can move. And in five years—ah!"

"What?" demanded Jeckie as she followed him to the door.

"You'll be mistress of a grand country house and a town mansion in Mayfair!" answered Mortimer, showing his teeth. "Wealth! Look beneath your very boots! it's just waiting there to be torn out of the earth."

Jeckie put Mortimer's cheque away in her safe, and went to bed, her avaricious spirit more excited than ever. Like all the folk in that neighbourhood, she knew how the coal-fields of that part of Yorkshire had been developed and extended of late; she had heard too, of the riches which men of humble origin had amassed by their fortunate possession of a bit of land under which lay rich seams of coal. There was Mr. Revis, of Heronshawe Main, three miles the other side of Sicaster, who, originally a market gardener, was now, they said, a millionaire, all because he had happened to find out that coal lay under an unpromising, black-surfaced piece of damp land by the river side, which his father had left him, and had then seemed almost valueless. There was Mr. Graveson, of the Duke of York's Colliery, on the other side of the town—he, they said, had been a small tradesman to begin with, but had a sharp enough nose to smell coal at a particular place, and wit enough to buy the land which covered it—he, too, rolled in money. And, after all, the stranger from London had shown his belief by putting five hundred pounds in her hands—it would cost her nothing if she made the venture. And if there was coal beneath Ben Scholes's forty acres, why not try for the fortune which its successful getting would represent?

After her one o'clock dinner next day, Jeckie, who by that time had a capable manager and three assistants in her shop, assumed her best attire and went out. She turned her face towards the Savilestowe Leys, a desolate stretch of land at the lower end of the village, and from the hedgerow which bordered it, looked long and speculatively across its flat, unpromising surface. She was wondering how men like Mortimer knew that coal lay underneath such land—all that she saw was coarse grass, marsh marigolds, clumps of sedge and bramble, and a couple of starved-looking cows, Scholes's property, trying to find a mouthful of food among the

96

prevalent poverty of the vegetation. That land, for agistment purposes, was not worth sixpence an acre, said Jeckie to herself; it seemed little short of amazing to think that wealth, possibly enormous in quantity, should be beneath it. But she remembered Mortimer's enthusiasm and his testimonials, and his cheque, and she turned and walked through the village to Ben Scholes's farm.

There was a circumstance of which Jeckie was aware that she had not mentioned to Mortimer when they discussed the question of buying Ben Scholes's bit of bad land. Ben Scholes, who was only a little better off than her own father had been in the old days at Applecroft, owed her money. Jeckie, as time went on, had begun to give credit; she found that it was almost necessary to do so. And that year she had let Ben Scholes and his wife get fairly deep into her books, knowing very well that when harvest time came round Ben would have money, and would pay up—he was an honest, if a poor man. What with groceries and horse-corn and hardware—for Jeckie had begun to deal in small goods of that sort, forks, rakes, hoes and the like, since years before—Scholes owed her nearly a hundred pounds. She remembered that, as she walked up the street, and she busied herself in thinking how she could turn this fact to advantage. Yet, she was not going to put the screw on her debtor; in her time she had learnt how to be diplomatic and tactful, how to gain her ends by other means than force. And it was not the face of the stern creditor which she showed when she knocked at the open door of Scholes's little farmstead.

It was then three o'clock, and Scholes and his wife were following the usual Savilestowe custom of having an early cup of tea. They looked up from the table at which they sat by the fire, and the wife rose in surprise and with alacrity.

"Eh, why, if it isn't Miss Farnish!" she exclaimed. "Come your ways in, Miss Farnish, and sit you down. Happen, now you'll be tempted to take a cup o' tea? it's fresh made, within this last five minutes, and good and strong—your own tea, you know, and I couldn't say no more. Now do!"

"Why, thank you," responded Jeckie. "I don't mind if I do, as you're so kind. I just walked up to have a word or two with Ben there."

Scholes, a middle-aged, careworn-looking man, who, in spite of everything, had a somewhat humorous twist of countenance, grinned almost sheepishly as Jeckie took an elbow chair which his wife pulled forward for her.

"I hope you haven't come after no brass, Miss Farnish," he said, with an air intended to be ingratiatingly seductive. "I've nowt o' that sort to spare till t'harvest's in, but there'll be a bit then to

97

throw about. We mun have a settlin' up at that time. Ye know me—
I'm all right."

Jeckie took the cup of tea which Mrs. Scholes handed to her,
and stirred it thoughtfully.

"I didn't come after any brass, Ben," she answered. "It's all
right, that—as you say, I know you. I wasn't going to mention it till
harvest comes."

"Why, now, then, that's all right!" said Scholes, facetiously.
"Them's comfortable words, them is. Aye, brass is scarce i' this
region, but we carry on, you know, we carry on, somehow. We
haven't all gotten t'secret o' makin' fortunes, like you have, ye know.
Us little 'uns has to be content wi' what they call t'day o' small
things."

"Aye, an' varry small an' all!" sighed Mrs. Scholes. "I'm sure!
It's all 'at a body can do, nowadays, to keep soul and body together."

"Why, mi lass, why!" said Scholes. "We've managed it so far.
All t'same, I could offen find it i' mi heart to wish 'at I'd one o' these
here rellytives 'at ye sometimes read about i' t'papers—owd uncles
'at dies i' foreign parts, and leaves fortunes, unexpected, like, to
their nevvys and nieces at home. But none o' my uncles niver had
nowt to leave 'at I iver heerd on."

"I came up to tell you how you could make a bit o' money if
you want to," said Jeckie. The conversation had taken a convenient
turn, and she was quick to seize the opportunity. "A nice bit!" she
added. "Something substantial."

Scholes pushed his cup and saucer away from him and looked
sharply at his visitor.

"Ecod!" he exclaimed. "I should be glad to hear o' that! But—
wheer can I make owt, outside o' this farm o' mine? It niver does no
more nor keep us. It does that, to be sure, seein' 'at there's nobody
but me and t'missis there, but that's all."

"Well, listen," said Jeckie. "There's that piece o' land o' yours,
down at t'bottom end o' t'village. I want to buy it."

Scholes' thin face flushed, and he rose slowly from his chair,
and for a moment turned away toward the window. When he looked
round again he shook his head.

"Nay!" he said. "Nay!—I couldn't sell yon theer! Why, it's been
i' our family over three hundred years! Poor enough it is, and
wean't feed nowt—but as long as I have it, ye see, I'm a landowner,
same as t'squire his-self! Why, as I dare say you've aweer, he wanted
to buy that forty acres fro' me a piece back—but I wodn't. No! He
were calculating to plant it, and to make it into a game preserve. It
were no use. I couldn't find it i' mi heart to let it go. No!"

"Don't be silly!" said Jeckie. "That's all sentiment. What good

98

is it to you? Them two cows 'at you've got in it now can scarce pick up a mouthful!"

"It's right, is that," agreed Scholes. "If them unfortunate animals had to depend on what they get out o' that theer they'd have empty bellies every night! But—(he dropped into his chair again and looked hard at his visitor)—since it's as poor as it is, what might you be wantin' it for? If it's no good to me it's no good to nobody."

"I've got something that you haven't got," answered Jeckie, in her most matter-of-fact tones. "You could never do aught to improve that land, because you haven't got the money to do it with. I have! I'll be plain with you. I'll tell you what I want it for. You know how I've developed my business since I started it—developed it in all sorts of ways. Well, I'm going in for market-gardening and fruit-growing, and that piece o' land'll just suit me, because it's within half a mile o' the shop. Sell it to me, and I'll have it thoroughly drained. That's what it wants; and make real good land of it, you'll see. You can't do that; it 'ud cost you hundreds o' pounds. I don't mind spending hundreds o' pounds on it. And—I want it!"

Scholes was evidently impressed by this line of argument. He looked round at his wife, who was gazing anxiously from him to Jeckie, and from Jeckie to him.

"Ye're right i' one thing," he answered. "It would make all t'difference i' t'world to them forty acres if they were drained. My father allus said so, and I've allus said so. But we never had t'money to lay out on that job."

"I have," said Jeckie. "Let me have it! It 'ud be a shame on your part to deprive anybody of the chance of making bad land into good when you can't do aught at it yourself! It's doing you no good; I can make it do me a lot o' good. And I'll lay you could do with the money."

Mrs. Scholes sighed. And Scholes gave her a sharp look.

"Aye, mi lass!" he said. "I know what ye'd say! Sell! But when all's said and done, a man is sentimental. Three hundred year, over and above, yon theer property's been i' our family. I' time o' owd Queen Elizabeth—that's when we got it. Lawyer Palethorpe, theer i' Sicaster, he has all t'papers. He telled me one day 'at of all t'landowners round here there isn't one, not one, 'at has land 'at's been held i' one family as long as what our family's held that. It 'ud be like selling a piece o' miself!"

"I'll tell you what I'll do," said Jeckie, utterly unmoved by Scholes's reasonings. "I'll give you a full receipt for your bill—close on a hundred pound it is—and a cheque for three hundred. That's giving you nearly four hundred pound. And you know as well as I do that if you put it up to auction you'd scarce get a bid. Don't be a fool, Ben Scholes! Three hundred pound, cash down, 'll be a rare help to you. And you'll have no bill to pay me when harvest comes."

Late that evening Mortimer tapped at the private door, and Jeckie admitted him. He followed her into the parlour.

"Well?" he said, without any word of greeting. "Anything come of it?"

"It's all right," answered Jeckie. "I've got it. Four hundred. I'm going into Sicaster with him to-morrow to settle it at the lawyer's. So that's managed."

CHAPTER III

COAL

Mortimer threw down his cap, and dropped into the easy chair which he had come to look upon as his own special reservation. He rubbed his hands together in sign of high satisfaction.

"Smart woman," he exclaimed admiringly. "Excellent! Excellent! Didn't I tell you that you'd be able to manage it? Good! Good!"

"Yes," said Jeckie, almost indifferently. "I did it. I knew how to do it, you see, when I came to to think it over. And I did it there and then, and paid the price—there's naught to do but the legal business, and that's only a matter of form. The land's mine, now." She moved across the room to her safe, unlocked it, took out an envelope, drew Mortimer's cheque from it, and quietly laid it at his elbow. "I shan't want that, of course," she added.

Mortimer looked up at her in surprise.

"But—I was to find the money!" he said.

"I've found it," answered Jeckie. "I've bought the land—it's mine, and whatever's underneath it is mine, too. So if there's nothing, there's nothing—and you'll lose nothing."

"Oh, well," said Mortimer, "as long as we've got it, it doesn't much matter who's bought it—we'll make that right later."

Jeckie gave him no reply. But in Mortimer's sorry acceptance of her announcement she made a sudden discovery as to his

100

character. Enthusiastic he no doubt was, and eager and full of ideas as to business. But—he was easygoing, apt to let things slide; ready to take matters as settled when they were all unsettled. Jeckie herself, had she been Mortimer, and bearing in mind the conversation of the previous evening, would have insisted on a proper and definite understanding as to the ownership of the forty acres. She smiled grimly as she relocked the door of her safe, and she said to herself when it came to a contest of brains she was one too many for this smart London fellow. The land was hers, and the mineral beneath it—so she said nothing; there was nothing to say.

"The thing is," said Mortimer, again rubbing his hands in high glee, "the thing is, now, to get to work. We must bore!"

"How's that set about?" asked Jeckie, who was now anxious to learn all she could. "What's done, like?"

"Oh, you just get some men and the necessary apparatus," replied Mortimer nonchalantly. "I'll see to all that. And I'll get a friend of mine down from London—I'll take a room for him at the 'Coach-and-Four'—a friend who's one of the cleverest experts of the day; he and I, between us, will jolly soon tell you what lies under that land. Of course, I haven't the slightest doubt about it, but it's better to have the opinion of two experts than one. My friend's name is Farebrother—he's well-known. He shall come down and watch the boring operations with me. I'll get the men and the requisite machinery at once, and we'll go to work as soon as you've got the legal business through—we'd better keep it dark until then."

"All that'll cost money, of course," observed Jeckie.

"Oh, a few hundred'll go a long way in the preliminaries," answered Mortimer. "I'll wait until Farebrother comes along before I decide which method I'll follow—the percussive or the rotatory. But I won't bother you with technical details; what you'll be more interested in will be results."

"This boring that you talk about, now?" said Jeckie. "It shows what there is underneath the surface?"

"To be sure!" assented Mortimer. "It's like this—you select your spot, and you put in (this is the rotary method) a cutting-tool which is a sort of hollow cylinder, with saw-like teeth at its lower edge, or an edge of hard minerals—rough diamonds, sometimes— and it's driven in by steam-power at two or three hundred revolutions a minute. As it's hollow, a solid core is formed in the cylinder—you raise the cylinder from time to time and examine the core, which comes up several feet in length. And you know from the core what there is down there. See?"

"I understand," said Jeckie. "I thought it must be something of that sort. Very well—I'll pay for all that. Get to work on it."

101

Mortimer again glanced at her in surprise. But she saw that there was no suspicion in his eyes as to her object.

"You seem inclined to launch out!" he said, laughing. "You were disposed the other way when I first mentioned this matter."

"It's my land," reiterated Jeckie. "So, to start with, anyway, I'll pay the expenses. As you said just now, we can make things right later. Mind you, I'm going on what you've said! If you hadn't assured me, you, as a professional man, that there's coal under that land, I shouldn't ha' bought it, and if there isn't—well, I know what I shall say! But I'm willing to pay the cost o' finding out. Only—I shall want to be certain!"

"If there isn't coal under your forty acres, may I never see coal again!" asserted Mortimer. "I tell you there's any amount there!"

"Then it's all right—and when we know that it is there, for certain and sure, it'll be time to consider matters further," said Jeckie calmly. "Go on with your boring and I'll pay. As you said, I say again—we can make things right later."

Mortimer was too elated at the prospect of opening out a new and possibly magnificent enterprise to ask Jeckie what her present ideas were as to how things should be made right in the event of coal being found in sufficient quantity to warrant the making of a mine. He went away and plunged into business, and in a few days brought his friend Farebrother down to Savilestowe—a quiet, reserved man of cautious words, who impressed Jeckie much more than Mortimer had done. But, cautious and reserved as he was, Farebrother, dragged hither and thither by Mortimer over the woods and meadows, uplands and lowlands, gave it as his deliberate opinion that there were vast quantities of coal under Savilestowe, and that Jeckie's forty acres of land probably covered a particularly rich bed.

"Get to work, then!" said Jeckie laconically. "I'll pay for the machinery, and I'll pay what men you want. Bring their wages bill to me, every Friday, and the money'll be there."

No one in Savilestowe, not even Steve Beckitt, nor any of the select company of the bar-parlour of the "Coach-and-Four," knew what was afoot, nor what the machinery which presently arrived in the village, and was housed in a hastily constructed wooden shed in the centre of Jeckie Farnish's forty acres, was intended for. But Ben Scholes, who had made no secret of his sale of the long-owned property, was able to enlighten his curious neighbours.

"Jecholiah Farnish," he said, in solemn conclave at the blacksmith's shop, shared in by several of the village wiseacres, "bowt that theer land fr' me for a purpose. It's her aim, d'ye see, to turn them forty acres into a fruit-orchard and a market-garden. But it's necessary, first of all and before owt else, to drain that theer land. I should ha' done it mysen if I'd iver hed t'brass to do it wi'. I dedn't—shoo has. And this here machinery 'at's arrived on t'scene it'll be for t'purpose o' drainin'—shoo's a very wealthy woman now, is Jecholiah, and shoo's bahn to do t'job reight. Pumpin' and drainin' machinery—that's what it'll be."

The general company, open-mouthed, took this as gospel—save one man, a jack-of-all-trades, who had travelled in his time. He shook his head and betrayed all the marks and signs of scepticism.

"Well, I don't know, Mestur Scholes," he remarked. "But I see'd 'em takkin' some o' that machinery offen t'traction wagons 'at it cam' on, and I'll swear my solemn 'davy 'at it's none intended for no pumpin' and drainin'—nowt o' t'sort!"

"What is it intended for, then?" demanded Scholes. "Happen ye know? Ye allus reckon to know better nor anybody else, ye do!"

"Nah thee nivver mind!" retorted the sceptic. "Ye'll all on yer find out what it's for afore long. But ye mark my words—it's none for drainin'—not it!"

Two or three weeks had gone by before the curiosity of the villagers received any appeasement. Whatever went on in the forty acres was conducted in secrecy in the big wooden shed which the carpenters had hastily run up. There, every day, Mr. Mallerbie Mortimer, his friend Mr. Farebrother, and a gang of workmen—foreigners, in the eyes of the Savilestowe folk—for whom Mortimer had taken lodgings in the village, conducted mysterious rites, unseen of any outsider. Once or twice the unduly inquisitive had endeavoured to enter the field, on one excuse or another, only to find a jealous watchman at hand who barred all approach. But the sceptic of the blacksmith's shop was a human ferret and one morning he leaned over the wall of Ben Scholes's yard and grinned derisively at the late owner of Savilestowe Leys.

"Now, then, Mistur Scholes!" he said triumphantly. "What did I tell yer about yon machinery 'at's been setten up i' that land 'at ye selled to Jecholiah Farnish? Pumpin' and drainin'! I knew better! I seen a bit i' my time, Mistur Scholes, more nor most o' ye Savilestowers, and I knew that wor no pumpin' and drainin' machinery. I would ha' tell'd yer at t'time, when we wor talkin' at t'smithy, what it wor, but I worn't i' t'mind to do so. Ye don't know what they're up to i' yon fields 'at used to be yours!"

"What are they up to, then?" demanded Scholes. "I'll lay ye'll know!"

"I dew know!" answered the other, with arrogance. "An' ye'll know an' all, to yer sorrow, afore long. They're tryin' for coal! I hed it fro' one o' t'workmen last neet; I hed a pint or two, or it might be three, wi' him. An' he says 'at it's varry like 'at theer's hundreds o' thousands o' pounds' worth o' coal under that land. That's what Jeckie Farnish wanted it for. Coal!"

Scholes, who was cleaning out the ginnel in front of his stable, straightened himself, staring intently at his informant. The informant nodded, laughed sneeringly, and went off. And Scholes, casting away his manure fork with a gesture that indicated rising anger and hot indignation, went off, too, in his shirt sleeves, but in the opposite direction. He made straight down the village to Jeckie Farnish's shop.

It was then nearly noon, and the shop was full of customers. Jeckie, who had long since given up counter work, and now did nothing beyond general and vigilant superintendence, was standing near the cashier's desk, talking to the vicar's wife. Scholes's somber eyes and aggressive look told her what was afoot as soon as he crossed the threshold. She continued talking, staring back at him, as if he were no more than one of the posts which supported the ceiling. But Scholes was not to be denied, and he strode up with a pointed finger—a finger pointing straight at Jeckie's hard eyes.

"Now then!" he burst out in loud, angry tones which made the vicar's wife start, draw back and stare at him. "Now then, Jecholiah, I've a crow to pull wi' ye! Ye telled me an' my missis 'at ye wanted yon land o' mind for to mak' a fruit orchard and a market-garden on, and I let ye hev it at a low price for that same reason. Ye're a liar! ye wanted it for nowt o' t'sort! Ye were after what you knew then wor liggin' beneath it—coal! Ye've done me! Ye're a cheat as well as a liar! Ye've done me out o' what 'ud ha' made me a well-to-do man. Damn such-like!"

Jeckie turned, cool and collected, to the vicar's wife.

"I'll see what I can do about it," she said quietly, continuing their conversation. "If I can put it in at a lower price, I will, though I'd already cut it as fine as I could. But, of course if it's for the mothers' meetings, I must do what I can." Then she turned again— this time to the angry man in front of her. "Go away, Scholes!" she said. "I can't have any disturbance here; go away at once!"

"Disturbance!" shouted Scholes. "I'll larn ye to talk about disturbance! Ye're no better nor a thief! Look ye here, all ye folk, high and low!" he went on, waving an arm at the astonished customers. "Do ye know what this here woman did? She finds out 'at there's coal under my land, and, wi'out sayin' a word to me about it, she persuades me to sell her t'land for next to nowt! Is that fair doin's? Do ye think 'at I'd ha' selled if I'd known what I wor sellin'? But she knew; and she's done me and mine. Ye're a thief, Jecholiah Farnish—same as what ye allus hev been—ye're sort 'at 'ud skin a stone if theer wer owt to be made at it! Damn all such-like, I say, and say ageean—and I'll see what t'lawyers hev to say to t'job!"

"You'll hear what my lawyer has to say to you," retorted Jeckie, who, the vicar's wife having hurriedly left the shop, was now not particular about letting her tongue loose. "You get out of my shop this instant, Scholes, or I'll have you taken out in a way you won't like. Here, you, boy, run across the street and tell the policeman to come here! What do you mean, you fool, by coming and talking to me i' that way? Didn't I give you t'brass for your land, cash down? And as to coal, I've no more notion whether there's coal under it than you have; there may be and there mayn't. But I'll tell you this—if there is, it's mine! And you get out o' my shop, sharp, or I'll hand you over to t'law here and now. I'll have none o' your sort tryin' to come it over me. Get out!"

Scholes looked Jeckie squarely in the face—and suddenly turned and obeyed her bidding. But he went up the street muttering, like a man possessed, and the vicar's wife, who had stopped to speak to a group of children, shrank from him as he passed, and went home to tell her husband of what she had heard and seen, and to voice her convictions that the knowledge that he had been cheated had affected Scholes's brain.

"Do you think she could really do such a thing?" she asked half incredulously. "If she did, it certainly looks—mean, at any rate."

"If you want my personal opinion," answered the vicar dryly, "I should say that Jeckie Farnish is capable of any amount of sharp practice. Coal! Dear me! Now I wonder if that's really what she's after, and if there is coal? Because, of course, if there's coal under her land there'll be coal under my glebe, and in that case—really, one's almost afraid to think of such a possibility. Coal! I wonder when we shall get to know?"

The whole village knew within another week; indeed, from the time of Scholes's indignant outburst at the shop, it was hopeless to conceal the operations at the waste land. Throngs of villagers were at the hedgerow sides from morning till night, eager for news; there, too, might be seen the squire and the vicar, and Stubley and Merritt, as inquisitive as the rest. The men engaged in boring forgathered of evenings at the "Coach-and-Four," and, despite Mortimer's warnings and admonitions, talked, more or less freely, over their beer. And one day at noon the rumour ran from one end to the other of the village street that coal had been found, and that there would be a rich and productive yield; before night the rumour had become a certainty—the squire himself had it from Mortimer and his fellow-expert that beneath Jeckie Farnish's forty acres there was what would probably turn out to be one of the best beds of coal in the country, and that it doubtless extended beneath the land of the other property owners.

The one person who showed no excitement, who refused to allow herself to be bustled or flurried, was Jeckie herself. Within twenty-four hours she was visited by the squire, the vicar, and Stubley—each wanted to know what she was going to do, each had a proposal for coming in. The squire wanted to start a limited liability company for founding a colliery to work the district, with himself as the chairman; the vicar was anxious about royalties on the coal which no doubt lay beneath his glebe lands; Stubley came to warn Jeckie to make sure. Jeckie listened to each and said nothing; it was impossible to get a word out of her that gave any indication of what she had in her mind. The only persons with whom she held conversation at that time were Mortimer and his friend Farebrother; with them she was closeted in secret every evening; Farnish, told off to act as watch-dog, had strict orders that no other callers were to be admitted. The result of the conference was that within a fortnight Jeckie had acquired a vast mass of useful information, which she carefully memorised. And, as Mortimer remarked, at the end of one of these talks, there was now nothing to do but to arrange the financial matters for beginning work. Money—capital—that was all that was needed now. To that remark Jeckie made no answer—she already had her own ideas about the matter, and she was resolved to keep them carefully to herself.

CHAPTER IV

BIRDS OF A FEATHER

Close countenance though Jeckie Farnish kept to all the world, her thoughts had never been so many nor so varied as at this eventful stage of her career. She spent many a sleepless night considering possibilities, probabilities, eventualities. She thought over ways and means; she reckoned up her resources. She tried to look ahead as far as possible; to take everything into account. But, in all her reflections and plans and schemings, there was one dominant note—the desire to make money out of her lucky discovery—money, more money than she had ever dreamed of possessing. She was in no hurry. She made Mortimer and Farebrother continue their boring operations until she became as certain as they were themselves. They had made these boreholes, so as to test the whole of Jeckie's property, and had kept a careful journal of the boring, which was punctiliously entered up—Jeckie made a point of inspecting that journal, and of examining the cores which the boring cylinders brought up and were duly labelled and laid out under cover. But she was not satisfied with this, nor with merely taking the opinions of Mortimer and his friend. At her own instance and expense she called in two acknowledged mining experts and a professor of geology from one of the local universities; to these three she submitted the whole matter, only impressing upon them that she wanted an opinion that could be relied upon. All three agreed with Mortimer and Farebrother—coal was there, under the otherwise unpromising surface of the forty acres, in vast quantity. So, as Mortimer was constantly saying, there was nothing to do but to arrange the financial side of the affair, and to get to work on the construction of the necessary mine.

Jeckie was not going to be hurried about that, either; she had her own ideas. In spite of Mortimer's exhortations and Farebrother's hints, she kept them to herself until she was ready to act. But upon one point she was determined, and had been determined from the very first. Neither squire, nor parson, nor Stubley, nor Merritt, nor any Savilestowe party was going to come in with her—no, nor was Mortimer, of whom, all unknown to him, she was making a convenience. She was going to keep this El Dorado to herself as far as ever she could—to be chief controller of its destinies, to be master. Nevertheless, knowing, after her various consultations with Mortimer and Farebrother, that she did not possess sufficient capital of her own to establish a colliery, she had decided to take in one partner who could contribute what she could not find. She had that partner in her mind's eye—Lucilla Grice.

Lucilla, as Jeckie well knew, had long been top dog in the Grice menage. Albert, from the day of his marriage, had become more and more of a nonentity; as years went by he grew to be of no greater importance than one of his wife's umbrellas; a thing that had its uses now and then, but could at any moment be tossed into a corner and disregarded for the time being. Lucilla managed everything. Lucilla invested the money which he got for his partnership and received the dividends; Lucilla kept the purse; Albert had no more concern with cash than the cob in his stable; all he knew of money was that he was allowed three-and-six a day to spend as he liked. Jeckie Farnish knew all this, and more. She knew that Lucilla's marriage portion of two thousand pounds, and

Albert's partnership money of five thousand, both secure and untouched in Lucilla's hands, had been added to of late by legacies from Lucilla's father, the Nottingham draper, and her maternal uncle, a London solicitor, which had materially increased Mrs. Albert Grice's fortune. The Nottingham draper had left his daughter ten thousand pounds—one-third of his estate; the maternal uncle, an old bachelor, regarding her as his favourite niece, had bequeathed to her all he died possessed of, some fourteen or fifteen thousand; Lucilla, therefore (Albert being ruled clean out of all calculations), was worth at the very least thirty thousand pounds. And there were psychological reasons why Jeckie fixed on Lucilla as the proper person to come in with her. From the very first she had recognised in Lucilla, a kindred spirit—a lover of money for money's sake. Jeckie had known it at their first interview; she had seen signs of it in their business dealings; she had been quick to observe that when Lucilla received her important influx of money from her father and uncle, whose deaths had occurred about the same time, she had not launched out into greater expenditure. She and Albert still occupied the same villa residence, just outside Sicaster; still kept the same modest establishment; still stuck to the one cob and the same dog-cart; still pursued the same uneventful course of life. And as she spent no more than she had ever spent, Lucilla, according to Jeckie Farnish's reckoning, must, since her receipt of the family legacies, have added considerably to her capital. But— and here was another and more important psychological reason— Jeckie knew, by instinct as much as by observation, that Lucilla, like herself, was one of those persons who, having much, are always feverishly anxious to have still more. There were few details of the life of that neighbourhood with which Jeckie was not thoroughly familiar, and she knew intimately the habits and customs of the Grice household. She was well aware, for instance, that Albert, who had now grown a beard and become a somewhat fat man, more easygoing than ever, went into Sicaster every morning to spend his three-and-six and pass the time of day with his gossips in the bar-parlours of the two principal hotels; he left his door punctually at ten o'clock for this daily performance and returned—even more punctually—at precisely one o'clock. It was, therefore, at half-past ten one morning that Jeckie, armed with an old-fashioned reticule full of papers, presented herself at the villa and asked to see its mistress; Lucilla, she knew, would then be alone.

Lucilla had a certain feeling for Jeckie; a feeling closely akin to that which Jeckie had for Lucilla; it centered, of course, in money. Lucilla knew how Jeckie had made money, and how Jeckie could stick to money, and for money and anything and anybody that had to do with money Lucilla had instincts of respect which almost amounted to veneration. Accordingly, she not only welcomed her visitor with cordiality, but showed her pleasure at receiving her by immediately producing a decanter of port and a sponge cake, and insisting on Jeckie's partaking of both.

"You'll have heard, no doubt, of what's been happening down our way?" said Jeckie, plunging straight into business as soon as she had accepted the proffered hospitality. "About finding coal under my land, I mean. It's generally known."

"I have heard," assented Lucilla. "A sure thing, they say. Well!—if you aren't one of the lucky ones, Miss Farnish! Everything you touch turns to gold. Why—you'll make a fortune out of it! I suppose it's dead certain, eh?"

Jeckie finished her port, shook her head as her hostess pointed to the decanter, and began to pull her papers out of the old silk reticule.

"Aye, it's as dead certain as that I'm sitting here, Mrs. Grice," she said. "That is, unless all them that ought to know is hopelessly wrong. To tell you the truth, and between ourselves, I've come to see you about it, and I'll give you the entire history of the whole affair. You'll ha' seen that smart London chap that's been staying at the 'Coach-and-Four' for some time now—Mortimer, Mr. Mallerbie Mortimer? Aye, well, it was him put me on to it. He's a mining expert—a member of the Institute of Mining Engineers—and he came down to these parts prospecting. He told me, in confidence, that there was coal, no end of it, under Savilestowe, and particularly under forty acres o' poor land that belonged to Ben Scholes. Well, I said naught to nobody, but I bought that bit o' land fro' Ben—I gave him next to naught for it and had it properly conveyed to me. And then I told this here Mortimer to bore, and he got machinery and men, and another expert fro' London—a man called Farebrother. And they sunk these borings, at different spots' i' my land, and the result was splendid. But I worn't going to go on their word—right as it is. I got two independent experts, t'best I could hear of, and a professor o' geology fro' Clothford University, and had them to go thoroughly into the matter. And they all agreed with the other two— they tell me that under my forty acres there's coal of the very best quality, that it'll take many and many a year to exhaust, and that there's a regular big fortune in it. So—there's no possible doubt. But cast your eye over these papers yourself—you'll be quite able to understand 'em."

Lucilla readily understood the typewritten sheets which Jeckie handed to her. They were all technical reports, signed by the five men whom Jeckie had mentioned—differing in phraseology and in detail, all were alike in asserting a conviction, based on the results of the borings, that coal lay under Savilestowe Leys in vast quantity and of the best quality. Lucilla handed them back with obvious envy.

"Well, if ye aren't lucky!" she exclaimed. "It's as I said—all turns to gold that you handle. Then—what's going to happen next! You'll be for a company, I suppose?"

"No!" said Jeckie grimly. "I'll ha' no more fingers in my pie than I can keep an eye on, I'll warrant you, Mrs. Grice! I've had no end o' suggestions o' that sort—the squire, and the parson, and Stubley, and Merritt, they'd all like to come in—the squire wanted to get up a big limited liability company, with him as chairman, and do great things. But I shan't have aught to do wi' that. I know what there is under my land, according to these papers, and as I say, it's a pie that I'm not going to have a lot o' fingers poked into. But, I'll tell you what—and it's why I come here—I don't mind taking in one partner, just one. You!—if you like the notion."

Lucilla blushed as if she had been a coy maiden receiving a first proposal of marriage.

"Me!" she exclaimed. "Lor', Miss Farnish!"

"Listen to me!" said Jeckie, bending forward across the bearskin hearthrug. "You and me knows what's what about money matters—nobody better. I know—for I know most o' what goes on about here—that you're now a well-to-do woman, what with what you had and with them legacies you've had left. Now, so am I, to a certain extent. What I propose is, let's you and me—just ourselves and nobody else—go into partnership to work this coal-mine. Farnish and Grice, Savilestowe Main—that's how it would be. You and me—all to ourselves?"

"Goodness gracious! It 'ud cost an awful lot of money, wouldn't it?" said Lucilla, in an awe-struck whisper. "To make a colliery! Why——"

"Aye, and think what we should get out of it!" interrupted Jeckie. "It'll take many a long year, they say, to exhaust what there is just under my land. And it'll not be so expensive as in some cases, the making of a mine. I've gone into that, too, and had estimates. It's the character of the, what do they call 'em—strata; that's the various stuffs, soils, and stones, yer know, they have to get through. They say this'll be naught like so difficult as some, and that we could be working in less nor two years."

Lucilla, perched on her sofa, was already regarding Jeckie with dilated and avaricious eyes. Her lips were slightly parted, but she said nothing, and Jeckie presently bent still nearer and whispered.

"There's hundreds o' thousands o' pounds worth o' that coal!" she said. "And we've naught to do but to get it out!"

Lucilla found her tongue.

"How much should we have to put in?" she asked faintly.

"Well, I've thought that out," answered Jeckie, readily enough. "Supposing we put in twenty-five thousand each, to make a starting capital o' fifty thousand? Then, as regards profits—as the land's mine, and the coal, too, you wouldn't expect to share equally. One-third of the profits to you, and the other two-thirds to me—that's what I think 'ud be fair, and right, and reasonable. Even then, you'd have a rare return for your outlay. You know I could find a hundred people 'at 'ud just jump at such an offer. The squire 'ud fair leap at it! But I came to you because I know that you understand money, same as I do, and I'd rather have a woman for a partner nor a man. But look here. I'm a rare hand at figures, and I've worked this out. You come to this table, and go into these figures wi' me."

Jeckie had only just left the villa residence, when Albert returned to the midday dinner. His wife said nothing of her visitor, and Albert was too full of his usual bar-parlour gossip to notice that Lucilla was remarkably preoccupied and absent-minded. He remained innocent and unconscious of what was going on, nor was he aware that Jeckie Farnish visited Lucilla during several successive mornings, and that on the last two, both women went into town, and were closeted for some time with, first, solicitors, and, second, bankers. Albert, indeed, never entered into the thoughts of either Lucilla or Jeckie; he was not even a circumstance to be taken into account. There was, however, a man in the neighbourhood who had Miss Jecholiah Farnish very much in his thoughts at this time. This was Farebrother, a more observant man than Mortimer, and Farebrother at last tackled his friend definitely as they sat dining one night in the parlour of the "Coach-and-Four."

"Look here!" he said, suddenly. "It's about time you knew what this Farnish woman's going to do. If you want the plain truth, Mortimer, I don't trust her."

"Oh, she's all right," exclaimed Mortimer. "A keen business woman, no doubt, but not the sort to——"

"My lad!" interrupted Farebrother, "you're always too optimistic, and too ready to believe in people. The woman's just the sort to do anybody out of anything—she did both you and Scholes over the land. It's hers—and so is all that's beneath it, to the centre of the earth. You should have bought it yourself."

"I?—a complete stranger!" protested Mortimer. "Impossible! There would have been suspicion with a vengeance!"

"Then you should have made an arrangement with her before

111

she got it," said Farebrother. "She's got it now—and all that it implies. And my belief is that she's up to something. The last two or three times I've been in the town I've seen her coming out of solicitors' offices—she's at some game or another. She'll do you out of any share that you want to get in this very promising mine unless you're careful, and if you take my advice you'll put it straight and unmistakably to her, and ask her what she's going to do."

Mortimer protested and explained, but when dinner was over he went round to Jeckie's private door, and after a slight interchange of casual remarks, asked her point-blank what she was going to do about starting a company to work the mine. Jeckie pointed to a large, legal-looking envelope which lay on the table.

"It's done," she said calmly. "There'll be no company. Me and a friend of mine have gone into partnership to work it—there's the deed, duly signed to-day. We're going to start operations very soon."

Mortimer felt his cheeks flush—more from the memory of what Farebrother had said than with his very natural indignation.

"But what about me?" he exclaimed. "Why—I gave you the idea! I said from the first that I'd find money towards the company and knew others who would. It was my idea altogether—mine entirely. I only gave you the chance of coming in—I——"

"Whose land is it?" demanded Jeckie, coolly. "Did I buy it? Is it mine? If you wanted it why didn't you buy it? I bought it; it's my land. And—all that's beneath it. Do you think I was going to do that for other folks? We do nowt for nobody hereabouts, unless there's something to be made at it, my lad! But, of course, I'll pay you and your friend for your professional services—you must send your bill in."

Mortimer rose from his chair and looked at the woman in whom, half-an-hour previously, he had expressed his belief.

"So you've done me, too?" he said, simply. "You know well enough what my intentions were about this mine—of which you'd never have known, never have dreamed, if I hadn't told you of it. Do you call that honest—to do what you are doing?"

"Send in your bill—and tell Farebrother to send in his," said Jeckie, in her hardest voice. "You'll both get your cheques as soon as I see that you've charged right."

Mortimer went away, worse than chagrined, and told Farebrother of his dismissal; Farebrother forbore to remind him of what he had prophesied.

"All right!" he said. "I see what it is. She learnt all she can from us—now she's going to be what such a woman only can be—sole master! All right!"

And being a practical man, he sat down to make out, what Jeckie styled, his bill.

CHAPTER V

THE YORKSHIRE WAY

During the course of the next morning Jeckie received a large oblong envelope delivered to her by the stable-boy of the "Coach-and-Four." It was handed to her over the counter of the shop, and she opened it there and then, in the presence of her assistants and of several customers, all of whom were surprised to see the usually hard, unmoved face flush as its owner glared hastily at the two enclosures which she drew out. Within an instant Jeckie had hurried them into the envelope again, and had turned angrily on the stable-boy.

"What're you waiting for?" she demanded sharply.

"Mestur Mortimer, he said I wor to wait for an answer," replied the lad. "That's what he telled me."

"Then you can tell him t'answer'll come on," retorted Jeckie. "I can't bother with it now. Off you go!"

The stable-boy stared at the angry face and made a retreat; Jeckie retreated, too, into her private parlour, where she once more drew out the two sheets of excellent, unruled, professional-looking paper whereon the two mining engineers had set down their charges for services rendered.

"Did ever anybody see the like o' that!" she muttered. "They might think a body was made o' money! All that brass for just standin' about while these other fellers did the work, and then tellin' me what their opinions were! It's worse nor lawyers!"

She had no experience, nor knowledge, even by hearsay, of what professional charges of this sort should be, for the two experts and the professor of geology whom she had engaged, in order to get independent opinion, had not yet rendered any account to her. But she remembered that they would certainly come in, and that she would just as certainly have to pay them, whatever they might amount to, for she had definitely engaged the three men, from whom they would come, writing to request their attendance with her own hand.

"And if them three charge as these two has," she growled, looking black at what Mortimer demanded on one sheet of paper, and Farebrother on the other, "it'll come to a nice lot!—a deal more nor ever I expected. And as if they'd ever done aught for it! I'm sure that there Mortimer never did naught but stand about them sheds, wi' his hands in his pockets, smokin' cigars without end—why it's as

113

if he were chargin' me so many guineas for every cigar he smoked! And if these is what minin' engineers' professional charges is, it's going to cost me a pretty penny before even we've got that coal up and make aught out of it!"

No answer, verbal or otherwise, went back from Miss Farnish to the London gentlemen at the "Coach-and-Four" that day. But, early next morning, Jeckie, who had spent much time in thinking hard since the previous noon, got into her pony-tray (an eminently useful if not remarkably stylish equipage) and drove away from the village. Anyone who had observed her closely might have seen that she was in a preoccupied and designing mood. She drove through Sicaster, and away into the mining district beyond, and after journeying for several miles, came to Heronshawe Main, an exceedingly flourishing and prosperous colliery which was the sole property of Mr. Matthew Revis, and was situated on and beneath a piece of land of unusually black and desolate aspect. Revis, a self-made man, bluff, downright, rough of speech, had had business dealings with Jeckie Farnish in the past in respect of some property in which each was interested, and of late she had consulted him once or twice as to the prospects of her new venture; she had also induced him to drive over to Savilestowe during the progress of the experimental boring. She wanted his advice now, and she went straight to his offices at the colliery. She had been there before, and on each occasion had come away building castles in the air as regards her projected development of Savilestowe. For to sit in Revis's handsome, almost luxurious private room, looking out on the evidences of industry and wealth, to see from its windows the hundreds of grimy-faced colliers, going away from their last shift, was an encouragement in itself to go on with her own schemes. Already she saw at Savilestowe what she actually looked on at Heronshawe Main, and herself and Lucilla Grice mistresses of an army of men whose arms would bear treasure out of the earth—for them.

Revis came into his room as she sat staring out on all the unloveliness of the colliery, a big, bearded man, keen-eyed and resolute of mouth, and nodded smilingly at her. He already knew Jeckie for a woman who was of a certain resemblance to himself—a grubber after money. But he had long since made his fortune—an enormous one; she was at a stage at which he had once been, a stage of anxious adventure, and therefore she was interesting.

"Well, my lass!" he said. "How's things getting on? Made a start yet with that little business o' yours? You'll never lift that coal up if you don't get busy with it, you know!"

He dropped into an easy chair beside the hearth, pulled out

114

his cigar-case, and began to smoke, and Jeckie, noting his careless and comfortable attitude, wished that she had got over the initial stages of her adventure, and had seen her colliery in full and prosperous working order for thirty years.

"Mr. Revis," she answered, "I wish I'd got as far as you have! You've got all the worst of it over long since. I've got to begin. Now, you've been very good to me in giving me bits of advice. I came to see if you'd give me some more. What's the best and cheapest way to get this colliery o' mine started?"

Revis laughed, evidently enjoying the directness of her question. He knew well enough that it did not spring from simplicity.

"Why!" he answered. "You've got them two London chaps at Savilestowe yet, haven't you? I saw 'em in Sicaster t'other day. They're mining engineers, both of 'em. Why not go to them—I thought you were going to employ them."

"I don't want to have naught more to do with 'em, Mr. Revis," said Jeckie earnestly. "They're Londoners! I can't abide 'em. They seem to me to do naught but stand about and watch—and then charge you for watching, as if they'd been working like niggers. I don't understand such ways. Aren't there mining engineers in Yorkshire that 'ud see the job through. Our own folk, you know?"

"I see—I see!" said Revis, with a smile. "Want to keep work and money amongst our own people, what? All right, my lass!—I'm a good deal that way myself. Now, then, pull your chair up to my desk there, and get a pen in your hand, and make a few notes—I'll tell you what to do about all that. And," he added, with a laugh that was almost jovial, "I shan't charge you nowt, either!"

An hour later Jeckie went away from Heronshawe Main filled to the brim with practical advice and valuable information. It mattered nothing to Matthew Revis if a hundred new collieries were opened within his own immediate district; he had made his money out of his own already, and to such an extent that no competition could touch him. Therefore, he was willing to help a new beginner, especially seeing that that beginner was a clever and interesting woman, still extremely handsome, who certainly seemed to have a genius for money-making.

"Come to me when you want to know aught more," he said, as he shook hands with his visitor. "Get hold of this firm I've told you about, and make your own arrangements with 'em, and let 'em get on with the sinking. With your capital, and the results o' that boring, you ought to do well—so long as naught happens."

Jeckie started, and gave Revis a sharp, inquiring look.

"What—what could happen?" she asked.

"Well, my lass, there's always the chance of two things," answered Revis, becoming more serious than he had been at any time during the interview. "Water for one; sand for the other. In these north-country coal-fields of ours, water-logged sand has always been a danger. But—you'll have to take your chance: I had to take mine! None of us 'ud ever do aught i' this world if we didn't face a bit o' risk, you know."

But Jeckie lingered, looking at him with some doubt in her keen eyes.

"Did you have any trouble yourself in that way?" she asked.

"Aye!" answered Revis, with a grim smile. "We came to a bed of quicksand—a thinnish one, to be sure, but it was there. Two thousand gallons o' water a minute came out o' that, my lass!"

"What did you have to do?" inquired Jeckie. "All that water!"

"Had to tub it with heavy cast-iron plates," replied Revis. "But you'll not understand all these details. Leave things to this firm I've told you about; you can depend on them."

All the way from Heronshawe Main to Sicaster, Jeckie Farnish revolved Revis's last words. Water!—sand! Supposing all her money—she gave no thought to Lucilla Grice's money—were swept away once for all by water, or swallowed up for ever in sand? That would indeed be a fine end to her ventures! But still, Revis had met with and surmounted these difficulties; no, she meant to go on. And she had saved a lot of money that morning by getting valuable advice and information from Revis for nothing—nothing at all—and she meant to get out of paying something else, too, before night came, and with that interesting design in her mind, she drove up to Palethorpe and Overthwaite's office, and went in, and laid before Palethorpe, whom she found alone, the charges sent in to her the day before by Mortimer and his friend Farebrother. Palethorpe, whose keenness had not grown less as he had grown older, elevated his eyebrows, and pursed his lips, when he glanced at the amounts to which Jeckie pointed.

"Whew!" he said. "These are pretty stiff charges, Miss Farnish!"

"Worse nor what yours are!" said Jeckie, showing a little sarcastic humour. "And they're bad enough sometimes."

"Strictly according to etiquette, ma'am!" replied Palethorpe, with a sly smile. "Strictly regular. But there——"

"Aye, there!" exclaimed Jeckie. "All that brass for just hearing them two talk a bit, and for seeing 'em stand about watching other fellers work! And I want to know how I can get out o' paying it?"

Palethorpe put his fingers together and got into the attitude of consultation.

"Just give me a brief history of your transactions with these gentlemen," he said. "Just the plain facts."

He listened carefully while Jeckie detailed her knowledge and experience of Mr. Mallerbie Mortimer and his friend, and, when she had finished, asked her two or three questions arising out of what she had told him.

"Now, you attend closely to what I say, Miss Farnish," he said, after considering matters for awhile. "First of all, would you like me to see these two, or would you rather see them yourself? You'll see them yourself? Very well; now, then, when you go, just do and say exactly what I'm going to tell you."

There was no apter pupil in all Yorkshire than Jeckie Farnish when it came to learning lessons in the fine art of doing anybody out of anything, and by the time she walked out of Palethorpe and Overthwaite's office she had mastered all the suggestions offered to her. And it was with an air in which cleverly assumed surprise, expostulation, and injured innocence were curiously mingled that she walked into the parlour of the "Coach-and-Four" that evening, just as Mortimer and Farebrother finished dinner, and laid down on an unoccupied corner of the table the two folded sheets of foolscap which they had sent her the previous day.

Farebrother gave Mortimer a secret kick, and spoke before his too easygoing friend could get in a word.

"Good evening, Miss Farnish," he said, politely. "Won't you take a chair, and let me give you a glass of wine; it's very good. I hope you found these accounts correct?"

"Thank you," replied Jeckie. "I'll take a chair, but I won't take no wine. Much obliged to you. And as to these accounts, all I can say 'at I never was so surprised in my life as when I received 'em! It's positively shameful to send such things to me, and I can't think how you could do it, reckoning to be gentlemen!"

Farebrother gave Mortimer another kick and looked steadily at their visitor.

"Oh!" he said, very quietly. "Now—why?"

"Why?" exclaimed Jeckie. "What! amounts like them? You know as well as I do 'at I never employed either of you! You haven't a single letter, nor paper, nor nothing to show 'at I ever told you or engaged you to do aught for me; you know you haven't. It's all the fault o' Mr. Mortimer there if there's been any misunderstanding on your part, Mr. Farebrother, but I'd naught to do with it. I know quite well what part Mr. Mortimer's played!"

Mortimer received a third kick before he could speak, and Farebrother, who was gradually becoming more and more icy in manner, asked another question.

117

"Perhaps you'll give me an account of Mr. Mortimer's doing?" he suggested. "I shall like to hear what you have to say."

Jeckie favoured both men with an injured and sullen stare.

"Well!" she said. "Mr. Mortimer came to me, unasked, mind you, and said he was having a holiday down here, and who he was, and that he'd a suspicion there might be coal under this village. He talked a lot about it in my parlour, though I'm sure I never invited him to do so. I didn't know him from Adam when he came to my house! It's quite true 'at I bought land from Ben Scholes on the strength of what he said, but he'd naught to do with that. I paid for it with my own money. And then he goes and sends me in a bill like that there?—a bill three or four times as much as yours, though, from what I've seen of both of you, I reckon you're a more dependable man than what he is, and——"

"Mr. Mortimer has been employed by you four times as long as I had," interposed Farebrother. "Therefore——"

"He was never employed by me at all!" exclaimed Jeckie, emphatically. "Where's his papers to show it? I always reckoned that he was just a Londoner down here for a holiday—that's what he told t'landlord and his wife when he came to this house—and that, being interested in coal, he was telling me what he knew or thought he knew. And I never gave him any reason to think that I was employin' his services, nor yours either, for that matter. It's naught but imposition to send me in bills like them!"

"Here, I can't stand this any longer!" said Mortimer, suddenly rising from his chair. He turned on Jeckie and confronted her angrily. "You know as well as I do that you constantly consulted me, and that you told me to get Mr. Farebrother down from London—"

"Have you aught to prove it?" interrupted Jeckie, with a knowing look in which she contrived to include both men. "You know you haven't! No! but I can prove, 'cause you're a great talker and over-ready with your tongue, mister, that you gave it out all over t'village 'at your friend Mr. Farebrother was coming down to have a holiday, too. And he came; and, of course, I'd no objection if you both gave me advice, and I should ha' been a fool if I hadn't taken it, but I never employed neither of you. Didn't I get my own advisers when the time came? I employed them, right enough, but not you. You know quite well, if you're business men, 'at you haven't a scrap of writing nor a shred of evidence to show that I ever gave you any commission to do aught for me. I just thought you were amusing and interesting yourselves, and giving me a bit of advice and information, friendly-like. But, of course, I'm willing to make you a payment, in reason, and if ten pound apiece 'ud be——"

Jeckie got no further. Before Mortimer could speak

Farebrother suddenly picked up the obnoxious accounts, tore them in two, flung the fragments into the fire, and, opening the parlour door, made Jeckie a ceremonious bow.

"We'll make you a present of all we've done for you, my good lady," he said. "Now, go!"

Jeckie went, grumbling. She had honestly meant to part with twenty pounds. It vexed her, temperamentally, to think of anybody doing something for nothing. She would have liked to pay these two ten pounds each. And she went home feeling deeply injured that they had scorned her.

CHAPTER VI

OBSESSION

Before noon the next day the two Londoners, for whom Jeckie Farnish had no further use, had shaken the Savilestowe dirt from off their feet, to the sorrow of Beckitt and his wife and the frequenters of the bar-parlour, and Jeckie told her partner, Lucilla Grice, of how cleverly she had done them. Lucilla applauded her cleverness; what was the use, she said, of paying money if you could get out of paying it?—especially as there was such a lot of spending to be done that she and Jeckie could not by any possible means avoid. The mere pointing out of that undoubted fact made Jeckie sigh deeply.

"Aye!" she said, almost lugubriously. "That's true enough!— we're just starting out on what can't be other than the trying and unpleasant part of the business—laying money out in bucketfuls with no prospect of seeing aught back for some time! However, there's no doubt about seeing it back in cart-loads when it does start coming, and now that I've got this advice and information from Mr. Revis—free, gratis, mind you!—we'd best set to work. Revis, he says that these engineers and contractors that he's recommended'll do the whole job twenty per cent. cheaper than those London chaps would ha' done, so you see I've saved a lot already. And now there's naught for it but to work—and wait."

"We shall have our hands full," remarked Lucilla sententiously. "But—let's start." Savilestowe—its mouth agape and eyes wide open—witnessed the start of the Farnish-Grice enterprise before many weeks had gone by. Until then—save for Jeckie's boring operations, which were, comparatively, hole-and-corner affairs—it had never been roused out of its bucolic life since the Norman Conquest. It had always been a typical farming village, a big and important one, to be sure, but still a purely rural and agricultural settlement. Within the wide boundaries of its parish—one of the largest in England—there were fine old country-houses in their parks and pleasure grounds; roomy and ancient farmsteads in their gardens and orchards; corn-lands, meadow-lands, woods, coppices, streams; industry other than that of spade and plough had never been known there. But now came a transformation, at which the older folk stood aghast. The quiet roads became busy and noisy with the passage of great traction engines drawing trains of wagons filled with all manner of material in steel and iron, wood, stone, and brick; vast and unfamiliar structures began to arise on the forty acres wherein Ben Scholes's half-starved cattle had once tried to add to their always limited rations; smoke and steam rose and passed away in noisome clouds over the cottages which had hitherto known nothing but the scent of homely herbs and flowers. And with all these strange things came strangers—crowds upon crowds of workmen, navvies, masons, mechanics, all wanting accommodation and food and drink. Hideous rows of wooden shanties, hastily run up on the edge of Savilestowe Leys, housed many of these; others, taken in by the labourer's wives, drove away the primitive quietude of cottage life; it was, as the vicar's wife said in her most plaintive manner, an invasion, captained by Jeckie Farnish and Lucilla Grice. The old order of things was gone, and Savilestowe lay at the mercy of a horde of ravagers who meant to tear from it the wealth which its smiling fields had so long kept safely hidden.

And now the Savilestowe folk talked of nothing but the marvellous thing that was going on in their midst. The old subjects of fireside and inn-kitchen conversation—births, deaths, marriages, scandals, big gooseberries, and two-headed lambs—were forgotten. There was not a man, woman, or child in the village who was not certain that wealth was being created, and that its first outpourings were already in evidence. Money was being spent in Savilestowe as it had never been spent within the recollection of the oldest inhabitant, and there was the more glamour about this spending in that the discerning knew whence this profusion came.

"There niver wor such times as these here 'at we're privileged to live in!" said one of the assembly which usually forgathered round the blacksmith's forge and anvil of an afternoon. "Money runs like water i' t'midst on us. I un'erstand at wheer t' 'Coach-and-Four' used to tak' six barril o'ale it now needs eighteen, and t'landlord o' t' 'Brown Cow,' up at t'top end o' t'village, says 'at he mun build a new tap-room for t'workmen to sit in, for his house is filled to t'brim wi' 'em ivery neet. An' they say 'at Farnish's shop hez more nor once been varry near selled clear out o' all 'at there wor in it, and 'at they've hed to send to Sicaster for new supplies. An' it's t'same wi' t'butcher—he's killin' six or eight times as many beasts and sheep as he used to, and t'last Frida' neet he hadn't as much as a mutton chop nor a bit o' liver left i' t'place. Now, there is some brass about, and no mistak'!"

"Why, thou sees, it's what's called t'circulation o' money," observed the blacksmith, leisurely leaning on his hammer. "It goes here and it goes theer, like t'winds o' heaven. Now, ye were sayin' 'at Jecholiah Farnish's shop's varry near been cleaned out more nor once—varry weel, if ye'd nobbut think a bit, that means 'at Jeckie wor gettin' her own back wi' summat added to it—that's what's meant by t'circulation o' money. We all on us know 'at this here army o' fellers, all at their various jobs, is paid bi Jeckie and her partner, Mrs. Albert Grice, all on 'em. Twice a week they're paid—one half on 'em o' Mondays, and t'other half o' Fridays. Varry weel, they get their brass—now then, they hev to lig it out, and it goes i' various ways—and a good deal on it goes back to Jeckie for bread and bacon and cheese and groceries, d'ye see? She pays out wi' one hand and she tak's in wi' t'other; they've niver had such an amount o' trade at her shop as they hev now. Stan's to reason!—ye can't hev three or four hundred stout fellers come workin' in a place wi'out 'em liggin' brass out. They mun ate and drink—same as what t'rest on us does. And so t'money goes back'ard and forrards."

"Aye, but theer's one i' t'place 'at'll tak' good care 'at some on it sticks in' her palm!" said an individual who leaned against the door and watched the proceedings out of a squinting eye. "Theer'll be a nice bit o' profit for Jeckie Farnish out o' all that extry grocery trade—tak' a bit o' notice o' that!"

"Varry like—but when all's said and done," answered the first speaker, "theer's no denyin' t'fact 'at all this here brass 'at's bein' paid out and spent i' t'village hes what they call its origin wi' her and t'other woman. They hef to pay t'contractors, ye know. And a bonny-like sum it mun be an' all, wi' all that machinery, and t'stuff 'at they've browt here i' building material, and t'men's wages—gow, I couldn't ha' thowt 'at her and Albert Grice's wife could ha' had so much brass!"

"Now, how much will they reckon to mak' a year out o' t'job when it's fully established, like?" asked a man who had shown his keen interest by watching each preceding speaker with his mouth wide open and his eyes turning and staring from one to another. "Is there a deal to be made out o' this here coal trade? 'Cause mi mother, 'at lives close to Mestur Revis' colliery, yonder at Heronshawe Main, as they call it, she niver pays no more nor five shillin' a ton for her coal. I reckon ye'd hev to sell a lot o' tons o' coal at that figure before ye'd get enew o' brass to pay for all 'at's bein' laid out here—what?"

"Thy mother lives close to t'scenes o' operations, fathead!" retorted the blacksmith. "She's on t'threshold, as it were—nowt to do but buy it as it comes out o' t'pit. But if thy mother lived i' London town, what dusta think she'd hev to pay for her coal then? I've read pieces i' t'papers about coal bein' as much as three and four pounds a ton i' London—what's ta think o' that?"

"Why, now, that's summat like a price!" assented the questioner. "I shouldn't hev no objection misen to sellin' coal at four pound a ton. But they hev to get it to London town first, hevn't they, afore they can sell?"

Before the blacksmith could give enlightenment on this economic point, the jack-of-all-trades, who, on a previous similar occasion, had warned Ben Scholes of what Jeckie was after in buying his land, put in one of his caustic remarks.

"Aye, and afore Jeckie Farnish gets her coal to London town—which there isn't no such place, 'cause London's a city—she'll hev to get it somewheer else!" he said. "Don't ye forget that!"

"I thowt ye'd ha' summat to say," sneered the blacksmith. "Wheer hes she to get it, like?—ye'll knaw, of course."

"I dew knaw," affirmed the wiseacre. "She'll hev to get it to t'surface! It's i' t'bowels o' t'earth yet, is that coal—it's none on t'top."

"What's to prevent it bein' browt to t'top, clever 'un?" demanded the blacksmith. "Aren't they at work sinkin' t'shafts as fast as they can?"

"Aye—and I've knawn wheer they sunk t'shafts deeper nor wheer ye heerd on!" said the clever one. "And then they niver got no coal! Not 'cause t'coal worn't there—it wor theer, reight enough wor t'coal. But it niver rase to t'top!"

"And for why, pray?" asked an eager listener. "What wor theer to prevent it?"

But the hinter at evil things, having shot his shafts, was turning on his heel, bound for the tap-room at the "Brown Cow."

"Niver ye mind!" he said darkly. "Theer's been no coal led away fro' Jeckie Farnish's pit mouth yit! An' happen ther niver will be!"

If he really had some doubts on the matter the Jack-of-all-trades formed a minority of one on the question of Jeckie Farnish's success. Everybody in the village believed that within a comparatively short time the pit would be in full working order, and coal would be coming up the winding shaft in huge quantities. And there were not wanting those in Savilestowe who were eager to get some share in the fortune which Jeckie and Lucilla had so far managed to monopolise. The squire, and the vicar, and Stubley, and Merritt as principals, and some of the lesser lights of the community as accessories, began putting their heads together in secret and discussing plans and schemes of money-making, all arising out of the fact that work was going ahead rapidly at the Farnish-Grice pit. Now, it was almost impossible for anything to be discussed, or for anything to happen in Savilestowe without the news of it reaching Jeckie—and one day she went to Lucilla with a face full of information and resolve.

"It's always the case!" she began, with a dark hinting look. "Whenever a big affair like ours is started, there's sure to be them that wants to get a bit of picking out of it by some means or other, fair or foul. I'll not say 'at this isn't fair, but it doesn't suit me!"

"What is it?" asked Lucilla anxiously. "Nothing wrong?"

"Not with our concern," replied Jeckie. "That's going all right, as you know very well—we shall be getting coal in another twelve month. No, it's this—it's come to my ears that the squire and Stubley and some more of 'em, knowing very well that there'll have to be a bit of housing accommodation provided, are forming themselves into a society or a company, or something, with the idea of building what they call a model village that'll be well outside Savilestowe but within easy reach. Now, you and me's not going to have that!"

"But—the miners'll have to live somewhere!" said Lucilla.

Jeckie gave her partner a queer look.

"Do you think I don't know that?" she said. "Why, of course! And I've made provision for it, though I thought we'd time enough. But now—before ever this lot can get to work—we'll start. We'll have our men in our own hands—on our own property."

"But how?" inquired Lucilla.

"I never told anybody until now," answered Jeckie, "but I have some land in Savilestowe that I bought years before I got that land of Ben Scholes's. There's about thirty acres of it—I bought it from James Tukeby's widow for next to naught, on the condition that she was to have the rent of it till she died. It was all properly conveyed to me, and, of course, I can do what I like with it. Now then, we'll build three or four rows of cottages on that—of course, as the land's mine, it's value'll have to be reckoned in our partnership account—and we'll let 'em to our own miners, d'you see? I'll have none of our men livin' in model villages under the squire and the parson—it's all

123

finicking nonsense. We'll have our chaps close to their work! Good, substantial, brick cottages—bricks are cheap enough about here— with a good water supply; that's all that's wanted. Model villages!— they'll be wantin' to house workin' fellers i' palaces next!"

"It'll cost a lot of money," observed Lucilla. She had never considered the housing of the small army of miners which would troop into Savilestowe at the opening of the new pit. "And you know what we're already laying out!"

"We shall get it all back in rents," said Jeckie. She pulled some papers out of the old reticule. "See," she continued, "I've worked it out—cost and everything; I got an estimate from Arkstone, the builder, at Sicaster, yesterday. There's no need to employ an architect for places like they'll be—just five roomed cottages. Come here, and I'll show you what it'll cost, and what it'll bring in."

Lucilla was always an easy prey to Jeckie, and being already deeply involved, was only too ready to assent to all the plans and projects which her senior partner proposed. Moreover, Albert, when the two women condescended to call him into counsel, invariably agreed with his one-time sweetheart; he had the conviction that whatever Jeckie took in hand must certainly succeed. He himself was so full of the whole scheme that he had long since given up his daily visit to Sicaster. Ever since the beginning of active sinking work at the pit, he had driven Lucilla over to Savilestowe every morning after breakfast, and there they had remained most of the day, watching operations; in time Albert came to believe that he himself was really a sort of ex-officio manager of the whole thing, and in this belief Jeckie humoured him. And so it was easy to gain Lucilla's consent to the cottage-building scheme (which eventually developed into one that included the construction of houses of the villa type for the more important officials), and once more the two partners paid visits to solicitors and bankers.

The money was rushing away like water out of a broken reservoir. As in most similar cases, the expenditure, when it came to it, was greater than the spenders had reckoned for. More than once Lucilla drew back appalled at the sums which had to be laid out; more than once the bankers upon whom the partners were always drawing heavy cheques, took Jeckie aside and talked seriously to her about the prospects of the venture; Jeckie invariably replied by exhibiting the opinions of the experts and the professor of geology, and by declaring that if she had to mortgage her whole future, she was going on. She would point out, too, that the work had gone on successfully and smoothly; there had been nothing to alarm; nothing to stay the steady progress.

"I'll see it through to success!" she declared. "Cost what it may, I'm going to put all I have into it. I've never failed yet—and I won't!"

The work in her forty acres and in the land where the rows of ugly cottages were being built came to fascinate her. She began to neglect her shop, leaving all its vastly increased business to a manager and several sorely-taxed assistants, and to spend all her time with the engineers and contractors, until she came to know almost as much about their labours as they themselves knew. She would wander from one of the two shafts to the other a dozen times in a day; she kept an eye on the builders of the cottages and on the men who were making the road that would lead from the pit to the main street of the village; she had a good deal to say about the construction of the short stretch of railway which would connect it with the line that ran behind the woods, whereon she hoped to send her coal all over the country. In her imagination she saw it going north and south, east and west, truck upon truck of it—to return in good gold.

But meanwhile the money went. More than once she and Lucilla had to increase their original capital. A time came when still more money was needed, and when Lucilla could do no more. But Jeckie's resources were by no means exhausted, and one day, after a sleepless night during which she thought as she had never thought in her life, she went into Sicaster, determined on doing what she had once vowed she never would do. The shop must go.

CHAPTER VII

THE LAST THROW

It was a conversation with Farnish that sent Jeckie, grim and resolute, into Sicaster, determined on selling the business which she had built up and developed so successfully. Until the day of that conversation the idea of giving up the shop had never entered her mind; she had more than once foreseen that she might have to raise ready money on the strength of her prosperous establishment, but she had not contemplated relinquishing it altogether, for she knew—no one better—that as the population of Savilestowe increased because of the new industry which she was founding in its midst, so would the trade of the Golden Teapot wax beyond her wildest dreams. But certain information given her by her father brought matters to a crisis, and when Jeckie came to such passages in life she was as quick in action as she was rapid in thought.

Farnish, since the beginning of his daughter's great adventure, had grown greatly in self-importance. Like Albert Grice, he believed himself to be a sharer, even a guiding spirit, in the wonderful enterprise. Long since promoted from his first position as a sort of glorified errand-boy to that of superintendent of transit and collector of small accounts, he now wore his second-best clothes every day, and was seen much about the village and at Sicaster. Jeckie had found out that he was to be trusted if given a reasonable amount of liberty; consequently, she had left him pretty much to his own devices. Of late he had taken to frequenting the bar-parlour of the "Coach-and-Four" every evening after his early supper, and as he never returned home in anything more than a state of quite respectable up-liftedness, Jeckie said nothing. He was getting on in years, she remembered, and some licence must be permitted him; besides, she had for a long time given him an increased amount of pocket-money, and it now mattered nothing to her how or where he laid it out so long as he behaved himself, and did his light work faithfully. They had come to be better friends, and she had allowed him, in some degree, to make evident his parental position, and had condescended now and then to ask his advice in small matters. And in the village, and in Sicaster, he was no longer Farnish, the broken farmer, but Mr. Farnish, father of one of the wealthiest women in the neighbourhood.

The problem of Jeckie's wealth—and how much money she really had was only known to her bankers and guessed at by her solicitors—had long excited interest in Savilestowe and its immediate surroundings. It was well known that she had extended her original business in such surprising fashion that her vans and carts now carried a radius of many miles; she had been so enterprising that she had considerably damaged the business of more than one grocer in Sicaster and Cornchester; the volume of her trade was at least six times as great as that which George Grice had ever known in his best days. Yet the discerning knew very well that Miss Farnish had not made, could not have made, all the money she was reputed to possess out of her shop, big and first-class as it was. And if Jeckie, who never told anybody everything, could have been induced to speak, she would have agreed with the folk who voiced this opinion. The truth was that as she had made money she had begun to speculate, and after some little practice in the game had become remarkably proficient at it; she had found her good luck following her in this risky business as splendidly as it had followed her in selling bacon and butter. But, it was only a very few people—bankers, stockbrokers, solicitors—who knew of this side of her energetic career. What the Savilestowe folk did know was that Jecholiah Farnish had made no end of brass; some of them were not quite sure how; some suspected how. Jeckie said and did nothing to throw any light on the subject. It pleased and suited her that people knew she was wealthy, and her own firm belief—for she was blind enough on certain points—was that she was believed to be a great deal richer than—as she herself knew, in secret—she really was.

It fell to Farnish to disabuse her on this point.

Farnish, returning home one night from the customary symposium at the "Coach-and-Four," found Jeckie peacefully mending linen by the parlour fire. It had come to be an established ceremony, since more friendly relations were set up between them, that father and daughter took a night-cap together before retiring, and exchanged a little pleasant conversation during its consumption; on this occasion Farnish, after the gin-and-water had relapsed into a moody quietude. He was usually only too ready to talk, and Jeckie glanced at him in surprise as he sat staring at the fire, leaving his glass untouched.

"You're very quiet to-night," she said. "Has aught happened?"

Farnish started, stared at her, and leaned forward.

"Aye, mi lass!" he replied. "Summat has happened! I've been hearin' summat; summat 'at's upset me; summat 'at I niver expected to hear." He leaned still nearer, and dropped his voice to a whisper. "Jecholiah, mi lass!" he went on, in almost awe-struck tones. "Folks is—talkin'!"

"Folks! what folks?" exclaimed Jeckie in genuine amazement. "An' talkin'? What about?"

"It's about you, mi lass," answered Farnish. "I heerd it to-night, i' private fro' a friend o' mine as doesn't want his name mentionin', but's a dependable man. He tell'd me on t'quiet, i' a corner at t' 'Coach-and-Four'; he thowt you owt to know, this man did. He say 'at it's bein' talked on, not only i' Savilestowe here, but all round t'neighbourhood. Dear—dear!—it's strange how long a tale tak's to get to t'ears o' t'person 'at's chiefly concerned!"

"Now then—out with it!" commanded Jeckie. "What's it all about?"

Farnish glanced at her a look which was half fearful, half-inquiring. "They're sayin' 'at you and Lucilla Grice hes come to t'end o' your brass, or close on it," he whispered. "Some on 'em 'at reckons to know summat about it's been reckonin' up what you mun ha' laid out, and comparin' it wi' what they knew she hed, and what they think you hed, and they say you mun be about at t'last end. An' they say, 'at it'll be months yet afore t'pit'll be ready for working, and 'at ye'll niver be able to keep up t'expense, and 'at ye'll eyther hev to sell to somebody 'at can afford to go on wi' it, or gi' t'job up altogether, and lose all t'brass—an' it mun be a terrible amount bi' now—'at you've wared on it. That's what's bein' whispered about, mi lass!"

"Aught else?" demanded Jeckie.

"Well, theer is summat," admitted Farnish. "They say 'at ye never paid them two London gentlemen 'at did such a lot at t'beginning o' things; 'at they went away thro' t'place wi'out their brass, an'——"

"That'll do!" interrupted Jeckie. "Is that all?"

"All, mi lass," assented Farnish. "Except 'at it's a common notion 'at ye'll niver be able to carry t'job through! Now, what is t'truth, mi lass? I'm reight fair upset, as you can see."

"Sup your drink and go to bed and sleep sound!" said Jeckie contemptuously. "An' tell any damned fool 'at talks such stuff again to you 'at he'd better wait and watch things a bit. Money! I'll let 'em see whether I haven't money! More nor anybody knows on!"

Farnish went to bed satisfied and confident; but when he had gone Jeckie sat by the fire, motionless, staring at the embers until they died out to a white ash. She was thinking, and reckoning, and scheming, and when at last, she too retired, it was to lie awake more than half the night revolving her plans. She was up again by six o'clock next morning, and at seven was with the manager of the works—a clever, capable, thoroughly-experienced man who had been recommended to her by Revis, of Heronshawe Main, and in whom, accordingly, she had every confidence. He stared in astonishment as Jeckie, who had wrapped head and shoulders in an old Paisley shawl, came stalking into his temporary office. "I want a word with you," said Jeckie, going straight to the point after her usual fashion. She shut the door and motioned him to sit down at his desk. "I want plain answers to a couple of questions. First—how long will it be before we get this pit into working order?"

The manager reflected a moment.

"Barring accidents, ten months," he answered.

"Second," continued Jeckie, "how much money shall we want to see us through? Take your time; reckon it out. Carefully, now; leave a good margin."

The manager nodded, took paper and pencil, and began to figure; Jeckie stood statue-like at his side, watching in silence as he worked. Ten minutes passed, then he drew a thick line beneath his last sum total of figures, and pointed to it.

"That," he said. "Ample!"

Jeckie picked up the sheet of paper, folded it, slipped it under her shawl, and turned to the door.

"That's all right," she said. "I only wanted to know. Get on!"

This it was that sent her, dressed in her best, a fine figure of a woman, just on the right side of middle age, into Sicaster that morning. But before she reached the town she called in at Albert Grice's villa. It was still early, and Albert and Lucilla were seated at their breakfast table. Jeckie walked in on them, closed the door, after making certain that the parlour-maid was not lingering on the mat outside, declined to eat or drink, pulled a chair up to the table, and produced the sheet of paper on which the manager had made his reckoning.

"Look here!" she said. "You know that this—what with that building scheme and one thing and another—is costing us a lot more nor ever we'd reckoned on; things always does. Now then, I've made Robinson work out—carefully—exactly how much more we shall have to lay out yet before that pit's in full working order. Here's the amount. Look at it!"

Albert and Lucilla bent their heads over the sheet of paper. Albert made a sound which expressed nothing; Lucilla screamed.

"Mercy on us!" she exclaimed. "I can't find any more money; it's impossible! Why——"

"Never said you could," interrupted Jeckie. "I'll find it; all t'lot. But ... bear in mind, when I've found that, as I will, at once, my share in our united capital'll be just eight times as much as yours. So, of course, your share in the profits'll be according. D'you see!"

Lucilla made no answer, but Albert immediately assumed the air of a wise and knowing business man.

"Oh, of course, that's right enough, Lucilla!" he said. "That's according to strict principles. Share in profits in relation to amount of capital held by each partner. You'll be able to find this capital?" he continued, turning to Jeckie. "It 'ud never do for things to stop—now!"

"I'll find it—at once," declared Jeckie. "Naught's going to stop. But your wife must sign this memorandum that the sharing's to be as I've just said, and we'll have the deed of partnership altered in accordance. After all, it'll make no difference to you. You'll get your profits on your capital just the same." She produced a typewritten document which she had prepared herself after her interview with the manager, and when Lucilla had signed it, went off in silence to the town. Her first visit was to the bank, where she asked for a certain box which reposed in the strong-room; she opened it in a waiting-room, took from it a bundle of securities, gave the box back to the clerk, and going out, repaired to a stock and share broker's.

Within half an hour she was back at the bank, and there, in the usual grim silence in which she usually transacted similar business, paid in to the credit of Farnish & Grice a cheque which represented a very heavy amount of money.

And now came the last desperate move. She had just sold every stock and share she possessed; she had only one thing left to sell, and that was the business in which she had been so successful. She walked twice round the old market place before she finally made up her mind. It was fifteen years since she had caused the golden teapot to be placed over the door of the house which she had rented from Stubley, and she had prospered beyond belief. There was no such business as hers in that neighbourhood. And there were folk who would be only too willing to buy it. She turned at last and walked determinedly into the shop of the leading grocer in Sicaster, a man of means, who was at that time Mayor of the old borough. If anybody was to step into her shoes he was the man.

He was just within the shop, a big, old-fashioned place, when Jeckie walked in, and he stared at her in surprise. Jeckie showed neither surprise nor embarrassment; now that her mind was made up she was as cool and matter-of-fact as ever, and her voice and manner showed none of the agitation which she had felt ten minutes before.

"I want a few minutes' talk with you, Mr. Bradingham," she said. "Can you spare them?"

"Certainly, Miss Farnish!" answered the grocer, an elderly, prosperous-looking man, who only needed his mayoral chain over his smart morning coat to look as if he were just about to step on the bench. "Come this way."

He led her into a private office at the rear of the shop and gave her a chair by his desk; Jeckie began operations before he had seated himself.

"Mr. Bradingham!" she said. "You know what a fine business I have yonder at Savilestowe?"

Bradingham laughed—there was a note of humour in the sound.

"We all know that who are in the same trade, Miss Farnish," he answered. "I should think you've got all the best families, within six miles round, on your books! You're a wonderful woman, you know."

"Mr. Bradingham," said Jeckie, "I want to sell my business as it stands. I want to devote all my time to yon colliery. I've made lots o' money out of the grocery trade, and lots more out o' what I made in that way, but that's naught to what I'm going to make out o' coal. So—I must sell. Will you buy?—as it stands—stock, goodwill, book debts (all sound, you may be sure, else there wouldn't be any!), vans, carts, everything? I'd rather sell to you than to anybody, 'cause you'll carry it on as I did. You can make a branch of this business of yours, or you can keep up the old name—whichever seems best to you."

Bradingham looked silently at his visitor for what seemed to her a long time.

"That's what you really want, then?" he said at last. "To concentrate on your new venture."

"I don't believe in running two businesses," answered Jeckie. "I'm beginning to feel—I do feel!—that it's got to be one or t'other. And—it's going to be coal!"

"You've sunk a lot in that pit, already?" he remarked.

"Aye—and more than a lot!" responded Jeckie. "But it's naught to what I mean to pull out of it!"

Bradingham continued to watch his visitor for a minute or two and she saw that he was thinking and calculating.

"I've no objection to buying your business," he said at last. "Look here—I'll drive out to Savilestowe this afternoon, and you can show me everything, and the books, and so on, and then we'll talk. I'm due at the Mayor's parlour now. Three o'clock then."

As Jeckie drove back to Savilestowe she remembered something. She remembered the day on which she had run down from Applecroft to get old George Grice's help, and how he had come up and found poverty and ruin. Now, another man was coming to see and value what she had created—he would find a splendid trade, a rich and flourishing business—all made by herself. But it must go. The pit was yawning for money—more money—still more money. And as in a vision, she saw sacks of gold, and wagon loads of silver, and bundles of scrip, and handfuls of banknotes all being hastened into the blackness of the shaft and disappearing there. It was as if Mammon, the ever-hungry, ever-demanding, sat at the foot, refusing to be appeased.

CHAPTER VIII

THE COMMINATION SERVICE

At five o'clock that afternoon, by mutual agreement, Jeckie Farnish sold to John Bradingham the stock and goodwill of her grocery business, and a few days later she paid in another heavy cheque to the credit of Farnish and Grice, and, at the same date, secured the alteration in the deed of partnership which made matters straight between her and Lucilla. There was something of a grim desperation in Jeckie's face as she walked out of the solicitor's office whereat this transaction had been effected; she was feeling something that she had no desire to speak of. But Lucilla felt it, too, and said it.

"Well!" she remarked in a low tone as the two partners walked away from the town. "I don't know how it is with you, but I've put my last penny into that pit! Me and Albert's got just enough to live comfortably on till we begin to get some returns, but I can't ever find any more capital!"

"No need!" said Jeckie, almost fiercely. "Wait! as I'm doing."

She herself knew well enough that she, too, had thrown in her last penny; there was nothing for it now but to see the additional capital flow out steadily, and to wait in patience until the first yields brought money. In the meantime, she was not going to waste money on herself and her father. Selling most of the furniture which she had gradually accumulated, and leaving the house behind the shop, which had become an eminently comfortable dwelling, she transferred Farnish and herself to a cottage near the pit, told him that there they were going to stop until riches came, and settled down to watch the doings of the little army of workers into whose pockets her money was going at express speed. Wait—yes, there was nothing else to do.

There was not a man amongst all that crowd of toilers, from the experienced managers to the chance-employed navvy, who did not know Jeckie Farnish at that stage of her career. She was at the scene of operations as soon as work began of a morning; she was there until the twilight came to end the day. Here, there, everywhere she was to be met with. Now she was with the masons who were building the cottages on her bit of land outside the Leys; now with the men who were constructing a solid road from the pit-mouth to the highway; now with the navvies who were making the link of railway that would connect Savilestowe Main Colliery with the great trunk line a mile off behind the woods; now, careless of danger and discomfort, she was down one or other of the twin shafts, feverishly eager to see how much farther their sinkers were approaching to the all-important regions beneath. Sometimes she had Lucilla in her wake; sometimes Albert; sometimes Farnish. But none of these three possessed her pertinacity and endurance; a general daily look round satisfied each. Jeckie, when she was not in her bed or snatching a hasty meal, was always on the spot. Her money was at stake, and it behoved her to see that she was getting full value for every pennyworth of it.

She was not the only perpetual haunter of Savilestowe Leys at that time. The men who worked there at one or other of the diverse jobs which the making of a coal-mine necessitates—all of them strangers to the place until the new industry brought them to it— became familiar with a figure which was as odd and strange as that of Jeckie Farnish was grim and determined. Morning, noon, and night a man forever hung around the scene of operations, a man who was not allowed to cross the line of the premises and had more than once been turned out of them, but whom nobody and nothing could prevent from looking over fences and through gaps in the hedgerows and haunting the various means of ingress and egress, a wild, unkempt bright-eyed man, who was always talking to himself, and who, whenever he got the chance, talked hard and fast and vehemently to anyone he was able to lay a mental grappling-iron upon; a man with a grievance, Ben Scholes. He was always in evidence. While Jeckie patrolled her armies within, Scholes kept his watch without; he was as a man who, having had a treasure stolen from him, knows where the thief has bestowed it, and henceforth takes an insane delight in watching thief and treasure.

The first result of Scholes's discovery that Jeckie Farnish had done him over his forty acres of land was that he took to drink. Immediately after leaving the sign of the Golden Teapot he turned in at the "Coach-and-Four," and found such comfort in drinking rum-and-water while he retailed his grievances to the idlers in the inn-kitchen that he went there again next day, and fell into the habit of tippling and gossiping—if that could be called gossiping which resolved itself into telling and retelling the story of his woes to audiences of anything from one to a dozen. Few things interest a Yorkshireman more than to hear how Jack has done Bill and how Jack contrived to accomplish it, and while Scholes never got any sympathy—every member of his congregation secretly admiring Jeckie for her smartness and cleverness—he never failed to attract attention. There were many houses of call in that neighbourhood; Scholes began a regular round of them; he had a tale to tell which was never likely to pall on folk whose one idea was to get money by any means, fair or foul, and the sight of his lean face and starveling beard at the door of parlour or kitchen was enough to arouse an eager, however oft repented, invitation.

"Nah, then, Scholes!—come thi ways in, and tell us how Jeckie Farnish did tha' out o' thi bit o' land—here, gi' t'owd lad a drop o' rum to set his tongue agate! Ecod, shoe's t'varry devil his-self for smartness is that theer Jecholiah! Nah, then, Scholes, get on wi' t'tale!"

Scholes had no objection to telling his tale over and over again, and there was not a pair of ears in all that neighbourhood which had not heard it; if not at first, then at second hand—nor was there a soul which did not feel a certain warmth in recognising Jeckie Farnish's astuteness; Scholes himself recognised it.

"Ye see, shoo hed me afore iver shoo come to t'house!" he would say. "Knew t'coal wor theer afore iver shoo come reck'nin' to want to buy mi fotty acre and mak' an orchard on't! But niver a word to me! Buyin', shoo wor, not fotty acre o' poor land, d'ye see, but what they call t'possibilities 'at ligged beneath it! T'possibilities o' untold wealth! As should ha' been mine. Nowt but a moral thief— that's what shoo is, yon Jecholiah. Clever' 'er may be—I don't say shoo isn't, but a moral thief."

"Tha means an immoral thief," said one of his listeners.

"I mean what I say!" retorted Scholes. "I know t'English language better nor what thou does. A moral thief!—that's what yon woman is. I appeal to t'company. If ye nobbut come to consider, same as judges and juries does at t'sizes, how shoo did me, ye'll see 'at, morally speakin', shoo robbed me o' my lawful rights. Ye see— for happen ye've forgotten some o' t'fine points o' t'matter, it wor i' this way——"

Then he would tell his tale all over again, and would afterwards argue it out, detail by detail, with his audience. In that part of Yorkshire the men are fond of hearing their own tongues, and wherever Scholes went the companies of the inn-kitchens were converted into debating societies.

One night, Scholes, full of rum and of delight in his grievance, went home and found his wife dead. As he had left her quite well when he went out in the morning, the shock sobered him, and certain affecting sentences in the Burial Service at which he was perforce present a few days later turned his thoughts toward religion. The truth was that Scholes, already half mad through his exaggeration of his wrongs, developed religious mania in a very sudden fashion. But no one suspected it, and the vicar, who was something of a simpleton, believed him to have undergone a species of conversion; Scholes, anyhow, forsook the public-house for the house of prayer, and was henceforth to be seen in company of a large prayer-book at all the services, Sunday and week-day. Very close observers might have noticed that he took great pleasure in those of the Psalms which invoke wrath and vengeance on enemies, and, on days when the choir was not present and the service was said, manifested infinite delight in repeating the Psalmist's denunciation in an unnecessarily loud voice. But no one remarked anything, and if the vicar secretly wished that his new sheep would not bleat quite so loudly, he put the excess of vocalisation down to the fact that Scholes was new to his job and anxious to obey the directions of the Rubrics. Moreover, he reflected, the probability was that Scholes would soon tire of attendance on the services, and would settle down to the conventional and respectable churchmanship of most of the folk around him.

Scholes, however, developed his mania. He suddenly got rid of his farm, realised all that he was worth, and went to live, quite alone, in a small cottage near the churchyard. From that time forward he divided his time between the church services and the doings on Savilestowe Leys. Whenever there was a service he was always in church—but so soon as ever any service was over he was off to the end of the village, to haunt the hedgerows and fences, and button-hole anybody who cared to hear his story. This went on for many an eventful month, and at last became a matter of no moment; Ben Scholes, said all the village, was a bit cracked, and if it pleased him to spend ten minutes in church, and all the rest of the day hanging about the outskirts of Jeckie Farnish's pit, why not? But in the last months of the operations at the new pit, the first day of another Lent came round, and the vicar, with Scholes and a couple of old alms-women as a congregation, read the Commination Service. Scholes had never heard this before, and the vicar was somewhat taken aback at the vigour with which he responded to certain fulminations.

"Cursed," read the vicar in unaffected and mellifluous tones, more suited to a benediction, "cursed is he that smiteth his neighbour secretly!"

"Amen!" responded Scholes, suddenly starting, as if a thought struck him. "Amen!"

"Cursed," presently continued the vicar, "is he that putteth his trust in man...."

"Amen, amen!" said Scholes fervently. "Amen!"

"Cursed," continued the vicar, glancing round at his respondent parishioner, and nervously hurrying forward, "are...."

"Covetous persons, extortioners!" exclaimed Scholes,

135

anticipating certain passages to come. "Amen, amen! So they are—amen!"

Then without waiting to hear what it was that the prophet David bore witness for, he clapped his prayer-book together with a loud noise, and hurried from the church; through one of the windows the vicar saw him walking among the tombs outside, gesticulating, and evidently talking to himself. When the service was over, he went out to him. "I fear the service distressed you, Scholes," he began, diffidently. "You are——"

Scholes waved his arms abroad.

"Nowt o' t'sort!" he exclaimed. "I wor delighted wi' it! I could like to hev that theer service read ivery Sunda'! I wor allus wantin' to mak' sure 'at a certain person 'at I could name wor cursed. An', of course, wheer theer's cursin' theer's vengeance—vengeance, vengeance!"

"Don't forget, Scholes, that it has been wisely said, 'Vengeance is Mine: I will repay, saith the Lord,'" answered the vicar, in his mildest tones. "You must remember——"

"Now, then, I forget nowt!" retorted Scholes. "I know all about it. But t'Lord mun use instruments—human instruments! Aw, it's varry comfortin', is what ye and me read together this mornin'—varry comfortin' to me. Cursed! 'Covetous persons'! Aw!—ye needn't go far away to find one!"

The vicar was one of those men who dislike scenes and enthusiasm, and he left Scholes to himself, meditating among the gravestones, and went home to tell his wife that he wished somebody would give the man a quiet hint that loud upliftings of voice were not desirable in public worship. But next Sunday Scholes was not in his accustomed place—the front pew in the south aisle—nor did he come to church again. The clauses in the Commination Service had set his crazy brain off on another tack, and from the day on which he heard them he forgot the temporary anæsthetic which religious observance had brought to him, and sought out his older and more familiar one—drink. He took to frequenting the "Brown Cow," a hostelry of less pretensions than the "Coach-and-Four," and there he would sit for hours, quietly drinking rum and water—as inoffensive, said the landlady, as a pet lamb in a farm-house kitchen.

For Scholes no longer talked about his grievance. He became strangely quiescent; sharper observers than the landlady would have seen that he was moody. He never talked to anybody at this stage, though he muttered a great deal to himself, and occasionally smiled and laughed, as if the thought of something pleased him. But one night, as he sat alone in a corner of the "Brown Cow," there came in a couple of navvies whom he recognised as workers at the hated pit, and a notion came into his mentality, which, crazy as it was rapidly becoming, yet still retained much of its primitive craftiness. He treated these men to liquor; they came to be treated again the following night, and the night after that; they and Scholes henceforth met regularly of an evening in their corner, and drank and whispered for hours at a time.

There came a day whereon these men and Scholes no longer forgathered at the "Brown Cow." Instead, they met at Scholes's cottage. It was a lonely habitation, a tumbled-down sort of place in the lee of the old tithe-barn, and had been empty for years before Scholes took it and furnished it with odds and ends of seating and bedding. It stood well out of the village, and could be reached unobserved from more than one direction. Here the two navvies with whom he had made friends at the "Brown Cow" began to come. Scholes laid in a supply of liquor for their delectation. And here, round a smoky lamp and a spirit bottle, the three were wont to talk in whispers far into the night.

Had Jeckie Farnish or Lucilla Grice known of what it was that these three men talked—one of them already obsessed with the belief that he was the Lord's chosen instrument of vengeance, the other two cunningly anxious to profit by it—neither would have slept in their beds, nor felt one moment's peace until Scholes and his companions were safely laid by the heels. But they knew nothing; nothing, at any rate, that was discomposing or threatening. Ever since the time of putting more capital into the concern the making of the colliery had gone on successfully and even splendidly. The two shafts, up-cast and down-cast, had been sunk to depths of several hundreds of feet without any encountering of more than the ordinary difficulties; the two great dangers, water and running sand, had not presented themselves. On the surface the building of the various sheds and offices had proceeded rapidly; some were already roofed in; in one the winding machinery and engines had been installed. The connection road was made; the link of railway finished; and on the high ground above the Leys three rows of ugly red-brick cottages were steadily approaching completion. The man who made his silent calculations that morning when Jeckie Farnish stood by him in grim silence came to her one day with a sheepish smile on his face.

"I was a bit out in my reckoning, Miss Farnish," he said. "But it was on the right side! At the rate we're going at now we'll be finished, and the pit'll be working from six to eight weeks sooner than I thought. You'd better hurry those builders on with the cottages; you'll be wanting to fill them before so long."

Jeckie needed no admonition to hurry anything. She was speeding up all the work as rapidly as she could, for good reasons which she kept to herself. Once more the outlay was proving greater than had been anticipated, and she knew that if the manager's final reckoning of ten months from the time of her sale of the grocery business had been kept to she would have had to raise more capital. She was secretly overjoyed when Revis, of Heronshawe Main, drove over one day, made a careful inspection of all that had been done, and was then being done, and corroborated Robinson's revised opinion—the pit would be at work six weeks sooner than she had thought.

"And I reckon you'll be rare and glad to see the first tubs o' coal wound, my lass!" he said heartily as he drove off. "I know I was!"

Jeckie nodded and smiled; she was too thankful for his opinion to put her feelings into words. That night she was wakeful—not from anxiety, but from satisfaction and anticipation. Two months more, and the money that had been sunk in that pit would be coming out of its depths again, multiplied, increased....

In the middle of that night a brilliant flash of lurid flame followed by a roar that shook her cottage to its foundations and left it rocking, sent her headlong from her bed. And as she stood sick and trembling, grasping at the lintel of her window, she heard, in the deadly silence that followed, a sudden outburst of the big bell of the church, pealing as if for victory.

CHAPTER IX

THE BELL RINGS

Jeckie Farnish was a strong woman; physically as well as mentally she was the strongest woman in all those parts. She had scarcely ever known what it was to feel a sudden giving way of strength; the end of a long day's toil usually found her fresh and vigorous, ready for and gladly anticipating the labours of the morrow. Nor had she ever known what it was to experience a mental giving way; the nearest approach to it—only a momentary one—had been on that day, long years before, whereon George Grice had turned his back on her and her father's fallen fortunes. She had felt mentally sick and physically weak then, as though all the strength had been dashed out of her mind and body. But the feeling had quickly passed under the reviving fire of her anger and resentment, and since then she had rarely felt a qualm that affected her in either sense—determination and resolution had always kept her going. There were folks in the parish who were fond of saying that she was moulded of beaten iron with a steel core in the middle—it was their way of expressing a belief that nothing on earth below or in heaven above could move or bend her.

But as the vivid flash of flame and the infernal roar which followed it passed away, Jeckie standing in her night-clothes between her bed and her curtained window, felt herself stricken from head to foot; she was sick, in heart and brain. She suddenly realised that she was shaking throughout her strongly-fashioned frame, that her knees were knocking one against the other, her feet rattling on the floor, her fingers working as from a terrible shock. And in the silence she heard her heart thumping and thumping and thumping—it made her think of the engines at the pit which pumped up the leaking water as the shafts were driven deeper and deeper into the earth. She tried to lift a hand towards her heaving breast; it dropped back, nerveless, to her side.

"Oh God!" she breathed at last. "What is it? What is it?"

The hurrying of folk in the street outside roused her out of her momentary paralysis, and with an effort she stumbled rather than walked to the window-place, drew aside curtain and blind, flung open a casement, and leaned out into the night. And at what she saw, a moan burst from her lips, and she began to tremble as with a violent attack of ague. For the night was one of brilliantly clear moonlight, and from her window she could see all across the Leys and the buildings upon which she had expended such vast sums. And over the newly made pit, so rapidly approaching completion, hung a great umbrella-shaped cloud of dun-coloured smoke, thick and rolling, and from the pit mouth itself issued spurts and flickers of bright flame, which, as she stared, horror-stricken, began to gather at one place into a steady, spreading blaze. Thitherwards men were already beginning to hasten from the open doors of the cottages, calling to each other as they ran. And above their voices, never ceasing, sounded the frantic ringing of the big bell of the church, maddening in its insistence.

She leaned farther out of the window and called to the folk who were hurrying past; called several times before she attracted attention. But at last a white face looked up and a voice hailed her—

the voice of one of the principal foremen in the machinery department at the pit.

"Miss Farnish!" he called. "Miss Farnish!—it's an explosion! The down-cast shaft! And look there!—the pit's on fire!"

He pointed a shaking arm across the flat expanse of land before the cottage, and Jeckie saw that the gathering flame about the mouth of the shaft had suddenly leaped into a great mass of lurid light. Its brightness illumined the whole area around it, and she saw then that the surface works which had steadily grown up around the excavations had either been blown away or were left in shapeless bulks of ruinous masonry. Towards these from all directions men were running like ants swarming about a broken down nest.

She turned away from the window, and with no other light than the glare from without, sought for and huddled her shaking limbs into the first garments that came to hand. And as she fastened them about her, scarce knowing how, a hand began to beat upon her door, and Farnish called to her, once, twice, thrice, before she realised that the sounds were human and had any significance.

"Jeckie, mi lass!" Farnish was calling. "Jeckie! Jeckie!"

"What is it?" she asked at last in a dull, strained voice, so strange in its sound that she found herself wondering at it. "What do you want?"

"Yon noise?" cried Farnish, who slept at the back of the cottage. "What's it about, mi lass? What's it mean?"

"The pit's blown up," answered Jeckie, with almost sullen indifference. "It's on fire, too. You can come in and see for yourself."

Farnish pushed the door open and entered; he was half whimpering, half moaning as he crossed the floor towards the window. But Jeckie, now wrapped in a thick ulster coat and tying a shawl round her head and neck, said nothing. Her heart had resumed its normal action by then; she was only conscious that she felt sick and faint. She stared stupidly at her father's figure, darkly outlined against the glow of the fire.

"God ha' mercy on us!" groaned Farnish. "A bad job! a bad job! Howiver can it ha' come about, and what mun be done? It's all of a flame, and——"

"Come out!" commanded Jeckie. "I must see for myself what's——"

She had laid a hand on the half-open door of the bedroom, when it was suddenly wrenched out of her grasp, and she herself thrown backwards across the bed by a second and apparently more violent explosion, which came simultaneously with another vivid burst of orange-coloured flame. Jeckie remembered afterwards

140

what curious and vivid impressions she had in that moment. As she herself was flung over the edge of her thick feather-bed she saw Farnish thrown away from the window, his arms whirling in the air like the sails of a wind-mill; she heard a musical tinkle of falling glass, making a sort of background to his startled outcry. And she saw things. The vividness of the glare lit up a glass-fronted case on the bedroom wall wherein was a stuffed squirrel; it also lit up a framed text of Scripture, set in a floral bordering of hideous design, and a little weather-glass, furnished with two figures, one of which, a man, came out for fine weather, while the other, a woman, emerged for wet; years afterwards she had vivid recollections of how these two quaint puppets were violently agitated at the end of their wires. And then there was gloom again, and silence, and she heard Farnish gathering himself up from the floor, moaning.

"Are you hurt?" she asked, dully and indifferently. "Is aught wrong?"

"T'window were blown right in on mi face," answered Farnish, "I'm bleedin' somewhere. What about yoursen, mi lass?"

Jeckie was seeking for matches and a candle. The candle had been blown out of its tin holder and had rolled into a corner. When she found and lighted it it was to reveal Farnish with a trickle or two of blood on his cheeks and scarce a pane of glass left in the window. She pointed him to a towel, and turned to the door. "That 'ud be the other shaft," she said in a low voice, and in a fashion that made Farnish afraid. "It's been a put-up job. I've enemies! But I'll best 'em yet! I'll not be bet!"

Without another word she went downstairs and out into the street, and Farnish, left alone, looked dolefully at his face as envisaged to him in Jeckie's mirror. Something glittered on one of his projecting cheekbones, and he groaned again as he picked out a sliver of glass. Then he wiped his face with the towel, and, still moaning and bewailing, descended to the living-room. In those days Jeckie no longer locked up the spirits, and he, accordingly, went to the cupboard, got out the gin, and mixed himself a stiff drink. And as he stood sipping it he muttered to himself.

"A bad job!" said Farnish. "A bad, bad job! All that theer brass—gone i' th' twinklin' of an eye, as the sayin' is! An' who can ha' done it?"

He, too, went into the street at last. By that time the whole village was out of bed and abroad, and while the more active of the men folk were flocking towards the scene of the explosion, the older men and the women were hanging in groups about the doors of the houses and cottages, gazing fearfully at the great cupola of smoke that hung over the Leys. Farnish joined one such group, the

141

members of which were already recounting with great zest their own particular private experiences.

"Our Sarah's little lad, Albert James, wor flung fair out o' t'bed and ageean t'wall!" declared one woman. "And his father's heead wor jowled ageean t'chest o' drawers! An' our cottage rocked same as if it wor a earthquake—I made sure 'at all t'place 'ud come tummlin' down about wor ears!"

"Aye, an theer isn't a pane o' glass left whole in our front windows!" said another. "Blown reight into t'kitchen they wor, and I would like to know who's goin' to pay for t'mendin'! This is what comes o' mekkin' coal-pits i' a quiet, peaceable place same as what this wor afore Jeckie Farnish started on at t'game! I allus did say 'at no good 'ud come o' t'job, and 'at we should all on us be blowed up i' wor beds some fine night, and if we hevn't been to-night it nowt but a merciful dispensation o' Providence 'at we hevn't! An' I hope 'at t'job's finished, and 'at we shall hev' no more on't—theer's nowt 'ud suit me better nor to see all t'coal-miners tak theer-sens off and leave us i' peace as we used to be, for I'm sure——"

"Hod this wisht!" broke in one of the few men who had kept back from the Leys. "That's talkin' like a fooil!—doesn't ta see 'at this here'll mean no end o' money lost to them 'at's mekkin' t'pit, and theer's Mestur Farnish stannin' theer? How is it, Mestur Farnish?— d'ye knaw owt about how it happened like?"

"I know no more about it nor what you do," answered Farnish, who was standing at the end of a group of cottages, staring blankly at the flame and smoke which glared and rolled in front. "It's a bad job—a bad job! An' what's yon theer bell ringin' for—is it somebody 'at's gone to ring for t'Sicaster fire brigade, or what?"

"Why, theer wor a young feller started off on his bicycle for that theer purpose, as soon as t'first explosion wor over," answered the man. "Besides, they wodn't hear our bell as far off as Sicaster— t'wind's i' t'wrong quarter, an' all. I been wonderin' what t'bell wor ringin' for, missen. How would it be if we stepped up to t'church, like?"

Farnish, realising the hopelessness of going near the pit, joined the two or three men who turned in the direction of the church. As they hurried up the street, a dog-cart dashed past them; the young man who had hastened to Sicaster for the fire brigade had called at Albert Grice's house on his way, and Albert and Lucilla, panic-stricken, were flying to what might be the grave of their hopes, and more than one man who watched them pass noticed that Lucilla was driving, and flogging the smart cob to the utmost limit of his speed, while Albert, pale and frightened, cowered in the lower seat at her side. Behind them presently came the Sicaster fire engine, its bell ringing clangerously as the steaming horses clattered through the village; in its brazen loudness the frantic ringing of the church bell was lost to hearing, and when Farnish and his companions came to the churchyard and comparative silence, it had ceased altogether.

"Whoever wor ringin' must ha' been ringin' for t'fire engine," muttered one of the men. "Ye see, he's stopped now 'at t'fire brigade's comed. It mun ha' been t'sexton." But just then the sexton, accompanied by the vicar, came hurrying through the little wicket-gate at the farther end of the churchyard. Encountering the other men at the porch, they stopped short.

"Who is in there, ringing that bell?" demanded the vicar. "Who's this?—you, Farnish? Did they send some one up from the pit to ring? If so, they must have broken into the church."

"Notwithstanding," interrupted the sexton, solemnly, "'at everybody in t'parish know 'at t'keys is in my possession, and close by!"

"I know naught about it," answered Farnish. "We come up here to find out who it wor, and what he wor ringin' for, ye see."

High over their heads the big bell once more gave tongue—loudly, clamorously, insistently. It rang out a score of times; then stopped as suddenly as it had begun. And one of the men, stepping back, as the rest, headed by the sexton, made for the porch, and looking up towards the head of the great square tower, let out a sharp exclamation.

"There's a man up there, looking ower t'parapet!" he said. "See yer!—there, wi' t'moon shinin' on his face! Look!"

The other men fell back, and shading their eyes from the bright moonlight, stared in the direction indicated. There, leaning over the battlemented parapet of the tower, immediately above one of the most grotesque of its gargoyles, appeared a weird and sinister figure—a man whose unkempt hair and sparse beard were being blown about his face by the light breeze. One of the younger men there, whose sight was keen, suddenly uttered a sound of recognition.

"Ecod!" he exclaimed. "It's Ben Scholes!"

The vicar uttered a sound too—dismal, and full of foreboding.

"Mad," he muttered. "Mad—undoubtedly! Scholes!" he went on, calling upwards to the figure silhouetted against the sky. "Scholes! What are you doing there? Come down, my good fellow, come down at once!"

But Scholes shook his floating locks, vigorously and emphatically.

"Naught o' t'sort, parson!" he answered, his voice coming with

143

curious force from his airy station. "T'job isn't half done in yet! Ye don't understand—how should yer? Ye see, it wor you 'at put t'idee into mi mind when ye read them comfortable passages t'other week, and I said 'Amen and Amen' to 'em. 'Cursed be covetous persons'— and sich like. I knew then, d'ye see, 'at I wor what they call t'instrument o' vengeance on yon theer Jecholiah. It hed to be, parson it hed to be! I wor doomed, as it weer, to blow her and her devil's wark to perdition, as t'sayin' is. Aye!—listen, all on yer—it wor through me 'at t'pit's been blown up! Three hundred pound o' good money I wared to get it blown into t'air. And I mun ring, I mun ring, all through the night, till t'sun rises on t'scene o' desolation; ring, d'ye understand, to show how t'Lord hes vengeance on bad 'uns like yon theer woman! Three hundred pound!—but I gat it done! Flame and smoke, parson!—I see'd 'em rise out o' t'pit. And then I rang, and rang, and rang—and I mun ring agen till t'sun rises ower yon woods. So may all them 'at cheats poor folk perish!"

"Mad!" repeated the vicar, looking helplessly round him. "What does he mean! And how can we get at him?"

"He means, sir, 'at he's paid some of them miners three hundred pound to blow t'pit up," answered the sexton, who was a sharp-witted man, "and as to gettin' at him, it's none to be done till he chooses to come down. There's naught but a straight ladder, and a man-hole at t'end on it, into yon belfry, and if he stands on t'trap door i' that man-hole he can keep all t'parish out as long as he likes. See you!—he's at it again!"

Scholes had suddenly disappeared from the parapet, and a moment later the big bell began clamouring once more.

"Didn't he say he mun ring till sunrise?" said the sexton. "He will ring!"

Farnish went hurrying home through the crowds in the village street. There was a light in the window of the living-room, and when he walked in, he found Jeckie, white-faced and grim, standing by a newly lighted lamp, staring at nothing. He went up and touched her timidly, and for the first time in her life she started, as if in fear. But Farnish was too full of news to notice that her nerves were gone.

"Jeckie, mi lass!" he said. "It's yon man Ben Scholes's 'at's at t'bottom o' this here! He paid some fellers three hundred pound to blow t'pit up—and he's gone mad wi' t'glory on it—mad!"

144

CHAPTER X

BLACK DEPTHS

The cottage to which Jeckie had removed her father and herself, and such household belongings as were absolutely necessary to their simple standard of comfort, faced due east; consequently, when the sun rose above the fringe of woods that morning its beams shone direct into the little living-room. And they fell full on Jeckie, who sat bolt upright at the table, her hands stretched out and tightly clasped on its surface, her eyes staring straight in front of her, her lips white and set. So she had sat for hours—motionless, silent. The tall clock in the corner had ticked away its record of minutes; the darkness had gone; the grey light had stolen in; there had come a glow in the skies and a gradual lighting of the window; finally, the sun had shown a ruddy, round face above the tapering pines and firs on the hilltop behind the Leys, and in the meadows and orchards the blackbirds and thrushes had begun to pipe and trill. But the breaking of a new day had caused no change in Jeckie Farnish's attitude. It was, said Farnish, talking of it after to his cronies, as if she had been turned into stone.

"Theer wor niver a word out on her, poor lass, after I'd told her what I'd gathered up at t'church porch," said he. "When she heeard 'at yon Ben Scholes had paid fellers three hundred pound to blow up t'pit she collapsed, as they call it, into t'chair and ligged her hand on t'table, and theer she sat, starin' and starin', hour after hour, till I wor fair afraid! I leeted t'lamp, and made t'fire, and brewed a pot a' tea, but I couldn't get her to put her lips to it. Wheer I laid t'cup at her side at four o'clock, theer it wor at seven—untasted. And not one word did she spake, all that time—nobbut sat and stared and stared i' front on her, as if she'd see summat. An happen she did see summat—how can I say?"

But Jeckie moved at last. As Farnish, well-nigh beyond his wits with fear and anxiety, stood by the hearth, watching her, a hurried step sounded on the flagged path outside the cottage, and Robinson, the manager, came hastening in, grimy and dishevelled. She stirred then; but it was only the stirrings of a burning eye and a dry lip.

"Well?" she said, in such a faint whisper that both men started and looked anxiously at her. "Well? Speak!"

Robinson threw out both hands with a gesture of despair. "It's worse than I thought!" he answered, huskily. "No use pretending it

145

isn't; it's far worse. We've made as thorough an examination as we could, and it's terrible to see what damage has been done. Work of all this time—many a long month!—all destroyed, in both shafts. They're blocked with wreckage! Brickwork, ironwork, everything's been blown out in both. The downcast's the worst. And—and that's not all!"

"What is all?" asked Jeckie. "Say it! I want to know."

Robinson glanced at Farnish, and Jeckie was quick to interpret the look. She turned on her father as if he had been a house dog.

"Go out!" she commanded. "Outside!—and shut the door. Now then," she demanded as Farnish hurried into the garden and pulled the door tight after him. "Say it straight out! What is—all?"

Robinson dropped into a chair and for a moment rested his head on his hands; when he raised it again his face was as white as Jeckie's.

"I've been down that down-cast shaft, through the wreckage, as far as I could—Hargreaves and I went down, an hour since," he replied. "You never saw such a sight!—those fellows must have used some explosive that's more powerful than anything we've ever used for ordinary blasting. Those heavy cast-iron plates that we used for that stretch of tubbing, now—twisted and curled as if they'd been sheets of paper—ribs, brackets, flanges—I couldn't have believed that such things could have been, well, just made into ribbons, as if they'd been no more than putty. The timbering and the masonry, of course, are just so much splinters and dust, but the ironwork—well, it beats me how it's happened! Still, in time, all that could be put right—there'd be long delay, to be sure, and awful expense—all would have to be done over again—it's like starting all over again, but——"

He paused, shook his head, shivered a little as if at some recollection, and for a moment seemed as if he had lost the thread of his story.

"Get on to what there is of the rest of it!" commanded Jeckie. "There's more!"

Robinson started; the last word appeared to spur him up.

"More!" he exclaimed, almost emphatically. "More? Yes more!—lots more. The worst of it! My God!"

"Will you get it out?" said Jeckie, in a low voice that betrayed her concentrated anxiety. "Say it, man. I want to know."

Robinson made an effort, and pulled himself together. He gave Jeckie a queer, sidelong glance.

"I went down, through the wreckage, as far as I could," he said. "And—there's been more than the mere blowing up of timber

146

and masonry, and iron fittings. We heard it, down there; heard it unmistakably—me and Hargreaves. I heard it; he heard it. Oh, yes; there's no doubt of it. The explosion must have blown out a tremendous lot of wall surface stuff in the lowest workings they'd got to, where they hadn't started any masonry or tubbing, you understand. Because—we heard! No mistaking it! Once—just once—I've heard it before. Never to be forgotten, that—no!"

"For God's sake, man, speak plainly!" said Jeckie. "Heard—what!"

Robinson glanced fearfully around him as he bent nearer to her. He spoke but one word, in a tense whisper.

"Water!"

Jeckie started back, and her drawn face grew white to the lips. She, too, spoke the word he had spoken, in a lower whisper than his.

"Water!"

Robinson edged his chair near to the table and tapped the edge with a forefinger on which there was both grime and blood.

"I tell you we heard it—me and Hargreaves," he said. "I say—no mistaking it. This explosion, now—it must have blown a pretty considerable hole into the lowest part of the shaft, where they've been at work this last week or two, and it's released—it may be a thin bed of quicksand that we didn't suspect, or water-logged sandstone or sand, or something of that sort, if you follow me, but there's the fact—water! It's running into the shaft at, I should say, the rate of thousands of gallons a minute; we could hear it fairly roaring down there. It's no use; it's there!"

"What'll happen?" asked Jeckie in a curiously hard voice.

"The shafts'll be flooded to the brim in twenty-four hours," answered Robinson. "To the brim!'

"You said shafts!" exclaimed Jeckie.

"It's running into the up-cast, too," said Robinson. "We examined that. There must have been—must be—an extensive bed of quicksand lying between both shafts. Anyhow, it's there. I tell you, they'll be flooded to the brim!"

Jeckie's mind went back to a certain conversation she had once had with Revis, of Heronshawe Main. He too, had met with an obstacle in water, and had surmounted it.

"But it can be pumped out?" she suggested.

"Aye!" assented Robinson. "But how long will it take as things are, and how long after that to get matters put as straight as they were last night, and how much will it cost? It's no use denying it—all that we've done, all that we'd arrived at, is just—ruined!"

Jeckie suddenly got up from the table. She went across to the window, and pulling aside the half-curtain that veiled the lower

147

panes, looked out across the Leys. The surface works of the new pit were either levelled with the ground or showing gaunt and ruinous against the sky-line; crowds of curious sightseers were grouped about them; above everything, a sinister blot on the otherwise sun-filled sky, a cloud of yellow smoke still hung, heavy and significant, as if loath to float away from the scene of destruction. And as suddenly as she had risen from her seat so she turned on Robinson with a quick movement and with a flash of her old spirit. "But the coal's still there!" she exclaimed. "The coal's still there—to be got!"

Robinson looked at her for a moment in silence. Of late she had taken him into her confidence, pretty deeply, and she suddenly saw of what he was thinking. Money!—always money! And she began to think, too, of the money that had gone into the pit, and of how much more would be wanted now to recover what had so gone. It was as if one had lost a sovereign down some grating in the street, and must needs pay another to get it back.

"I say the coal's still there!" she repeated with fierce insistence. "To be got, do you hear? It's got to be got—that water'll have to be pumped out, and everything put in order again, and do you think I'm going to lose all I've laid out?" she went on, suddenly beating her fist on the table. "We must get to work at once!"

Robinson moved his head from side to side; something in the movement suggested difficulty, perhaps hopelessness.

"It's for you to decide," he said, dully. "It'll cost—I don't know what it won't cost. If you'd hear that water pouring in! And as things are, the shafts cumbered up with ruin; we can do nothing to stop it."

Jeckie snatched up her ulster, and began to put it on.

"Come on!" she said, turning to the door. "I'm going there myself."

Robinson sighed heavily as he pulled himself out of his chair and followed her into the sunlight. And he sighed again and shook his head as they set out across the Leys in the direction of the wrecked pit.

"There's naught to be done at present," he said, dejectedly. "It'll be days before we know the full extent of the damage. And we shall have to wait till we find out how high this water's going to rise—we don't know yet what weight there is behind it, down there. We're all in the dark."

"Something's got to be done!" declared Jeckie. Badly shaken though she was, a flash of her old indomitable spirit still woke to life at odd moments. "We can't stand about doing nothing," she went on. "The coal's there, I tell you!"

There were plenty of people standing about, doing nothing, on the edge of the scene of disaster, and among them Albert and Lucilla

148

Grice. Lucilla was in tears, and Albert was in apparently heated argument with some of the officials, who turned to Robinson as he and Jeckie drew near.

"Mr. Grice is blaming us because he says there ought to have been a watch kept over these shafts," said one of them. "I've told him there were watchmen."

"Then how comes it that somebody could get down there and place these explosives where they did," demanded Albert. "Don't tell me! There's been no proper watch kept at all, or this couldn't ha' happened. And all my wife's money invested in this!—and blown to pieces!"

He gave Jeckie a sidelong glance, as if laying the blame on her shoulders. He chanced to be in her way where he stood, and she unceremoniously elbowed him aside.

"Your wife's money!" she snarled as she passed him. "What's her bit o' money compared to what I've put in? Come on, Robinson—I'm going down that shaft as far as I can—to find out how things are."

"It's dangerous," said Robinson. "We risked a lot, me and Hargreaves."

"Where you've been I can go—and I'm going," declared Jeckie. "Come on—we'll go together."

The others, standing round, watched Jeckie's descent into the tangled mass of iron, wood, masonry; she herself, following her manager, cared nothing for danger, and was only intent on listening for the dread sound of which he had spoken. And, at last, when they had made their way a good two hundred feet into the shaft, penetrating through broken and twisted plates and girders, Robinson paused and held up the lantern he was carrying as a sign that they could go no farther.

"Listen!" he said in a whisper. "You'll hear!"

Jeckie steadied herself among the wreckage, looking down the darkness beneath it. And suddenly, in the silence that hung all round them, she heard, far below, in the gloomy depths which her imagination pictured the steady, heavy rush of water. It was unmistakable—and once again she felt sick in heart and brain, and weak of body.

"It's increased in volume since I was down," muttered Robinson as he stood at her side. "It's as I said before—the pit'll be flooded out. There's no help for it. It must be rising fast, that water."

He tore away a loose piece of iron from the wreckage close by, and dropped it through the twisted mass beneath their standing place. The sound of its heavy splash came almost at once.

"You hear!" he exclaimed. "It's within thirty or forty feet of us

149

now! It'll be up here before long; it'll rise to the brim. There's nothing to be done, Miss Farnish—we'd best make our way up again."

When Jeckie climbed out of the last mass of wreckage at the mouth of the shaft, it was to find Revis standing close by, talking to the men who hung about. He came up to her with a face full of grave concern.

"This is a bad job, my lass!" he said in low tones. "I'm as sorry for you as I can be!" He turned from her to Robinson. "Water rising?" he asked.

"Aye, fast as it can!" answered Robinson. "There must have been a tremendous lot released right down where they'd got to. And we were close on to the seam, too!"

"Rising in both shafts?" inquired Revis.

Robinson gave him a significant look.

"Both!" he answered.

Revis drew him aside; the others, watching them, heard the two men talking technicalities; Jeckie caught chance terms and expressions here and there—"water-laden bed"; "dangerous feeder"; "water-logged trias"; "drainage tunnel"; "Poetsch's method"; "Gebhardt and Koenig's method"; "Kind-Chaudron system"; "winding and pumping"—she understood little or nothing of it, and at that moment did not care to inquire; all that she realised was that the work into which she had put so much energy, and whereon she had laid out all her beloved money, was in danger of utter ruin. She let Albert grumble and growl to the men, and Lucilla weep fretfully; she herself stood silent and motionless, watching Revis and the manager.

Revis came to her at last, motioning Albert and Lucilla to join them. He looked graver than before.

"This is a very bad job!" he said in a low voice. "There seems to be no doubt that this explosive, whatever it was—and it must have been of extraordinary force—has tapped an exceptionally heavy lot of water. The mine'll be flooded—that is, these two shafts will. It's a good job you hadn't got the whole thing finished and opened out, for in that case, if this explosion had happened, you'd have had all the workings flooded, and there'd probably have been serious loss of life. As it is——"

Jeckie interrupted him—the question of what might have been had no interest for her.

"Can't the water be pumped out?" she asked. "You had trouble yourself that way?"

"Aye, you can pump!" agreed Revis. "But—you don't know what amount of water there is yet. It looks to me, from what

Robinson says, as if there was a sort of subterranean lake down there. Pump, aye!—but ... a long and terrible job. And—now don't be frightened!—the thing is—will it be worth it?"

"The coal's there!" exclaimed Jeckie, dogged and determined.

Revis looked from her to the Grices. Lucilla was grasping a tear-soaked handkerchief and gazing at him in the last throes of despairing anxiety; Albert stood with his lips a little open, expectant of wisdom from the man of experience.

"Yes," said Revis, at last. "But—it's no use shirking difficulties—this may be a quicksand that forms a thick cover all over the measures of whatever extent they may be. The fact is—you don't know what's happened down there, nor where you are."

"The coal's there!" repeated Jeckie. "It's there, I say! We've got to get it."

CHAPTER XI

THE SENTENCE

On the evening of that eventful day—a day of comings and goings about the ruined colliery—Farnish stayed later than usual at the "Coach-and-Four." There had never been so much to talk about in the whole history of Savilestowe as there was that evening, and he, as father of Jeckie Farnish, was a person of consequence in the debate which was carried on in the bar-parlour to the latest hours allowed by the licensing laws. But he went home at last, to find the cottage in darkness; there was not even the gleam of the last ashes of the usual wood fire to welcome him when he opened the door which admitted to the living-room. "I misdoubt yon poor lass o' mine is still hangin' about them shafts!" he muttered, as he began to feel around him in the darkness. "It's nat'ral on her part, an' all, but it'll do no good, no good!" Then he struck a match, drawn from a box which was always handy at the corner of the mantelpiece, and as he turned to where the lamp was kept, saw Jeckie. She sat in an easy chair at the other side of the hearth, but in no lounging attitude, such as is commonly affected by folk who sit in easy chairs. Instead, she was bolt upright and rigid, and for a moment Farnish wondered if she had been stricken with paralysis, or was dead. But a

151

sudden flash of her keen eyes showed him that she was alive enough.

"Why, Jecholiah, mi lass!" he exclaimed, as he lighted the lamp. "What's this here? Sittin' there i' t'darkness?—no light, no fire! Ye mo'nt tek on so, Jecholiah—it's o' no use, and bad for a body."

"Who said aught about takin' on?" answered Jeckie, with a sombre stare at him. "I was thinkin'—can't one think in t'dark as well as in t'light?"

"I dare say they can, mi lass," assented Farnish. "I done it misen, more nor once, and a varry bad thing it is—what ye happen to think i' t'dark's allus magnified, as it weer. Let me get you a drop o' summat, now?—and then go to yer bed and try for a bit o' sleep— ye need it."

"You can get something for yourself," answered Jeckie. "I want naught!" Farnish had no objection to this invitation. He got out the bottle of gin, mixed himself a tumbler to his liking, and sitting down in his own chair, wagged his head over the glass.

"I been tryin' to collect a bit o' information," he said. "Yon theer Ben Scholes—as were at t'bottom o' this unfortunate episode, as t'term is—he's clean disappeared. They laid wait for him to come down out o' t'church tower; watched for him most o' t'day, but he niver come, and as t'afternoon were drawing to an end, some on 'em stormed his citadel. Went up t'ladder to t'chamber i' t'tower wheer they toll t'bells—but t'bird hed flown. An' now they're sayin' 'at Scholes knew some secret way in and out o' t'church, and 'at he's off wi' them fellers 'at he bribed to blow t'pit up. Howsomeiver, Jecholiah, mi lass, t'police is on t'track of all on 'em, and ye'll hev t'satisfaction o' seein' malefactors browt to justice. There is them 'at I've been talkin' wi' 'at says 'at i' their opinion it's a hengin' matter— high treason, or summat o' that sort, but chuse how, it'll mean 'at they'll be clapped i' gaol for t'rest o' their lives, and never come out no more. So ye mun cheer up!"

Jeckie glowered at him in the dim light of the lamp.

"What good'll that do me?" she demanded, contemptuously. "Will it repair t'damage they've done? I don't care whether they catch Ben Scholes or no! Him and them other devils can go where they like, for all I care! I want to hear naught about 'em. They've done their job. It's over!"

"Aye, why, mi lass," expostulated Farnish. "But theer's what t'scholars terms poetic justice. It 'ud be nowt but right if these here chaps were browt to it. Now, it 'ud nobbut be t'proper thing if they could be henged—and happen drawn and quartered, same as yere done i' t'good old times—on t'scene o' their misdeeds. But I doubt

152

whether that theer 'ud be allowed nowadays—we'm all too soft-hearted. Hev a drop o' comfort, Jecholiah, mi lass, and then get to your bed."

"No!" retorted Jeckie. "I haven't done thinking."

Farnish left her thinking, and went to bed himself, and slept soundly. But the habits of a lifetime had made him an early riser, and he was up again and downstairs as the grey dawn broke over the village. And there he found Jeckie still sitting just as he had left her, some hours before, and in the light of his chamber candlestick he saw something that made him start back in amazement.

"The Lord ha' mercy on us, mi lass!" he exclaimed in awe-struck accents. "What's come o' your hair? Look at yoursen!"

The feminine instinct never wholly dies out, and Jeckie lifted herself to her feet, and, taking the candle from her father's hand, looked into the old mirror which hung above the mantelpieces. Then she saw what he meant. Her hair, thick, luxuriant still, and till the day before black and glossy as in her days of young womanhood, was now patched freely with grey strands, and here and there with unmistakable threads of white. She stood, looked, turned away, and set down the candle.

"Aye!" she muttered, as if to herself. "Aye!—and there's a lot o' thinkin', and plannin', and schemin' to do yet!"

None knew that better than she did. Of all the folk who from personal motives or from sheer natural curiosity discussed the present and future situation of the unlucky mine, none were so keenly aware of the real state of things as its principal proprietor. Lucilla might weep and bewail, and Albert indulge in platitudes which he fondly believed to be oracular sayings of the deepest wisdom, but Jeckie, essentially practical and businesslike, knew what the real problem was. There was so much capital left. It would have sufficed amply, if things had gone on as they were going on before the explosions. But now the pit was ruined in its upper and lower workings, and an immense amount of labour in pumping, clearing, and restoring was absolutely necessary before it could be brought back to the state in which it had been when Scholes achieved his revenge. Could she last out?

It was not in her to be idle. She sought the opinion of numerous experts; she went carefully into the all-important question of the money; at last she went to work once more. It was a fell and sinister enemy that had to be encountered first, for the shafts, as Robinson had prophesied, were flooded to the brim. But there the water had paused in its upward progress, and she gave the word to start on its clearance. Henceforth the village saw nothing but the progress of this grim fight. There was now no more clanging of steel and iron about the place; no more work at the rows of cottages which should soon have been filled by miners and their families; there was nothing but the ceaseless clearing of the shafts from the dark flood which had been released from its unsuspected source in the bowels of the earth—and the fear lest, when all this was accomplished, some further eruption might not break out and render all the labour in vain.

And as before, when hope was high and the fruition of her toiling and scheming seemed certain, so now, when all was doubt and anxiety, Jeckie Farnish haunted the scene from early morning till the evening shadows fell. She aged rapidly in those days; the patches of white thickened in the dark hair; the keen eyes grew harassed and hunted; about the firm mouth lines and seams appeared which nothing would ever smooth away again. She grew strangely silent; it seemed to those whose business brought them into touch with her that all she did throughout the day was to watch and watch and watch. She said little to Farnish; she ate and drank mechanically—no more, observed Farnish to his cronies, than kept the health in her body, now growing thin and gaunt; and at night she sat alone in the cottage, always staring at the fire which her father took care to keep going; if it had not been for him, he said, there would have been no fire, for she had no interest in anything but the ceaseless clearance of the dark floods which were being drawn and pumped away. It was useless, too, he said, to sit with her and attempt to cheer her up; she just sat, staring before her. So Farnish continued to attend the nightly symposium at the "Coach-and-Four," and in the living-room of their cottage Jeckie sat motionless, her eyes fixed on the bit of red glow in the grate, thinking.

She was so sitting one night, long after darkness had fallen, and when there was no light in the place beyond a rapidly dying lamp and the dull gleam of the fire, when, behind her chair, she heard the latch of the door lifted, and a footstep which she knew to be a man's. She believed it to be Farnish, who had come in an hour before his time, and she took no heed. But then fell silence, a strange and frightening silence, and at last she turned her head and looked. And there, half in shadow, half in the light, staring at her out of glowing eyes, stood Scholes.

The man whom Jeckie had so cunningly dispossessed of his lawful rights, had always been more or less of an unkempt, carelessly attired individual—the sort of man who neglected hair and beard, and wore his clothes as if they had been thrown on with one of his own pitchforks. But as he stood there now, motionless, staring at her, he reminded Jeckie of pictures which she had seen;

pictures of prophets, hermits, anchorites. His head was bare, and his untrimmed, uncombed locks fell about his ears and shoulders; even in that dim light she could see leaves and straw in them, and in the straggling beard which mingled with them. The rest of him, as she saw it, was wrapped in an ancient, weather-stained ulster coat, in rags at all its extremities, and tied about the waist with a piece of old cart rope. He carried a long staff of hazel in one hand; the other clawed meditatively at his beard as he stood fixedly staring at the woman who, in her turn, stared at him over her shoulder. And, suddenly, Jeckie forgot hair, beard, the strange garb, and saw nothing but the man's burning eyes, which never shifted their intense gaze from her face. Before many seconds had elapsed she would have given much to withdraw her own gaze—twice she tried to close her eyelids, in the vain hope that this was a phantom, a bad dream. But Scholes held her; and at last he spoke, in a queer, hollow voice which sent a thrill of fear through her. For Jeckie Farnish, like all country folk of her sort, and in spite of her hard-hearted, practical temperament, was intensely superstitious, and it seemed to her that this was either Scholes's ghost or that if he were really there in the flesh he had become endowed with supernatural powers. And as he spoke she cowered before him, trembling in every limb.

"So ye're sittin' theer, Jecholiah, all bi yersen, doin' nowt but thinkin'!" said the queer voice. "An' to be sure, when all's said and done, that's t'inevitable end of all them 'at compasses evil. Ye've nowt to do now but think, and think, and think! Here's t'end of all your schemin' and contrivin' and sellin' yer soul for brass! Wheer's yer brass, now? Gone!—and ye'll niver see one penny on it agen— niver! Ye're doomed, Jecholiah! Ye've been doomed to destruction ever since that day when yer carried yer bad heart into a poor man's house, wi' full determination to cheat him. Ye reckoned to be buyin' one thing when ye knew well 'at ye wor buyin' another. An' what ye wor doin' then wor this—ye were sellin' yer soul to t'Devil! Ye cheated me to mi face; but ye can't cheat him 'at put it into yer mind to cheat me! An' theer's others powers beside him, and I've been their instrument. I wor nowt but an agent i' bringing you to destruction. For ye're destroyed, Jecholiah! Ye can work and tew, tew and work, labour and better labour, at yon black water, but ye'll never clear it; it's t'flood o' vengeance 'at's come down on yer! If ye'd been content to mak' yer brass honest and straight, nowt would ha' happened to ye; and ye'd ha' had all 'at yer've lost. Lost! lost! lost! Sit theer, and stare and stare at yer bit o' fire till it dies out; yer last hopes'll die wi' that, for niver one penny o' yer brass will ye iver see out o' that land 'at once were mine and 'at ye cheated me out on. Ye ran t'race i' yer own way, Jecholiah, and ye're beaten!"

The burning eyes and strange figure suddenly vanished into the gloom from which they had appeared, and at the same moment the light of the lamp, which had been growing fainter and fainter while the queer voice sounded, gave one leap, showed Jeckie that she was alone in the living-room, and died out. Then came blackness, for at the same time the red ashes in the grate sank into sombre grey, and with the blackness an intense silence. She knew then that what she had seen was Scholes's ghost, and with a lifting of her hands to her head and a sudden catching of her breath, she half rose, and in the action fell forward across the hearth.

Farnish, coming home an hour later, found her lying there unconscious. And, in unconsciousness or semi-consciousness, she lay in her bed for a long time, hovering between life and death. One season had merged into another before Jeckie came to herself. Farnish and his younger daughter were at her bedside when her eyes first opened with full intelligence, and for a moment she believed that the old days at Applecroft were back again, and that they were all together. But in the next she remembered and realised, and after one quick glance at Rushie she turned her face to the wall with a gesture that seemed to implore silence.

It takes much to kill a woman of such a constitution, and Jeckie began to mend. But it was long before she spoke a word to any of those who came about her as to the events that had led up to her illness. It was to Farnish that she spoke at last; he had never failed in constant attendance on her, and sat for hours in her room, watching her, waking or sleeping. And as he sat by her side one grey afternoon she suddenly turned her eyes on him with a flash of their old power.

"How long have I been here?" she demanded.

Farnish, mindful of the doctor's orders, tried to evade a direct answer.

"Ye'd best not to bother about that theer, mi lass," he said, soothingly. "Ye're mendin' varry weel now, and t'doctor says 'at if ye're nobbut kept quiet, and hev nowt to worry yer, ye'll soon be up and doin', so——"

"I shall have plenty to worry about if you don't tell me what I want to know," insisted Jeckie. "How long have I been ill? Out with it!"

"Why, then, a matter o' two or three month, mi lass," replied Farnish. "But ye've been well looked to. Me an' yer sister Rushie, we've been wi' you all t'time—she's been a reight good 'un, has Rushie—never left t'place, and——"

Jeckie made a movement of impatience.

"What's gone on across there?" she demanded, pointing a wasted hand to the window. "What have they done? How are things?"

Farnish, who sat by the bedside twiddling his thumbs in sign of deep perplexity, shook his head.

"Now, Jecholiah, mi lass!" he said, with a poor attempt at firmness. "That's t'varry thing 'at t'doctor said ye worrn't to be allowed to talk about. So——"

"If you don't tell me, I'll get up and see for myself!" she retorted. "You'd better say!"

"Why, then," answered Farnish, "if I mun say, all I can say is, 'at you were took badly Mestur Revis he's hed all t'affairs i' hand. He come forrard and said 'at he'd tak it all on his shoulders, i' your interest. And he's t'only man 'at can rightly say how things is—I can't. I know nowt, mi lass—'ceptin' what I've telled you."

"I must see him," said Jeckie.

"Ye mun ha' t'doctor's consent first, mi lass," replied Farnish.

She lay quiet for some time after that; then she suddenly asked a question which made Farnish stare at her.

"Has naught been heard of Ben Scholes?"

Farnish made a curious exclamation.

"Scholes!" he said. "Aye, for sure! He wor found dead, i' Wake Wood, some time ago; they say he'd evidently been i' hiding theer, and theer he'd died. Queer, worrn't it, mi lass?"

But Jeckie made no answer. She knew now, for certain, that it was Scholes's ghost that had come to her, and that all was lost.

CHAPTER XII

THE SECOND EXODUS

Those who ministered to her in her convalescence found it difficult to understand Jeckie Farnish's curious apathy and indifference to the things about her. Once her sister was out of danger, Rushie had gone home to Binks and her children; Binks was by that time a bustling tradesman in Sicaster, and had prospered so well that Rushie wore a real sealskin coat and sported gold chains and diamond rings. It had been Binks's idea that his wife should go to the rescue when Jeckie was taken ill; blood, said Binks, with the air of a Solomon, was thicker than water when all's said and done, and bygones should be bygones, and in no half-measures. So Rushie waited on Jeckie hand and foot, and Jeckie, after she had come to herself, watched her going about the sick room and said nothing. At that time, indeed, she said nothing to anybody, and when Rushie had returned, leaving her sister in charge of Farnish and a neighbour-woman, she said less. Farnish began to wonder if her illness had affected her mind, and voiced his doubts to the doctor; the doctor made him leave Jeckie alone; she would speak, he said, as soon as she wanted to.

There came a time when Farnish was obliged to speak, whether Jeckie wanted to hear or not. He approached her bedside one day in a shamefaced, diffident manner, looking doubtfully at her.

"Jecholiah, mi lass," said Farnish, "theer's a little matter 'at I mun mention to yer, though I'm sure I wouldn't trouble yer wi' it if it could be helped. But ye see, mi lass, when ye were ta'en badly an' could do nowt for yersen, I hed to tak things i' hand, and of course, I hed to lay out money. I knew wheer you kep' a certain supply down theer i' t'owd bewro i' t'kitchen corner, and I hed to force t'lock and lay hands on it. That's three months and more since, and for all I've been varry careful about layin' it out, it's come to an end, as all such commodities, as they term 'em, does. What mun I do, mi lass?"

Jeckie made an effort of memory, and remembered how much money there had been in the old bureau of which her father spoke— something between forty and fifty pounds, as far as she could recollect. She made a rapid calculation and found that Farnish had spent between three and four pounds a week during her illness. There was nothing extravagant in such expenditure at such a time. But she gave him a sharp, searching look.

"You made that do? You have borrowed aught from anybody?" she demanded.

"Surely not, mi lass!" protested Farnish. "No!"

"Not from them Binkses?" questioned Jeckie.

"Nowt from nobody, Jecholiah," said Farnish. "It's panned out very well, ower fourteen weeks. There's happen a pound or so left. But——"

"Go downstairs, and come up again when I knock on t'floor," said Jeckie. "I have a bit in my box."

Farnish went away in his usual obedient fashion, and when he had gone, Jeckie, who hitherto had been unable to get out of bed unaided, made shift to rise, and to wrap a shawl round her

158

shoulders. Weak as she was, her first action was characteristic—to totter to the door and lock it. That cost her trembling limbs an effort; she had to summon all her small reserve of strength and to pause once or twice in order to cross the floor to a heavy, iron-clamped box which stood in one corner of the room, staying again on the way to extract a key from a certain hiding-place beneath the carpet. And when this box was unlocked she found it difficult work to lift out and lay aside the various things that lay within; it took some time before she had got down to the bottom and had there unearthed a smaller box, wherein, months before, when she had been obliged to face possible contingencies, she had placed a personal reserve fund. The key of that box was in an old satchel kept within the larger one; she found it at last and laid bare her secret store.

Weak and trembling as she was, Jeckie could not forbear the satisfaction of counting over this money. She had deposited there a thousand pounds in banknotes, and fifty in gold, and she slowly counted paper and coin. It was all there, all safe, and she took ten pounds in gold, put the rest back, and with many tremblings and restings, locked up the two boxes, unlocked the door, knocked loudly on the floor, and climbed back into bed.

"There's ten pound," she said when Farnish came up in response to her summons. "Make it go as far as you can."

She turned her face away then, as if wanting no talk on the matter, and Farnish took the hint and the money and went quietly away. It astonished him, as Jeckie grew stronger, that she asked no questions about his expenditure; once upon a time, she would have made him account for every penny. But now she seemed indifferent; she was indifferent, indeed, to everything, and there came a time when she showed no interest in the doctor's visits, as if she cared nothing whether he was doing her good or not. But all that time she was steadily improving, and at last the doctor told her, in Farnish's presence, that there was no need for him to come again and that she could get up.

"Ye'll be glad to take a look round, no doubt, mi lass," observed Farnish, when the doctor had gone. "It'll liven you up."

Jeckie made no reply. The neighbour-woman got her up next day, helped her to dress, and bustled about in the hope of making her comfortable at her first rising. When Jeckie was dressed this good Samaritan went downstairs and returned with an easy chair and cushions.

"I'll put this here agen t'winda, Miss Farnish," she said with cheery officiousness. "Ye'll be able to look out theer ower t'pit, and see what they're a-doin' on theer. Nowt so lively as it wor afore

159

t'accident, but theer is things bein' done theer, an' happen ye'll like to get a glimpse on' em, for, of course, ye mun ha' been anxious, an'——"

"Put that chair in that corner!" snapped Jeckie, with a sudden gleam of her old temper. "An' hold yer wisht about t'pit! When I want to talk about t'pit, I'll let you know."

The woman had sufficient sense to see that her charge was irritable, and she made no answer; she had enough wit, too, to place the easy chair in a corner of the room from which it was impossible to see out of the window. And in that corner Jeckie spent the first period of her convalescence, at first doing nothing, afterwards occupying herself in mending her linen.

Farnish came upstairs every now and then, always with some question—was she wanting aught? But Jeckie never wanted anything; she ate and drank whatever was put before her without remark and with apparent indifference, and so the days went by. And during the whole of that time she never asked her father a question save once.

"Where," she asked suddenly, one day, as Farnish hung about the bedroom in his usual aimless, good-intentioned fashion, "where did they bury Scholes?"

"Why, i' t'churchyard, to be sure, mi lass!" answered Farnish, glad to break the silence which he found so trying. "Wheer else? Ligged him i' t'same grave as his missus—ye'll know t'spot; halfway down that new piece o' ground 'at they took in fro' Stubley's ten-acre a few years sin'. Aye, he wor buried all reight theer, wor Ben—same as anybody else. Why, mi lass?"

"Naught!" answered Jeckie, and relapsed into her usual silence.

The same silence continued when she at last went downstairs. And there Farnish noticed that she never went near the window of the living-room; it, like that of her bedroom, overlooked the ill-fated colliery. For awhile she accepted the help and ministrations of the neighbour-woman; then one day she gave her some money and with the curt remark that in future she and her father could fend for themselves, dismissed her. She began to go about the cottage then, and to do the household work, and Farnish, who was somewhat shrewd as regards observation, noticed that one night, when the darkness had fallen, she fitted two muslin blinds to the window of the living-room and the window of her chamber above; the light could come in through them, but no one could see out.

"It's t'same as if our Jeckie niver wanted to set her eyes on yon theer pit an' its surroundings niver no more!" observed Farnish, narrating this curious circumstance to his principal crony. "Shutten 'em clean out, as it weer!"

"An' no wonder, considerin' how things has befallen," remarked the crony. "If things hed turned out wi' onny affair o' mine as that's turned out wi' her, d'ye think I should want to hev' it i' front o' my eyes, allus remindin' me o' what had happened? Nowt o' t'sort!"

"Aye!" said Farnish, reflectively. "But—she knows nowt, as yet."

There came a time when Jeckie had to know. One morning, when she was fully restored to health, though now a gaunt and haggard woman, grey-haired and spiritless, Farnish, who had been out in the village, came in as she was washing up the breakfast things in the scullery and approached her with evident concern.

"Jecholiah, mi lass," he said, in a low voice, "theer's Mestur Revis outside, i' his trap. He's called at t'doctor's as he came through Sicaster, and t'doctor says you're now fit to hev a bit o' business talk. And Mestur Revis is varry anxious to come in and hev it, now. How will it be, mi lass?"

Jeckie finished polishing her china before she answered, and Farnish stood by, silent, anxiously waiting.

"Happen I know as much as Revis or anybody else can tell," she said at last in a queer voice. "And happen I got to know it in a way 'at neither Revis nor you, nor anybody, 'ud understand. But— tell him to come in."

Farnish went out to the colliery proprietor, who sat in his smart dog-cart, meditatively surveying the scene on the other side of the road. There were no signs of activity now about the pit on which Jeckie had set such hopes; the surface buildings stood as ruinous as the explosions had left them; on the hillside the cottages intended for the miners were just as they were when all work had come to an end on them; over the whole surface of the Leys there was ruin and desolation. And Revis had just shaken his head and heaved a deep sigh when Farnish emerged from the cottage.

"She'll see you now, if you'll please go in, Mestur Revis," said Farnish. Then he looked half entreatingly, half wistfully at the big man. "Ye'll break it gentle to her, sir?" he added. "She's in a queer state of mind, to my thinking."

"Leave it to me, my lad," said Revis, as he got out of his dog-cart. "I'll make it as easy as I can for her."

He went up the path to the cottage door, tapped, and walked in. Jeckie sat in her accustomed corner, in the shadows, but Revis saw how she had changed, and it was with a curious mixture of pity and wonder and interest that he went up and held out his hand to her.

"Well, my lass!" he said, with a sympathetic effort to put some cheeriness into his voice. "You've had a bad time of it, to be sure, poor thing! But—you're better?"

"Well enough to hear aught you've to say, Mr. Revis," answered Jeckie. "And—sit down and tell me straight out, if you please. You know me!"

Revis gave her a searching look and pulled a chair in front of her.

"Aye!" he said. "I think I know! Well, it's not cheering news, but you'd better know it. You know already that I've done what I could to look after things for you while you've been ill?"

"Yes, and I'm obliged to you," answered Jeckie. "You were always a good friend."

"It was this way," continued Revis. "When you were taken ill that brother-in-law of yours, Binks, came to me and asked me if I couldn't do something to help. I came over and consulted with him and your partner and her husband. We went right into things. Of course you know that when your illness came you were just at the end of your capital?"

"Who should know better!" exclaimed Jeckie, bitterly.

"Well, that was so," asserted Revis. "So—everything stopped, with those shafts still half-full of water, and——"

"I know how they were, and how all else was," interrupted Jeckie. "You can't tell me anything about that!"

"To be sure!" said Revis, humouring her. "Well, the question was—was it worth while putting more capital—it would have had to be a lot more capital!—to clear the mine, get all going again, and go on? Now, I had some talk with two or three influential men in the district, and we decided to come to your help if we could see that all the money you and Mrs. Albert Grice had put in, and all that we should have to put in would be got back—that, in short, the results would justify the expenditure. In other words, what amount of coal is under this property and close to it? You understand?"

For the first time for many long months a faint flush of colour came to Jeckie Farnish's haggard cheeks, and she spoke with some show of interest.

"You mean to say that there's a doubt?" she asked.

"We'll leave doubts out," answered Revis. "That was the real problem. I put aside all the investigations that you made before you started, and made some of my own, at my own expense. You know what a thorough man I am about such things. Well, I made, at once, more borings, in different parts, not only of your property, but in

162

the land round about. I've known the truth now for a week or two; it's an unpleasant one. There's without doubt a good bed beneath your land, but a small one. What you'd have got out of it would possibly have given you back your capital and a bit over. But there's none elsewhere! And your pit's been so ruined by that explosion, and there's such a body of water that——"

"I understand," said Jeckie, interrupting him with a significant look. "It's useless!"

"If you want plain words, my lass—yes!" answered Revis. "To get that pit cleared and to go on again would cost far more than you'd ever get back. I reckoned everything up, with your partner's assistance—you know she'd power to act for you if you couldn't— and things were just here—what with paying everything up to the time of stoppage and so on, you've just come to the end of your capital, and—there you are! It's a very sad thing, but it's one of these things that have to be faced."

"The workmen and all the rest of them?" asked Jeckie.

"All paid off—gone, weeks since," replied Revis, laconically.

"And the stuffs about those shafts—material—the building material at those cottages, and all that?" she inquired.

"Sold—to settle things up," said Revis. "Your partner had power to do all that, you know, as you couldn't. We all made the biggest effort we could for you and for her. To put things in a nutshell—you owe nothing to the bank or to anybody, and the whole concern is just a ruin which anybody can take up and remake if they like. I would have liked, but it isn't worth it."

Jeckie looked steadily at her visitor for a long time.

"Then," she said at last, in a low voice that was curiously firm, "then—I've nothing?"

Revis shook his head.

"Nothing," he answered. "Nothing! except the forty acres that you bought in the beginning."

He was surprised to hear Jeckie laugh. He was something of a student of human nature, this big, bluff man, but he could not gauge the precise meaning of that laugh, and he looked at the woman before him, in some slight alarm, which she was quick to recognise.

"I'm not going mad, Revis," she said. "I was only thinking that at the end of all that I've got—forty acres! Those forty acres!"

"How much did you give for them?" he asked, inquisitively. "A lot? I'd an idea it was for next to naught that you got them."

Jeckie suddenly got up from her chair, and turned towards the hearth. She stood looking into the fire for some time, and when, at last, she glanced at her visitor there was a look in her eyes which Revis never forgot.

"What did I give for them?" she said in a low, concentrated voice. "Man!—I don't know—yet!—what I gave for them!"

Revis stood staring at her for a moment of wonder. Her answer was beyond him. And as he had no reply to it he turned to go. But Jeckie stopped him.

"Wait a minute," she said. "A question—Lucilla Grice and her husband?"

"They've left the neighbourhood," replied Revis. "They sold their house and furniture and went away. I don't know where they've gone."

Jeckie said no more, and Revis went out, said a few words to Farnish, and drove off. And Farnish went indoors, and found Jeckie already setting about the preparations for their early dinner. He was astonished to find that she began to be talkative that day; still more astonished that, when evening came, she cooked a hot supper, encouraged him to eat, ate heartily herself, and before they went to bed mixed a goodly tumbler of grog for each of them. It was, thought Farnish, like old times, and he went to his chamber in high content.

But as the grey dawn broke a few hours later, Farnish woke to find Jeckie, fully dressed, standing at his bedside. He stared at her in astonishment.

"Get up; get dressed; come down; we're going away," said Jeckie. "Don't talk, but do as I tell you. There'll be some breakfast ready by the time you're down."

Farnish obeyed; he was still as clay in his elder daughter's hands. And an hour later, still obedient though wondering, he followed her out of the cottage, and up the empty street of Savilestowe, past what had once been Grice's, past what had once been the Golden Teapot, past the last house, past the last tree. At the top of the hill, and as the morning broke, he turned and looked back, having some strange intuition that he was being taken away from a place which he had known long and would never see again. He stood looking for some minutes; when he turned, Jeckie, who had never once looked back, was marching stolidly ahead.

CHAPTER XIII

THE LUSTRE JUG

Some eight or nine years after the morning on which Jeckie Farnish and her father had walked out of their native village for the last time, never to be heard of again in those parts, a man, who had just arrived by train at Scarhaven, the time being seven o'clock of a bitterly cold November evening, turned away from the railway station and betook himself, shivering in the north-east wind that swept inland from the sea, towards a part of the town wherein cheap lodgings were to be found. In the light of the street lamps he showed himself to any who chanced to look at him as a not over-well clad, somewhat shabby man, elderly, greyish of hair and beard, who carried an old umbrella in one hand and a much worn hand-bag in the other. Not the sort of man, this, anyone would have said, who had much money to spend—nevertheless, when, after some ten minutes of hard walking, he came to the end of a badly lighted street in a dismal quarter, he turned into the bar-parlour of a corner tavern and ordered hot whisky and a cheap cigar. In the light of the place his shabbiness was more apparent, yet it was shabbiness of the genteel sort. His overcoat was threadbare, but well brushed; his boots, patched in more than one place, were sound of sole and firm of heel and had been well cleaned and polished; his linen was clean and he wore gloves. A keen observer of men and things would have said, after inspecting him, that here was a man who had known better days.

Under the cheering influence of his whisky and his cigar, this man shook off the chill of the streets and the sea wind and began to feel more comfortable in flesh and bone.

He settled himself in a corner of the bar-parlour and picked up a newspaper from an adjoining table, there was a good fire in the grate close by, and he glanced at it approvingly as at the face of an old friend, and occasionally stretched out a hand to it. In this fashion he spent half an hour; at the end of that time he pulled out a watch, and here again a keen observer would have noted something of significance. The watch hung from a cheap steel chain, of the sort that you can buy anywhere for a couple of shillings, but the watch itself was a good, first-class article of solid gold, old, no doubt, but valuable. He replaced it in his pocket with an air of indecision; then, apparently, making up his mind about something, he had his glass replenished, and for another half-hour he sat, gradually growing warmer and more courageous. But soon after eight o'clock had struck from a neighbouring church tower, he rose, buttoned his overcoat about his throat, and, picking up bag and umbrella, made for the door. Ere he had reached it another moment of apparent indecision came over him. It ended in his returning to the bar and asking to be supplied with a bottle of whisky. He counted out its price from a handful of silver which he drew from his hip pocket, and, placing the bottle in the bag, made his exit and went out again into the night.

It was a badly-lighted street down which this man turned—a street of small, mean houses, wherein there were few lights in the windows and the gas lamps were placed far apart. Consequently, he had some difficulty in finding the number he wanted, and was obliged to look closely within the doorways to get an idea of its exact situation. But he got it at last, and knocked—to wait until a slight opening of the door revealed a dimly-lighted, narrow passage, and a girl between the lamp and himself.

"Mrs. Watson in?" he asked, making as if to enter. The girl shook her head.

"Mrs. Watson's dead, sir—died three years ago," she answered. "Name of Marshall here now."

The inquirer appeared to be seriously taken aback.

"Sorry to hear that," he said. "I used to get a night's lodgings with her in years past. Do they let lodgings here now?"

"No, sir," said the girl, "but there's plenty of houses where they do, both sides of the street. You'll see cards in the windows, sir."

The man thanked his informant and went away—to look for the cards of which the girl had spoken. There were plenty of these cards in the windows. He could see them, dismal and ghost-like in the gloom, and very soon he paused, irresolute.

"One's as good as another, I reckon," he muttered at last. "And when you can't afford an hotel——"

Then he knocked at the door by which he was just then standing. There was some delay there, but when the door opened there was a strong light in the passage behind it, and he found himself confronting a tall, gaunt, white-haired woman, gowned in rusty black, over whose shoulders were thrown an old Paisley shawl. He looked uninterestedly at her—one landlady was pretty much as other landladies.

"Can you let me have a room and a bit of supper and breakfast?" he began. "I used to put up at Mrs. Watson's, lower down, but I find she dead, so——"

Then he suddenly stopped, hearing the woman catch her

breath and seeing a quick start of surprise in her as she leaned forward to stare at him. And he, too, leaned nearer, and stared.

"Good Lord!" he muttered. "Jeckie! Jeckie Farnish! Well, I never!"

Jeckie held the door wider, motioning the applicant to step inside.

"I knew you, Albert Grice, as soon as you spoke," she said, in a dull, almost sullen voice. "Come in! I can find what you want. Where's your wife?" she went on, as she pointed him to a hat-stand. "Is she here, waiting anywhere, in the town, or is it just for yourself?"

Albert set down his umbrella and bag, and began to take off his coat.

"Lucilla's dead," he replied, shortly. "Five or six years since. I'd no idea of coming across you! I was here, once or twice— business, you know—for a night, some years since, at that Mrs. Watson's——"

"Come this way," said Jeckie. She walked before him down the narrow passage to a living-room at the end, a homely, comfortable place, where there was a bright fire, something cooking on the range, and, in an elbow-chair at the side of the hearth, an old, white-bearded man who smiled and nodded as Albert walked in. "You remember him," continued Jeckie, pointing to Farnish. "He's lost his memory—he wouldn't know you from Adam!—he's forgotten all about Savilestowe, and he thinks he's a retired farmer—wi' lots o' money!" she added, grimly. "Speak to him—but take no notice of what he says—he talks all sorts o' soft stuff."

Albert went up to Farnish and offered his hand.

"Ah, how do you do, sir?" he asked. "Hope I see you well, sir?"

"Ah, how do you do, sir?" responded Farnish, with another infantile smile. "I hope you're well yourself? Friend o' my dowter's, no doubt, sir, and kindly welcome. Jecholiah, mi lass, what'll the gentleman tak' to drink—ye mun get out the sperrits—and there'll be a bit o' tobacco in the jar, somewhere, no doubt."

"Sit you down," said Jeckie, motioning Albert to another elbow-chair. "There's some hot supper in t'oven; plenty of it, and good, too, and we'll have it in a minute, and then he'll go to his bed—he's quiet and harmless enough, but his mind's gone—at least his memory has."

"Does he ever take a glass?" asked Albert, staring curiously at Farnish. "I see he's got his pipe handy."

"Oh, I give him a drop every night before he goes to bed," said Jeckie, already bustling about the hearth. "That does him no harm."

Albert went back into the passage and returned with his bottle

167

of whisky. Seeing a corkscrew hanging on the delf-ledge, he drew the cork, mixed two tumblers of grog, and handed one to Farnish and offered the other to Jeckie.

"Nay, drink it yourself," said Jeckie. "I don't mind one after supper, but not now. You haven't made it over strong for him?"

"It'll not hurt him," replied Albert, pointing to the label on the bottle. "Sound stuff, that. Best respects, sir!"

"And my best respects to you, sir, and many on 'em," answered Farnish. "Allers glad to see a gentleman o' your sort, sir— friends o' my dowter's."

"He thinks all my lodgers are friends 'at come to see us," observed Jeckie. "Poor old feller!—he's been like that this three year."

Albert sat sipping his drink and watching father and daughter. Farnish had become white and doddering; Jeckie's hair was as white as his, and she was as gaunt as a scarecrow, and looked all the more so because of her height and her strong-boned figure, but she was evidently as bustling as ever, and not without some spark of her old fire. And before long she set a smoking-hot Irish stew on the table, and bade Albert to fall to and eat heartily; there was always plenty of good, plain food in her house, she added, dryly, and nobody went with their bread unbuttered. So Albert ate and grew warm and satisfied, and, when, later on, Jeckie was seeing Farnish to his bed, he sat by the fire, and drank more whisky, and wondered, in vague, purposeless fashion, about the vagaries of life.

Jeckie came back to him at last, and dropped into the chair which Farnish had left empty. Albert indicated his bottle.

"Well, I don't mind a drop," she said. "A woman 'at works as hard as I do can do with a glass last thing at night. I've some good stuff o' my own in that cupboard—you must try it when you've finished your glass."

"Good health, then," said Albert. He looked speculatively at her as he lifted his glass. "I was never more surprised in my life," he went on, confidentially, "than when you opened that door! For—it's all a long time ago!"

Jeckie, holding the tumbler which he had given her in both hands, stared meditatively at the fire for some time before replying.

"Aye!" she said at last. "I've had more lives nor one i' my time! You've never been back there?"

"Never!" answered Albert. "Have you?"

Jeckie shook her head.

"There's naught could ever make me do that," she said. "It was over and done with. Once I thought of emigrating and starting afresh, but there was him"—she nodded towards the stairs. "I had to think of him. So I came here, and furnished this bit of a house, and started taking in lodgers—chance folk, like yourself. It's been—well, just a comfortable living. T'old fellow upstairs is satisfied, especially since he lost all his memory. And that's the main thing, anyhow, now. There's naught else."

Albert said nothing, and there was a long pause before Jeckie spoke again. Then she asked a question.

"What might you be doing?"

"Bit o' travelling," replied Albert. "The old line—a patent food. No great thing; but, as you say, it's, well, just a nice living. For a single man, keeps one going; and I can manage a cigar now and then, and a drop o' that," he added, with a knowing sidelong glance at the bottle. "I don't complain."

Jeckie shrugged her shoulders.

"What's the use?" she said.

Albert suddenly rose, went out into the passage, and came back with a packet in his hand, which he presented to her.

"This is the stuff," he said. "Invaluable for children, invalids, and old people. You might try it on your father; it's grand stuff for old 'uns when they've lost their teeth. Lately I've done very nicely with it. What I want is to get a bigger connection with leading firms in some of these towns. I'm going to try a whole day here to-morrow. I've only one of these Scarhaven firms on my list at present. Now, you'll have an idea about where I should go, eh? Happen you can suggest...."

They continued talking for an hour or two, facing each other across the hearth, two broken things, with a past behind them, and a bottle between them, each secretly conscious of mutual knowledge, and neither daring to speak of it. They talked of anything but the past, any trifle of the moment; yet the consciousness of the past was there, spectre-like, and each felt it. And, at last, as the clock struck eleven, Jeckie rose and lighted a candle.

"I'll show you your room," she said. "You can depend on the bed being well-aired; I'm always particular about that; and there's everything you'll want. And I'll have a good breakfast ready at half-past eight."

When she had shown Albert to his room she went downstairs again, and, gathering the Paisley shawl about her, sat in front of the fire, staring at it and thinking, until the red ashes grew grey, and the grey ashes white. It was past midnight then, but she had so sat, and so heard the clocks strike twelve for many a long year.

"As sure as I'm a born woman," she muttered, she rose at last, "it was Ben Scholes's spirit 'at I saw that night! And I were none

169

wrong when I said to Revis 'at I didn't know what I gave for that land! for who knows what I'll have to pay for it yet! But I've kept paying, and paying, and paying, on account; but what about t'balance?"

She went slowly and heavily upstairs and looked in on Farnish. The old man was fast asleep, his hands clasped over his breast.

"He's all right," she muttered as she left his room. "He never had any great love of money."

Albert found a good breakfast of eggs and bacon ready for him when he came down in the morning, and did justice to it. Jeckie stood by the fire and talked to him while he ate, but again there was no reference to the past. And before nine o'clock he had got into his coat and hat, to start out on his round.

"I want to get done by four," he said. "I must go on to Kingsport to-night. So now—what do I owe?"

"Why if you give me three-and-six, it'll do," answered Jeckie. With the coins which he gave her still in her hand, she followed him to the street door and looked out into a grey sea-fog that was rolling slowly up the street. She continued to look when he had said good-bye and gone quickly away ... she watched his disappearing figure until the sea-fog swallowed it up. She went back to the living-room then, and took down from the mantelpiece an old lustre-jug which she had treasured all through her life, since the time of her girlhood at Applecroft, and in which she now kept her small change. And as she dropped the three-and-six in it, the lustre-jug slipped from her fingers, and was broken into fragments on the hearthstone. Presently, she picked up the fragments and went out into the yard behind the house and threw them away on the dustheap; bits of pot, not more shattered than her own self.

The End

170